Higher Ground
Book 1

Higher Ground

BOOK 1
SEARCHING

RICK SURKAMER

DANCIN BEAR LLC

Higher Ground
BOOK 1 - SEARCHING

ISBN 979-8-9894970-0-3 paperback
ISBN 979-8-9894970-1-0 ebook

Cover and Interior Design by:
Chris Treccani
www.3dogcreative.net

'SEARCHING HIGHER GROUND', BOOK ONE OF THREE IN THE TRILOGY "MISSION HIGHER GROUND"

Followed by "Living Higher Ground" and "Defending Higher Ground"

"Beginning today we embrace the vision of hope and goodness, so we may be all the world may need us to be. In doing so we may then let ourselves define the journey to that place called Higher Ground."
Galt the Redhead

WHAT IS HIGHER GROUND ?

The pursuit of a state of being that allows us to achieve our full human potential, and with it brings an obligation to help others to find their way as well.

Publisher's Note:

Our story is told through a young woman and man who grow to adulthood separately, then come together for a shared purpose. Our first main character, Galt, appears in book 1 as a young teenager, and we follow his growth and adventures into becoming a man. Book 1 is the foundation for the climax and successes achieved in books 2 and 3. It is written as an in depth background for Galt. One also represents the foundations of how he and SHE become lovers, partners, family, and leaders in America. Our second main character is a spiritual advisor to him, and is simply referred to as SHE in book 1. Together in books 2 and 3 of the trilogy, she appears in her final human form, as Ali Jai or AJ. A young adult woman who with Galt strives to grow their abilities to thrive on the Higher Ground ,and then to defend it. Along the way taking daring actions, then sharing lessons, assistance, and guidance on a path to Higher Ground. Achieving that end through their individual abilities and joint love for each other. In this way, 1+1=3.

Our story teller is proud and humbled to be able to share this most noble of pursuits, drama, and achievement of finding the way to the Higher Ground.

Our story teller aims at the singular purpose of sharing a tale that he hopes will be of some guidance or insight to others. He has chosen to tell this tale through characters he finds himself befriending in a spiritual way. It is a fairy tale, as simple as this may seem. Through a fairy tale of their adventures, love, and growth, it is assumed that this is the best possible way to help men and women of all ages with their own journey, challenges, losses, and achievement to the Higher Ground.

Know that no character is a true-to-life person. Our author or story teller has no intent to hurt, embarrass or make anybody popular. The intent is to take personal experiences and lessons he has observed and use this fairy tale to share them. This growth of our characters are in three stages. All the main characters have one goal in mind:

To persevere, achieve and then help others to find the **_Higher Ground._**

To reiterate, our founding character, GALT will be developed in book I. This book is fundamental to the themes within all three books and supporting sub plots. The second leading character, SHE, as referenced, will reveal her human form in book II as AJ or Ali Jai. Both are loaded with ups and downs, and forces of evil that many will understand in their lives as well.

In book III, the true optimization of spiritual and practical life lessons comes together. It is here where they best demonstrate how the pursuit of Higher Ground can be of benefit to others. Though both have this purpose, they both embrace a simple trinity: Through balance of the body, mind, and soul, one can first know of it, then expand it, and then share it.

It is the hope that the reader will embrace these lessons and teachings as they grow with our characters, with the understanding that what they get out of reading is entirely up to them. One must choose what they learn, retain, and/or grow from coming to know our male and female main characters. In other words, it is up to you. You have to WANNA. It is in book 3 where the reader will see the beginning of a new world in America. Where wealth is a commitment to others, and evil receives ZERO tolerance.

They will cross many places, forested, deserted, complicated, and joyful, but bridging youth-to-adult responsibilities, and ultimately the hierarchy and ego dynamic, rooted in both our characters' unique Self and Territory expression. They will jump time, and bring it all back.

For it is we as the two creators and partners who have chosen to reach Higher Ground by sharing their learnings, individually and collectively. Never losing track of the enablement of others to achieve Higher Ground. The singular objective is to share and perhaps help others through the experiences of our two main characters.

It is the story tellers advise that you read Book I and II as if they are one book with a wonderful plot. We have chosen to sell both at one price so as to assure you have a complete and thoughtful experience with our work.

So with that, on this day, May 15, 2018, let us open our hearts and share the way to *Higher Ground*.

NOTE:
THANKS TO THE "SPIRITUAL ADVISOR"
FOR BEING THERE .

OUR MAIN CHARACTER GALT:
The name is of Old English derivation, Meaning "From the High Ground"

People with this name have a deep inner desire to use their ability in leadership, and to have personal independence. They would rather focus on large, important issues, and delegate the details. They build their lives on a solid foundation of order and service, they value truth, justice, discipline, and may be quick-tempered with those who do not.

"For Man is nothing else, but what he makes of himself.
- Since we are not created nor born with an essence or intrinsic individual nature
- We discover that we exist, and we create ourselves by our own free choices.
- We are nothing except what we make of ourselves through our actions. "

–Jean Paul Sartre

Author's Final Note: "I ask you to read this first story of Galt. One that covers his youth and background experiences. All lay the foundation for his Discovery of Higher Ground, the pursuit to it, and finally the joy of finding a partner to grow with. Two who are highly motivated to share the path with others. The first book of the trilogy, is a book of background. A book written to establish the sharing of our main character's most intimate youth to early manhood and discovery of the power of Higher Ground. If this tale is of interest to you, we encourage you to read on in book 2 and 3 of this adventure to the Higher Ground. It is hoped it will help the reader to live a better life by achieving a balance within body, mind, and spirit. Sharing this balance with people you come to love. It is an adventure that grows from very personal to very global.

We hope you enjoy the Trilogy of Higher Ground.

TABLE OF CONTENTS

CHAPTER 1:

Meet Galt ...

. . . man-child at age fifteen, and full of . . . he isn't sure.

S trawberry blond, freckles abound, skinny and chubby at different times, big-boned.

Galt had just watched *Lawrence of Arabia* for the first time, he found himself in a very unusual place. He was still fifteen but was feeling pretty good about finally getting a handle on what "success criteria" is called for as a sophomore in a Chicago suburban North Shore high school. He played football, wrestled, had raised his mediocre grades up to honors level, and yet still was not socially engaged with the in-crowd at the school. This is not to say he didn't have friends, as he did—many—who were both diverse, male and female, different ages, and bright. However, he aspired for that in-crowd. That crowd looked cool and demonstrated what "in" looked like.

He was fortunate to have the support of his parents in this life adventure, as they assured good social and moral values be taught, as well as the right pair of penny loafers, crew neck sweater and matching socks to go with his khaki pants. Clearly he had the uniform thing down.

Then along comes somebody who moves his cheese at a time that almost seems to be chosen by powers greater than him. Because, despite this stage of being close to what is expected and cool, he had just returned from a dinner with his family in the kitchen, in which his father and mother had shared the following with him:

"How would you like to have your own room?" Answer: "Heck, yes," as his personal, introspective, and academic habits did not seem to mesh with one of his younger brothers. Ben was only a year or so younger, but as he was still in eighth grade he felt the need to continuously deter his older brother from this monastic state of temporary nirvana he seemed to have reached in the evening. In fact, his father even went as far as to say:

"How would you like your own shower and bathroom?"

Answer: Heck yes!

"How would you like to live on a lake, and have open land all around you?"

Hmmm. "Dad, we live on a lake, the great lake of Michigan, with a beach unparalleled even by our neighbor in Forest on the Bluff."

"Ah, yes, son, but this lake is yours and has sailing and tennis next to it. We may even buy a motorcycle to explore the open country in our backyard."

"Wait, Dad; where is this?"

Mom went silent and looked away.

"It is in Milwaukee."

WTH?

All Galt could think was, "Where is Milwaukee?" And, was this another family-rooted tease that his dad and grandfather had been so good at using to throw the kids off, always with the intent to help them grow. Good healthy teasing that counters what you may have gotten comfortable with, but then allows you to consider other alternatives. Then there was what his father called "kidding on the square," a message in a tease…

So. Back to the dinner table.

Dad: "I have been offered a new role, and promotion in my company's Wisconsin region, and the commute is too far for us to remain in the leafy incubator we call Bluff Lake. It is time for our family, including Mom, brother Ben, brother Wes, brother Dirk, and sister Ada to all load up with Rex, our perfect kidney-colored springer spaniel, and move to the land of yah heh!" Or something like that…

All then, starting with Galt, came to the realization this wasn't another vacation, or tease that the elder men were so good at, but rather a clear call to move. A redo every damn thing he had worked to establish as his out-riggers, as an emerging and aspiring-to-be-perfect son. In one of the most sought-after communities in America. To a place called Milwaukee, or another neighboring community that had another Native American name.

"How far is this, can you get a faster car, an apartment, can't we stay here with Mom till we are done with high school, meaning me, and can't you make this work by getting an apartment there?"

Mom stepped in: "We are a family, and we all go with Dad, and we all will have a wonderful adventure."

We all had moved before; in fact, Galt had attended three kindergar-tens in his younger days, a point of interest as our story evolves and how that "trifecta" had a significant impact on his ability or interest to explore anything past knowing just enough to be ready for the next adventure. More on that story later.

Anger swelled, as he knew that this meant the end of an era. as he had just watched *Lawrence of Arabia*, and had, for the first of many times, watched Peter O'Toole as the famous British map-making officer. The scene that kept coming back to him was with Lawrence and his face-off with his Arab leader, played by Omar Sharif.

It is one of many amazing scenes in this classic film, and one that Galt would draw from throughout his career, in management meetings and one-on-ones; in those dramatic moments in business where the opportu-nity to head for the Higher Ground presents itself.

The setting is WWI, in the Middle East, where Britain is facing Axis (German, Turk) advancements, and a chaotic relationship with the sup-posed many Arab tribes. Lawrence, based on a true-to-life story (always the case with Galt's favorite action films), is a British map expert in the

North African HQ in Cairo. He becomes increasingly frustrated with his limited role, and feels he must aspire for something more. He is ready for that moment to take steps up to his *higher ground*. Based on the depth of his map knowledge, the commanding officer has just assigned him to take an assignment to head deep into the desert and find the leader by default of the many diverse tribes, who are battling the Turks themselves, and report back. That's it, just report back. Being Lawrence, and seeing a seminal opportunity to shift the balance of the war to the rightful Arab tribes, he has now decided to "expand" the scope of his mission on his own. He bonds with one of the Arab's chosen leaders, Sharif Ali (played by Omar Sharif). They have befriended each other over death and strange debates about "what is written and what is not." However, they are beginning to find each other in a position to help their own cause.

He knows the positions of the enemy, and the ground by map only. He does not know the tribal power, other than there is one who controls all, and he knows of the city of Aqaba, a harbor city controlled by Turks, which holds a grip on waterways and logistics for supply to the enemy. An impenetrable stronghold on the sea at the tip of modern Jordan and Israel. It is a lynchpin in the Axis strategy, and a dilemma in that it is impossible to be taken by a traditional "frontal" attack due to the massive guns pointing to sea. Lawrence has spent the last days wandering the desert with his newly adopted aid, an illegitimate young Arab man, who is loyal to Lawrence to the end. We get a glimpse of his inner self, as he, too, was of an illegitimate birth. Lawrence is troubled by the lack of strategy and coordination by the many Arab tribes. Yet there is one leader who has taken a liking to his honesty and insights. He is Prince Feisal, who was to be later proclaimed as the king of the Arabs in 1916. He is of Syrian and Iraqi descent, and is the informal leader whom the British attempt to work with. He speaks to Lawrence of his frustration with his tribal independence, lack of weapons, and frustrating relationship with the British. They do share a common goal, to defeat the Axis allies, the Turks. As he leaves, he shares with Lawrence one final thought after an evening of discussing all the issues…

"We need a miracle, Lawrence."

"We need a miracle!", thinks Galt.

Lawrence takes this miracle challenge to heart. He begins his own self-isolation in the desert, where he has not eaten or drank water for a day. He has spent his time sitting, then walking, on the dunes, in the desert winds. Considering this new relationship with Omar, and how to unite these many factions in a noble cause, one that will provide a platform for the war to achieve a higher ground of freedom for all tribes. Although it is becoming clear at this point, his interest is tilting to the Arab Bedouin's future, and not necessarily that of Britain. He emerges from the desert with his vision to attack Aqaba from the rear, by crossing the desert of Nefud, a place even the tribes believe God has no role in. The prince calls Lawrence crazy. Lawrence then responds that their guns are locked and pointing in only one direction, and thus unable to defend this city from the deadly desert. Lawrence's strategy is also to assume that he is gathering the alliance of the Howeitat, a Bedouin tribe who has a reputation for being killers and plunderers. Offending Omar, Lawrence reminds him that they are great fighters, an argument that he cannot defend against. Auda Abu Tayi, the leader played by Anthony Quinn, is the tip of the sword and all-powerful leader of this tribe. (Through his life, Galt will reflect on the marvel that is Omar, Peter, and Anthony all fighting for the screen.)

In conclusion, the takeaway for our man-child Galt was simply this: Upon sharing the strategy, Omar says, "Impossible to do ...this is madness."

O'Toole says simply, "Aqaba is over there," as he leads Omar out of the tent into the hot sun, pointing across the desert and arid mountains.

O'Toole then says even more profoundly, "It is only a matter of going."

Omar stares and says, "You are mad."

End scene.

Galt loved this scene for three reasons:

1. It has never been done this way, and is counter-intuitive. Not like Galt thinks today at fifteen going on sixteen.

2. Peter O'Toole simplifies the concept of commitment and how to just simply end resistance. As "It is only a matter of going," Galt feels resistance as his primary helper, not his enemy.

3. This campaign, if he can convince Sharif Ali (Omar), will forever bond them and the Arab desire for freedom in their vast, boundaryless lands.

4. His commanding officers in Cairo have no clue what he is cooking up. *Radical.*

This scene is locked into Galt's head as reality hits what his father and mother have just declared to be the next mission for the family. This is how Galt's mind works. The drama of life, the lessons, the alternatives to his regimented existence fascinate him. Perhaps to be used in later life. But at the moment, all he can generate is no way, and tears. First tears in many years. Even summer football with his coach Bartkowski can bring these types of tears. Although much is owed to the coach, as he as well has shown Galt how to make big changes counterintuitive to most, and facilitate incremental change, if not seminal change, concepts that our Galt will come to live, and finds inspirational.

The mission to Milwaukee will prove to be one of the greatest things to ever happen to him, and have profound impacts throughout his adult life. He is to become an addict for what on the outside appears to be random behavior, or just like a bee, moving from one of life's flowers to the next. But this is life, and how he becomes conditioned to enjoy and be challenged by constant shifting change, to the point where he becomes addicted to it.

CHAPTER 2:

How a Nerd Develops and Blossoms, With No Sequence at All...

As a young man in his old home in the Chicago region, Galt has been a baseball card collector, game designer, advanced wargame player (Avalon Hill Stalingrad, Battle of the Bulge, Risk), sandbox master, sometime-athlete, and loyal friend. Red in color, with many freckles, his strawberry blond is his calling card in these early years. He never feels different, never an evil bone, but wants to strive to be as good as he possibly can. Friendship becomes the key as well as creation of that which is inside all. He has a near death experience, and the loss of friends, and family, too, will shape how he handles and reacts to the Milwaukee move as well.

Having attended three different kindergartens, as his father and mother crisscross northern Illinois on their way to their favorite home resting on the bluff over lake Michigan, he has an early lesson in change: If one is so concerned with the change that envelopes one, that person can nearly have a chance to survive it, must use it less to thrive. Something inherited or genetic is inside this Galt that allows him to become very calm during moments of great change, or trauma. It is a trait he will always be fascinated with as his life on earth extends.

It is here "on the Bluff" that he learns the power of friendship, and the amazing joy great trusted friends can bring. These early years of kindergarten to eighth grade in this leafy village also teach him that these beliefs about friendship aren't always easy for others to adopt. No matter how kind or friendly you can be, you will find that others don't always see you or new people in the same light. Instead, they have filters they have developed through life, or due to the unknown around them. Regardless of why, it is a barrier our Galt refuses to let get in the way.

Kindergarten to third grade is a remarkable pace, as all four years seem to blend together, other than the differential of the wonderful teachers he has. Even today, Galt will find that many of the people he meets in his third and last kindergarten are people he will never forget. It is in these three years, in a new home, with his family and amazing neighbors, next to a vast, 200-acre estate of mighty oaks, he learns of adventure and the outdoors, both of which are always experienced with friends. It is also on this dead-end street he learns to love all the seasons that come to the Midwest, building forts in the winter of snow, in the summer of box and wood, in the spring, mini forts in the sandbox, and in the fall, of leaves. Forts are those places where the firstborn of four can find his separate peace. Find himself.

Sports are assigned to him, but he never pursues them. As he is raised in his later grades in a protestant church on Sundays and the related classes, he comes to believe that the three dimensions of our being are how we must see ourselves, those being the mind, body, and spirit.

Thus sports are the tool his parents encouraged him to develop to have a sound body and learn to understand the spirit it requires to be successful, take defeat, and be a teammate. The church family dinner table is where the way is taught for the spirit, with its many good lessons. Finally, the mind is developed through schoolwork. The family unit can be that structure that brings all three together at any one time, allowing him to understand how all are meant to fit together. A triangle he adopts, as a powerful measure of most things in his life. It is there that the Rule of Three first comes to him. He recognizes that these simple three dimensions of thought, communication, and organization of complex topics in simple terms, work for him. Why, he does not know. (Someday, as he grows and progresses to his later stage of thirty-three and a third, he will have the chance to meet and explore this and many other intuitive lessons and paradigms he has adopted, through the friendship he grows with a spiritual guide of sorts. It isn't his giant rabbit, but if he were to share it, he likely would be sent to a child psychologist for help. Her name is only She. He has no idea who She is, or what She is at this stage, but with time all of the love he has felt will come together in this imaginary person. Love he has always given to those around him, that is of the deepest sincerity, but that is then compounded in his experience into their friendship and amazing dynamic. All to come later.)

Galt has grown in his ability to use strategy through games, and as one of his unique abilities. He plays these advanced board war games with kids down the street that are three to four years older than he is. These Avalon simulations of historical campaigns are games that can last up to a week or two, and have many, many variables. He plays to win, he thinks. In the end, his takeaway is that the game's interaction and the outcomes of various scenarios are what matters. This is not the game of Risk we know of or have heard of in an REM song about Andy Kaufman. Although Risk does play a role in his strategy development, it is more as a sport versus a pure rich strategy game. To master Risk is simple if one knows the few criteria needed to put the odds of the dice in your favor. Besides, a game using dice is a game that can't be won by good strategy only. However, dice can help one to learn how to adapt. Monopoly is a great example of a game one can learn to adjust on the fly, with financial accountability due to the throw of the dice.

So with games, some sports with friends, such as wiffle ball and touch football, coupled with a forest, remarkable early elementary teachers, dead-end streets, and great friends and family, our Galt has many, many opportunities to be successful and happy by modern definitions. What he doesn't know is that this life is only the beginning of what is out there for him, beyond even what it has given him. For it is at puberty that he somehow begins to challenge all these amazing gifts he has received, the warm home, family, and hood, none of which prepare him for what is to come at this transition—a transition that lasts for three years.

Learnings:

1. Nothing replaces friendship for growth and happiness.
2. We have an opportunity when young to learn and study the world, in academia, hobbies, sports or faith. All will have an impact later in life, so embrace *whatever it is*.
3. Family matters.

CHAPTER 3:

Puberty *Takes Way Too Long*

By sixth grade, our Galt was a very well-adjusted suburban boy, although his red hair and freckles still made him stand out. But knowing he had a different look to himself, and that self-awareness, brought with it some opportunity to expand his world as well. For it was on the brink of his puberty stage that he had his first encounter with the opposite sex, in a way he could not quite understand, but would never forget. He was only in sixth grade, but a grade locked into his history forever.

Her name was Jordan, and she lived just down the street. Her family was the only family of color in the Village on the Bluff. Her older brother was one of the amazing athletes at the high school; Galt would go to see him on Saturdays. He was also one of the three teens Galt would have as role models for him, including the two across the street from his home. Jordan and Galt had become friends, as they had with her next-door neighbor, Noah. Noah would become Galt's partner through many man-child experiences, and thus introducing a black girl into the mix seemed only natural. Only this time, it was different. She and Galt became fast friends, friends in every sense. Twelve going on thirteen, and suddenly a female friend entered the life recipe, a good friend, always there to talk and walk to school with Noah. But one day, in the spring of sixth grade, on the way home, just outside of her driveway, the friend thing got cloudy.

It was a warm, early spring day, and the flower buds had just begun to show, but more importantly, it still carried the stark look of a dry winter, as the mighty oaks that lined the village in all directions still remained dormant to the eye. Truly not, but dormant to the eye. Guided through puberty, Noah had already run home to his mother's call, and thus this was how Galt found himself, this moment when Jordan decided to tell him she was in love with him, and then grabbed his lower back and pulled him in for one of the most shocking and amazing first experiences of his young life. Her kiss was to not be forgotten in that it was so rich and full. Yet *brand new* to his senses. He didn't know quite what to do, as it seemed to go on further than he imagined a "peck" would go, as the "peck" had been his only understanding of that magical rainbow of kisses. He then, in his awkward, red-haired way, said, "*Thank you!*" and ran off as fast as he could home. He went into the kitchen, a kitchen his mother made so special, and after checking to make sure that all the younger siblings were not in earshot, and only the kidney spaniel Rex's eyes could see, he blurted out to Mom, "Jordan Patron kissed me on the lips Mom, and she wouldn't let me go! It wasn't just a peck, but a long kiss."

Mom gave out a great smile, as she did in those moments of both sad and happy transitions, as her love for all that life could be and brought you was much rooted in our young Galt as well. She then said, "How do you feel about that?"

Galt, of course, did not have a profound answer, but stumbled to, "I kind of liked it, Mom."

She gave him a hug, and said into his ear, "It won't be the last, but your heart and what we have taught you will be there to help as your guide, not *if*, but *when*, something like it happens again."

So it began for Galt the nerd, ball-card collector, sort of a sports guy, and lover of complex board games, in his room another dimension of life came to be. Friend or "What now?" became a dilemma he would wrestle with for a while.

Oddly or sadly, this act was to be the only of its kind with Jordan. Their friendship was never quite the same, and he also had as a result developed another set of lights shining on his outside world. It was not long after that spring that he met one of the great loves of his young life, one that was remarkable and yet never ever came to its full potential for both.

It was a few weeks later that in his sixth-grade homeroom he came strolling to his desk where the S's sat, as the sun broke through the windows. He put his books down, looked up, and saw directly behind him the most amazing pair of blue eyes he had ever seen. In fact, up to this point, Galt had never looked at the color of the eye, but suddenly color mattered.

Her name was Madison, and she had an accent that was full of courage, vibrato, history, and was very different from that of the Village on the Bluff. Her smile was right at him, as he tried to sit down after saying hello quickly and with some high pitch in his voice. Know this, that our poor Galt had yet to see the growth of the carrot hairs of his head in the other regions of his body that one would associate with growing up as a man. But he sure was beginning to feel more action inside, even more than those Saturday mornings in the family room, watching old Flash Gordon movies with Dale Arden or Princess Aura, with loyal Rex by his side, as they both ate Rex's dog cookies. Yep, Galt ate dog cookies with his pet, and he did enjoy them. These Saturdays in that basement family room also had some rich memories of booze and mixers, as well as dips on the bar down there. The piano had stains from drinks, and cigarette ashes in the tray. Slot machine was quiet, as was the huge stereo his father had built, but it was clear that Fridays, Ma and Pa had a wonderful time down there in that finished, all-American basement, with their neighbors and their old past. All while Galt, with his brothers and sister, slept quietly upstairs. But in the instant that he gazed at Madison, that flash to Flash Gordon and those beautiful women was now to be an instant memory, as Madison, from Boston, had now entered into the world of the Village on the Bluff.

At this point in the school year, call it April of 1964, the Beatles had been born, and everybody who was anybody . . . was going steady. Commissioned by the gift of a cheap necklace charm usually purchased from a local variety store in the village. This was not to be a Cracker Jack style, but an odd Buddhist symbol on a chain. Yep; that was a popular item. It was while attending the Beatles' first movie, *Hard Day's Night*, that he decided to make some gesture to her.

So as the days went by, and this feeling of what to do to keep up, but also how and what to do about this replacement for Dale Arden, he suddenly quit trading his baseball cards, and purchased that necklace charm. Held it in his pocket for two days as he was contemplating how all those advanced-for-thirteen-and-up war games had shaped his ability to take strategy theory, and then apply it to the real world of early infatuation, aka . . . love?

So he just decided the best approach was a frontal attack. He waited till the morning lunch break when most kids were able to walk home, and as all returned to mill about in the courtyard of his junior high, he went straight at her. Galt had observed that one of the "Mr. Cools" of the school had also begun to talk to Madison more and more every day. He knew if he didn't strike, all might be lost.

So he did. He went straight up to her when her friends had walked away into the call of the afternoon school bell, and on that glorious April day, said, "Madison, will you go steady with me?"

Her answer came as fast as he had executed his frontal attack, and took him by surprise.

"Yes Galt, I was hoping you would ask."

Galt felt a rush with those words that were unique to that moment, and never have been, or could be duplicated.

He said, "Here is this necklace for you with this Buddhist thing, and it means we are steady, now."

She said, "Thank you," and put it on.

Then Galt, in his greatest moment to date of awkward behavior, ran away into the school...only to find her walking behind him into their desks that were next to each other, for the next two months. It was a great moment for Galt, but also one of the beginnings of a retro tour to being a boy again. He walked her home, maybe once or twice after school, and maybe after that they spoke once again. He had done it, but now retreated to his baseball cards, games, guy friends, and maybe the Beatles songs he now played on his Silvertone Sears record player. But this was not to be the end of the story for the Madison and Galt joint venture. There would be at least three more returns to "going steady," but always with a strange break in the momentum, due to both of their unique quests for life and all it had to offer. More will come later as our Galt adventures away from the nest in later years. But for now, those seventh and eighth grade and freshman first terms are very challenging to our now sprouting pubescent redhead.

Lessons:
1. Love is confusing, very confusing if it is love.
2. It is also remarkable.
3. It brings our differences together and can help us better understand each other.
4. Skin color is irrelevant. But friendship can lead to love.

CHAPTER 4:

Being a Man-Child

As Galt continued to reflect over the next few days after Ma and Pa had shared this big move to a place he had never been, he also reflected on what this place he had been fortunate to live and grow in meant to him. In addition to the love he was introduced to outside the family and friends, he also began to understand that there are different kinds of friends. Remembering there were those who you both want to go to the same objective, and are friends of comfort and ease. Others take you with them on a ride that you would never have experienced. Finally, there are friends that you discover later in life whom you can do both with!

So it began for Galt, as he made great friends with both kind and gentle guys and girls. With the guys, it was a shrinking segment; however, as he approached his last two years in the Village on the Bluff in junior high, clearly this type of friend did not provide the elixir his emerging soul needed. For he was learning that we don't just find those friends who lead us into the places we have never considered venturing, but rather we must want to go inside of our souls, as our restless souls arise and begin to ask that damn question Galt was asking on his fourteenth birthday: *Why am I such a good boy? Am I missing something?*

That wake-up to the other side of his spirit was timed perfectly for his moment when he brought his old friend back into his life. This pal, Noah, had been the kind of friend he would sleep over in their trailer and maybe watch late-night movies on TV and eat Hostess snowballs and drink Nehi black cherry soda. But that was only the beginning with Galt and Noah. There would be generation after generation of connecting again and again, and to a different side, to the wild side of life.

It began when they were having one of those sleepovers in Noah's grandfather's trailer parked next to the house. The evening was coming, and Noah, never the one to miss any opportunity, saw one Saturday a few weeks back the condition of Galt's folks' party rec room, with all the open booze, etc. So, the day before, when they were to have been at band practice, they cut out, knowing Galt's mom was not home, and most certainly not his hard-working, corporate champion dad. Noah was convinced they could take one of those many semi-empty tonic or ginger ale bottles, empty them down the sink in the wet bar, and then cook a recipe from the gods, pouring off just the slightest bit of joy-juice formula for a grand old evening the next night. Bourbon, vodka, tequila, gin, and some ugly liquor was mixed in with only a few ounces of Canada Dry ginger ale. Filled up, they did, the whole thirty-two-ounce bottle with three to four ounces from every bottle of something Galt's folks held dear and served to their Friday night friends. Carefully putting the caps on as they had been found, the liquor bottles were then put back in the exact place. Noah was good, but how he had achieved these skills at such an early age was unclear to Galt. But he went along on this new path with fear and adrenaline pumping.

So it came, Friday night in the trailer with the rabbit-ear TV, and junk food—and oh, yeah—almost thirty-two ounces of what Galt would come to call from later experiences celebrating in a women's private dorm, while the Kohoutek Comet passed over, Wapatuli Punch!

They began that first evening of losing their alcohol virginity, a night that was full of awful tastes, choking outside the trailer, the makings of a stomach lining later on as the bottle approached being half gone. It was to be the first and last time that Galt would drink liquor, puke, and then drink more. It was also a moment when death was probably another twelve to sixteen ounces away at the bottom of the thirty-two-ounce Canada Dry bottle.

Next day was not to be remembered. No clue. He only remembered the evening choking it down and that first step he took out of the trailer. Maybe at best he had made many mistakes, but this time it seemed like a hole had been dug below the trailer door, and it led to hell. He took that step and never found solid ground, and went head-first into his projectiles and of course dirt and weeds that had grown around the old family trailer. It was not a natural experience, or one that was good for the grass, as most certainly the makeup of the Wapatuli and stomach acid was tough fertilizer for the soil and wild grass. All the time Noah was whispering at full volume, "Don't make so much noise; you will wake up my father!" Father Jake was not the one anybody wanted to wake. As he was always respectful of Galt, and appreciated his and Noah's friendship, he was not one to take bad behavior easily. But it was only a matter of minutes and the bouquet of Galt's event found its way into Noah's nostrils, and he was out the door, too. Cheetos, Jays chips, red licorice, Twinkies, and Playboy magazines had no use to either of them from that point on. Fact is, Noah's Mom, an amazing angel herself, offered the breakfast after a knock on the door in the morning, and soon realized after observing the weeds sticking to them, and with faces that neither of them would find fit for anything but being left alone, and hidden from Noah's father.

That fall night, under a full moon, was a coming-out party of sorts for both Noah and Galt. There would be more full-moon events, in most cases due to his recall and connection with that time of the season and what it brought to him. There were so many more with Noah that they may not all be covered in this writing, but here are a few more, just to give a feel for these seminal moments for the development of a man-child, and how damn hard it can be!

It was that same fall; Halloween, and again Galt and Noah took to their usual amazing rounds of candy-gathering in the Village. The Village was a treasure of giving folks, tightly fitted together, and very generous on trick-or-treat night. But as they were now the eighth graders, and in their last year of trick-or-treating, all they did to prepare was:

1. Buy lots of Cranks shaving cream at Albert's pharmacy, as it shoots farther and more accurately than any major brand.
2. Paint their faces.
3. Take numerous toilet paper rolls from both of their homes, and, last but not least,
4. Gathered *eggs*, TP and ran ready and hot.

So this Halloween?

Fall of '65, when the night was cold but clear, and the mighty oaks that lined the Village were stripped of most of their leaves, but not all. (Note: but not all.)

It began with a war with some of the enemies from the other side of the tracks, a tougher gang on the surface, but they did not know of Noah's wisdom in choosing shaving cream weapons. We nailed them from afar, as their Burma shave shot helplessly into the night and grass ahead of us, like an old man's prostate would demand. Clearly a first night's victory, and not one we had any reason to feel bad about. Galt was still being managed by the good boy inside, and from time to time the good boy would rule. This was a win-win event for good and bad. But the night was not over.

Next up was the rational toilet papering of the most sought-after girl by both of them. Noah had his and Galt had his. Both had danced with these wonderful and beautiful girls at the community dances, but both could not compete with the more prepped and ready-to-win guys who had experienced puberty and voice drop faster and more aggressively than both of them. It became clear that they needed to make their mark and show in a pagan method how they commanded the ground of these girls, and that no other man-child need apply. So what did they do? Hell, yes, the toilet papered their big oaks, elms, etc. with white laces of bountiful patterns. Feeling pretty good, but a bit guilty, Galt was laughing and enjoying this with Noah, when he got an inspiration (or had planned it out already . . . he always seemed to be spontaneous but always had something else up his sleeve, like a great rock band concert with two encores . . .). This time it was… a lighter he had. That was not far from the tail of one of the longest and best throws Galt, the little league defensive no-hitter catcher of the year, had winged through Noah's gal's home trees. He was proud of this toss, until Noah did his "flame-meets-TP demonstration'.

BAM! The whole old mighty oak lit up like the Sears Tower in downtown Chicago. Flames crawled up the TP, finding their way through the whole tree and dead leaves. Galt immediately felt his good boy come exploding out and scenarios, a skill he would later use in business, began to emerge in his imagination. Burning a beautiful tree, then the roof, then the house where Noah's wanna-be girlfriend lived, then people, killing them. Shit, this was not good.

All the while Noah stood in awe, saying very calmly to Galt, "Relax, leaves won't burn, and neither will the house." But, "Isn't it cool?" he kept repeating . . . then he slapped me on the back as the flame died, and more lights went on in the house, and said, "Let's get our butts out of here now, and run."

Exhaustion and stress came on as we stopped for a breath in park woods near our little league diamond, the one where both of us had so many healthy and fulfilling athletic experiences as innocents. Noah then said, "Galt, we have one more. then we take our booty of candy and head for the barn."

Galt thought he couldn't get the words out, as he followed Noah to the next crime scene. What on God's green earth could he be considering? The "Good Galt" said go home, and the growing strength of "Dark Galt" said, "Find out, you woosy".

So Galt reached a rational state about halfway to the police station in the park paths, and said, "Where are we going, and to 'consider' doing what?"

Noah just said, "Follow me, Galt, it will be *great.*"

It was only a few steps to the curb across the street from the village police station, where the lights were on this evening, and the cars were parked. Out of his backpack came the fresh eggs. As soon as Galt could figure out what Noah was considering, there were two launched grenades of white eggs in the air, hurtling towards the police station.

SPLAT! as the first egg hit the roof of the cruiser. Slap went to the other egg on the front door. Great throws under most other sporting conditions, but in this case, it was terror to Galt.

Two were not enough for Noah, and he put two into Galt's hands and said, "Your turn, brother."

It was like a switch turned off all Good Galt, and a wild and crazy Galt came out. A Bad Galt who didn't even give due consideration to the loft and just threw to the station and village hall, perfect tosses. As if some smart-ass was trying to steal second off his left-handed pitcher in a little league game last August. BOOM, nailed it, right on the 2nd base bag.

Noah was proud as the first yoke dripped down the door, and the second down the window, but also said, "We better go fast." But it was too late. The police chief, Frankie Night, was standing right behind us. Not the last time we would find him right behind us due to our initiative to become dangerous outlaws in the village of our sheltered childhoods. Frankie had been a bit, if not more than, Galt and Noah in his youth as well. So he came at them with a different approach than most. He called them on it of course, but he asked, as they believed he had not seen their throw. He had come walking back after their tosses from the park, but guessed that we were the culprits, and maybe the kleptos he had heard of that wild and crazy night. He just looked at Noah, and with his army fatigue coat, full of eight more eggs, the officer slapped him on the chest twice and made sure he had crushed each of those yokes into Noah's chest so they dripped down to his pants and underwear. Clearly a guilty plea was the only way out when he asked if they were responsible in a sarcastic way. Both had learned from their good parents that at these moments of truth, truth was always best, confessing to the eggs, but not the tree lighting ceremonies. He confiscated all the candy, telling them they had now used up the one break. He closed by saying he hoped they would come back tomorrow and wash the cruiser, or else. He turned and walked back to the station, and his car and building were covered with dripping egg yolks.

Galt and Noah had just begun this year of glory, compressed into just a fall, winter and spring before the big step to another zip code and town's high school. The one where all the kids of great wealth and size attended. It was either that or prep school. An easy choice for most parents of the Village by the Bluff.

To help better understand this transformation, or temporary state for Galt, we need to head back again, to earlier days, to understand the pillars that had been given to him. Those pillars served to not only stop him from becoming a father, but also to remind him of the value of being kind, and most importantly, that life can be a great adventure, without breaking the law and others' property.

It was the three major events in those years leading up to sixth grade that probably had the biggest impact on his pillar of good human spirit.

The first was that he was fortunate that he had grandparents on his mother's side that lived only an hour's drive away, in the old ring of the great city to the south. As well, not far from them, were also his father's father and sister. Both of them lived together and were like his mother's parents, always available for Galt to come visit and stay the weekend when Mom and Dad went off on one of their glorious adventures, a practice in itself that helped his parents keep their busy life and raising of five kids in balance. It was to be a toss-up as to which of these relatives, his grandparents and aunt, provided the best weekend for a young boy, but the scales may have tipped to his mom's folks. You may ask where the other Grandmother was. More on that and her life in Wyoming later.

His weekends with Grandma and Grandpa were amazing events. These were spent in his grandparents' two-flat, of which the upstairs was empty, ever since his mother and father had moved out when he was three to one of the many spots Galt and his growing sibling crew would live until settling in the Village on the Bluff. The weekends were a foodie's delight, as his grandmother loved to eat out, but also kept sweets at home, and Galt had the breakfasts with his grandfather. A quiet and assuming man, Grandpa was a man of great interest in using his hands to create, love, and always forgive. He was the kindest of souls, and would smoke his Lucky Strikes at their small kitchen table as he shared his Grape Nuts mixed with 40% Bran Flakes with Galt. Asking about school, interests, as he would smother his and Galt's cereal in whole milk. It was always a great day with Grandpa, as then the Cadillac would be warmed up outside. Grandma would sleep in, and they would head out to the car wash down the street, often for the third or fourth wash of the week for Grandpa's pride and joy. A pride and joy he would replace every three years at most. They took many adventures around the Chicago region, to monuments to WWI, museums, and family graves. Those were where his family had settled. This west side of the city provided a tight and loving environment for Galt, as did their small two-flat. Grandpa left him with this one lesson, and one that stays today: "No matter how difficult, or challenging some task or project may appear, there is always a way to get it done, there is always a way". All of it would serve Galt well in his professional career. Grandpa demonstrated his will and philosophy mostly with his hands and mind working together, but also through his patience with his grandmother who had her own history of depression and mental illness.

We would be remiss if we didn't share that his grandmother also taught Galt a lesson to never be forgotten, but maybe not always well practiced: Be reflective of all your experience in life, but strive to never be judgmental. That may have been the Danish heritage she had, connected back to the protestant reformer Kierkegaard, a man who himself only shared his beliefs in hopes others would embrace it, never judging those who stuck to their Catholic faith. Galt had heard these stories from his grandmother over lunch or dinner, and never forgot them.

The second major impact was the time he was also blessed to spend with his dad's father, a man of many secrets, but always at his best when Galt visited. He kept a small bungalow as well on the west hood of Chicago and beyond. There he chose to raise Galt's father and aunt, completely on his own, as Grandma, a native of western Wyoming, had never settled down beyond bearing their two children, and oddly a love for Grandpa that never died. But, she was a wildcat, and believed to be part Native American. Later in life this was to be proven by Galt's use of Heritage.

com, that she was in fact one-quarter Blackfoot Native American, and some French. She had left her husband, Grandpa Warren, and returned to where he had first met her. He had been on a hunting trip with his WWI Marine fellow vets. In those days there was no knowledge of PTSD. He had been decorated to the limit of his chest on his uniform, and served in some of the most challenging and dark battles in France, a marksman whose ability to use his inherited knack for a rifle served him and his country well. His own grandfather had also been a master of guns, but one who made them downtown Chicago, a trade Grandpa chose not to follow. Instead he brought Grandma Magdalene back to Chicago, and chose to provide for his family by driving a bread truck delivery route for almost forty years. She found this dashing Marine vet, with his red hair and big personality, to be quite attractive, and a way for her to escape her ancient and trap-like world of Glasgow and the Missouri breaks. She also may have hurt him in other ways, but still he tried to keep her. She would not rest, and went back to the edge of the northern Rockies. He was now to be a father, provider, and mother to his two young children. He kept his bread route and worked any and all shifts across the vast Chicago region, so as to be able to wake up at one AM, go to the bakery, and run his route till noon. In this way, he was able to be home when the kids got back from school. Galt's father and aunt were a team of sorts, and very close as a result. Thus it was in this condition, with an aging Marine and his aunt of thirty-something still at home with her father, that Galt would also visit for the weekend, as his mother and father would continue to chase their love affair as well.

Grandpa Warren and his Aunt Bernadette were amazing company. He would enjoy his stays with them. But it was a very different experience for growing Galt. Aunt B. would work long hours, while Grandpa, who had retired, was able to spend the day with Galt. Grandpa was disciplined and strict, but also took time to teach and share his basic survival tenets, many of which Galt used the rest of his life. These included:

a. Show up, and give it your best every time. There is no room for anything less, as the light of life can be turned off at any time.

b. Play a sport as long as you can. Grandpa was an avid golfer all the way to his death. He taught Galt's own father to be a good golfer as well as a bowler, and his father had tried with him. Both sports his Grandpa Warren enjoyed. Galt appreciated this much, and later in life, when going through Grandpa W.'s stuff after his death, he found that his green blazer fit Galt like a glove, as his bowling ball fit Galt's hands and his bowling shoes Galt's feet. The clubs also became Galt's, as they too were perfect. Grandpa wasn't all work and tough lessons, however. His favorite was to take Galt to an aging amusement park in the city, with the oddest sideshows of that era, and more importantly the wildest roller coasters—the BOBS, a wooden experience of rattles, speed, wind in the face, and a Galt who could not stop laughing while it traversed across those rickety rails and frames.

Aunt Bernadette was so full of love, and the perfect balance to Grandpa W.'s discipline lessons for Galt. One thing for sure, Galt never visited this home without also taking on his share of chores, a complete contrast to the leisure life of a weekend with his mom's folks a few miles away. Chores and daily regimen is how we give ourselves the best shot at a successful day on earth. This, too, stuck with Galt as his circle of life continued to grow.

The final seminal event that helped shape our Galt and his adoption to manhood during this wild and wooly year of eighth grade was his folks' adventure vacation to the west a place Galt had never seen except through his love of Western series like *The Rifleman* and *Lassie*, and Western movies like *High Noon* and *Shane*.

His father was able to take almost two weeks off for a glorious trip in the family's Ford Country Squire; the beauty of a car, with white paint, wood siding, and red leather interior. Room for him and his brother Ben in the back seat, and his baby sister Ada on the way-back (Wes and Dirk are yet to be brought into this amazing crew). Luggage strapped to the roof, they departed in early August 1963, with many short-term objectives, but one primary goal: to see what this 1963 World's Fair in Seattle was all about. The journey meant a full hot day with no AC across the farmlands of the Midwest, to a very cool hotel with a swimming pool somewhere in western Iowa. The first trip down a slide into the water was the takeaway here, one he would strive to enjoy in even larger surroundings. The bigger the slide the more exhilarating it would be for Galt. Thanks to Grandpa Warren, this was a piece of cake, to slide down three turns into an Iowa pool. But this was only the beginning. The ride was to include the following:

a. **Crossing the prairies in a Ford Conestoga.** Rapid City, Badlands, Black Hills, and the remarkable Mount Rushmore—a place that would remain one of Galt's favorite places to visit—along with the short stop off the highway to Devil's Tower.

b. **Into the high ground for the first time:** Following the map, the family then ventured to Yellowstone for all the highlights there, then took a hard turn north, to find the missing Grandma Magdalene in a lost valley on the Montana/Idaho border, where she had chosen to hide out for the next thirty-five years. Darby, Montana was a truly amazing place, as was this beautiful woman who, as old as she was, looked to be almost perfect. She was to Galt as kind and warm as he could imagine. Explanation of the circumstances of her departure had never been completely shared by his father, but he knew this was not normal for her to be here. However, our eleven-year-old Galt knew then that all could be forgiven by the next generation, who may not have the scares; and she desired the same. Galt's first time into hot springs of natural flow, and hiking around the remnants of major earthquakes, was a humbling and opening experience for our young Siddhartha. He felt home here, a warmth of embrace from the powerful vistas that would forever haunt him. There was no doubt his small share of the Blackfoot spirit within his soul. All he knew was this place of the West was an endless space of exploration and beauty.

c. **To the Emerald City:** The journey was a bit sad, as leaving this newfound Grandmother was not easy, but truly his father had found some peace for the balance of the trip.

The desert the family had never thought of or could have imagined in central Washington was never forgotten by any of them. This massive heat plain, before climbing over the splendor of the Cascades down into the "Emerald City" and the Pacific Ocean, was so damn hot that Galt and his siblings were miserable. Creating some angst in the car, by rolling down the windows to allow the 100-degree hot furnace to blow in the wagon, was the only option. His father was hell-bent on getting to Seattle and the wonders of the world fair. Lesson: this was none.

d. **The Needle:** Nothing before or since would reproduce the feeling of the Space Needle for Galt. Although later in life he would follow the elevator and stairs to the top of the Eiffel Tower, if anything the Needle was a first-born to that wonder of the world. The ocean, the seafood, which Galt had never enjoyed to this point, suddenly exploded in his mouth with unique flavors and texture, a lesson he took to the rest of the world: Not only embrace what the obvious is in the places you travel, but also the food they offer to you, for it is a catalyst to the culture.

California, Here We Come:

The Pacific Coast highway, the gigantic trees they drove through, as well as the art and vibe of San Francisco, dug deep into the Galt memory banks. This northern half of Cali also had that amazing feel of home or welcome to his soul, as had Montana and his grandparents' two-flat. All were places about which he would later in life say, "I feel I have lived here, and could again." It was his way to define this feeling he would have from these spots on the planet. San Fran, even in the fog, was special.

Contrasted so were the southern coast and towns such as Pismo. Where his father—and Lord knows how he knew to do this without the internet—pulled off Highway 1, drove down a sandy and long grass maze to a beach and waves that Galt had never seen, even on the sacred lake Michigan. It was the Pismo, and it was a place where a long-haired blond guy, suddenly maybe a hero to our young Galt, took a skinny longboard off into the surf and rode like the best downhill ski run back in the Midwest. But this was blue salt water, and the surfers were in swimsuits, with smiles on their faces as they rode in and out. Who were these people and what was this place? He did not understand, but the word Pismo seemed like the best way to file it.

The natural gateway to the fantasy of southern California, Pismo was no reflection of what was to follow. Hollywood, the back lots of the production companies, Disneyland! Knotts Berry Farm, among others. Waking up to San Fran fog/smog, and watching what we thought would be an awful day turn into beauty as the sun burned it off. Acting caught our young Galt's eye too, as he wondered if this "work" could be actually just that, to see his TV fantasy unwind with stage settings and live humans was a bit concerning, but also a lesson, that *what you see may not be what it is.*

Across another blazing desert they plowed, with Ma and Pa in the front. The trusty Ford Squire roared through it, as Ma kept telling us how wonderful and historic this place was (not), but then out of nowhere came these lights; this place is named after meadows?

Las Vegas

The original strip was all there was, but it was plenty. Galt was asked to attend to his two younger siblings outside on the street corner, as Ma and Pa ventured into the Golden Nugget to play games. Galt accepted this assignment with pride and great attention to detail. It was a good duty and he felt a bit grown up as the older brother, maybe for the first time. But his good fortune on this gigantic loop of a family vacation was to have another cool moment that next morning. Eating breakfast after sleeping in a two-bed strip motel in Vegas, the diner had a silver dollar machine by the door. Galt felt the stir of the wild inside as he asked his dad if he could try just once. Pop looked to the old chef and owner behind the grille and counter to see if it was ok. He said, "You *bet,* and good luck, Buckaroo."

Because at this point, Galt, his brother Ben, and little sister had been awarded various cowboy wear, be it hats, shirts, boots from Ma and Pa's winnings. Looking like an aspiring rodeo buck, young Galt swaggered up to the dollar machine with one silver coin in his hand. Pointing to the slot, he somehow felt this would be his only shot, so off it went, and a good tug down too. Click-click-click-click…all four cherries jumped onto the screen as the machine began to truly rattle, dropping silver like hail over Iowa in April. Gigantic silver coins, so many he couldn't count, poured into the tray. The chef just started laughing and saying he wanted to take Galt downtown with him. Galt walked away with $100 in silver that day. Dad took most, but explained to him that this was his return for loaning him the money, that the bank will always get its share, but the profits are yours. But don't forget Galt, that this was only luck, not earned. So that lesson Galt took away too.

The Lands of Enchantment

At this point a road rash was setting in Galt's body, and mind. Soul was fatigued, but still could gorge on more of this place called the American Southwest. All were feeling the time to head home was near. But Pop wasn't done. He had a deadline to return to his corporate job, suit and pressed shirt and tie, that coming Monday, and it was Friday. Yet that did not deter the family. They hit the Grand Canyon, and to this day Galt still can't fathom how it happened, and the time frames for it. Then onward to Albuquerque, to visit an adobe home on a shady street. A mystery, as Mom sat in the car as Dad went into the home and spent a half hour, then came out with some level of peace again on his face, as he had after he left Grandma Mag's back in Montana. What was this place of adobe and heat, with odd visits, and seemingly far from everywhere?

Years later, speculation was that it was either a distant cousin, a stepsister, or an old lover. Mom would never say, and her not going in with him just made it even weirder. The family visited the Navajo, the towers of Monument Valley, the village shops, and the home of the Dina people. This hit Galt hard; their story was so sad, and yet they held onto this pride that they seemed to have some connection to their land that European descendants would never know. He felt he needed to be here, and as he walked out, a voice spoke to him. It was a young woman's voice with a Dina accent. SHE was only to say one thing: *Do not be afraid, Galt, you and I will meet again, and someday you will return back here for good reason.* He would never forget this moment, overlooking the Monuments.

The family hit the panhandle and Oklahoma reservations...

...like a jet stream burning all the way to Missouri and a small town, the last stop for the push back to the Village on the Bluff. The country was reminiscent of the Midwest, but also had an odd western feel to it. Galt had begun to have a sense of the dry west and the moist central nation, but this was a hybrid. As they toured Westminster College, Pop was in charge. They learned this was where he had attended flight school during the final days of WWII. In his way, he had decided to make his highly-decorated father, Grandpa Warren, proud, leaving the day after his high school graduation, and enlisting into the naval fighter flight program. He had done well, they were told, till a fistfight broke out in the dorm. Galt's dad jumped in to try and break it up to save all from being rusted from the elite program, and was sent back to boot camp. Unfortunately, and to Grandpa Warren's deep disappointment, Pop and all were thrown out of the program. Third man in, peacemaker, it didn't matter, and he was out.

Galt took another lesson away here on this sojourn. We can fail, and it can happen even as we believe we are doing our best, but it is not, "Did we fail?" It is what we decided to do after that matters. Galt felt a bit confused by his Dad's teachings here, but with time it would make more sense to him, as his warm and cuddly journey in life would see failure of this magnitude, and perhaps more. But this lesson was filed "unknown" to him at the time, to be retrieved in darker days that would come.

So it is with these three life-changing experiences we begin to better understand what it is inside of Galt that pulled him to the "try it, fail, *do your best and explore*" approach, all tearing at him in different directions in that year of eighth grade and the year of being a man-child manifested itself the most.

The nerd continued to blossom with no sequence at all. Random, or just life? Probably both. We all need to beware of the tyranny of "either/or."

When they drove into the driveway, he felt that his home was going to be forever for the first time. Away from the terrorist and never boring times with Noah, Galt found himself drawn also to his street pals, the guys who grew up with him on his dead-end road, the road that faced straight into the eyes of a 200-acre gigantic oak forest. This was a rarity for a suburban region, and buttressed by the estate called "Tall Oaks," that was built to resemble an English fortress in the countryside, by a second-generation son of a turn-of-the-century media baron. Galt was to have many great adventures in those woods and in that house in these final years of phase one of "man-child," adding to the softer and more intellectual side of life. Both dead-end street pals were alike in many ways, and yet also different. Anthony was one of seven kids from the neighbors across the street. He was a gentle soul, and also enjoyed much of the games, arts, and music that his parents also encouraged Galt to appreciate. Both actually went to private art classes together, and shared in their progress. Both enjoyed the woods and the many strange adventures it brought them. The other pal was William Wallace, a new move-in at seventh grade, and a bit of Noah was in his soul, as well as a kindness and standard of good behavior, taught to him by his thirty-five-year veteran, Marine major father, who had been transferred to the military operation to the north of Galt's hometown. Both William and Anthony formed a nice triangle with Galt. Peace and adventure, but more constructive were their actions. Skate boards made from scratch on tracks built on the twenty-percent-slope road they lived on was one of their greatest thrills. That hill was unusual for this ridge on Lake Michigan. In fact, it was the highest ground in the county, and this sidewalk and street down to the forest was the best track for skateboarding any kid could desire. They were always modifying the boards to be wider, smaller, faster, and of course painted and decaled as they felt each must be cooler than the next. They played baseball, which was also the time when all four would come together. They, too, were friends with Noah, but not to the extreme of friendship bonds that Galt and Noah would experience and some of which was described prior. Clearly they knew to walk away, and also didn't quite understand why Galt had this "wonderlust" in him as well to meet the Noah challenges and advance into that place of wild and crazy.

Galt, William, and Anthony were at their best when they were listening, talking, and playing music. All three were in the junior high band, but all three also found great joy in the new forms of rock-and-roll that were surfacing from the blues, folk, jazz, and country of the late 50s and 60s. Galt played the trumpet, while Anthony played the drums. William had a passion for his violin, but also could let it rip for a thirteen-year-old on his older brother's Fender electric guitar. Music brought so much variety and respect for all forms into their lives, from Herb Alpert playing a "Taste of Honey" by the Beatles, to the Ventures, Jan & Dean, and Safaris, with their California surfing dreaming tunes. Attendance for all three with Anthony's older brothers and sisters at the local college for an Association concert was a huge event for Galt. Never before had he experienced this big live scene that a concert can bring. He had attended the symphony and opera in the city with his band field trips, but never this rock-and-roll concert scene til that Friday night in June in the old hockey rink at the college. "Along Comes Mary," "Cherish," "Windy" . . . he found himself still playing them all and singing them for years to come, bringing out his vinyl of their greatest hits even in his last third of life. This was music. Chorus, strings, electric guitars, percussion, and horns. Could there be any better form of music? Well, along came Blood Sweat and Tears, God Bless the Child, Chicago Transit Authority. . . Only the beginning; Electric Flags' "Killing," Weather Report and their classic, "Pursuit of the Women With the Feathered Hat," and even Sturgill Simpson, "Call to Arms" performance on Saturday Night Live, where country, horns, rock, blues, and even funk is blended to be one of the most powerful live performances on a TV stage ever. It would never end for Galt, this love of all types of music and especially when the best spices from the music drawer were assembled into beautiful sound and also life-guiding lyrics.

It is important to note that Galt as a student, striving to fill that third dimension of his protestant triangle of Mind, along with Body and Soul, was an exceptional student at an early age, always inhaling lessons and various disciplines as was shared with him in the early years of kindergarten through sixth grade. But it was the beginning of the slide into "Why Am I Doing This?" syndrome in seventh grade, and that syndrome, "Clearly there is no reason for doing school work well," in eighth grade, that helps us understand that all three wheels were coming loose for our man-child. He would find himself in these moments of doubt and fear of his path.

His pals Anthony and William couldn't understand the dichotomy of Galt. But they also appreciated how the three found this love of music, art and the woods to be their time away from the discipline and love of family, and the exploration of their softer sides. Galt truly was lucky among his friends in these years. But the days of growth to be ready for high school that fall, and a class in typing (wow, that was critical . . . seriously), were to have a few more moments of great risk and terror, but also lessons with Noah. Noah, his dark archangel, led him into the grips of the Irish Twins.

The Consequences Are Finally Understood

The Irish Twins were two fellow eighth-graders, who could have been brothers in how they anticipated, looked like, broke rules and pushed the envelope with each other. Pat O'Brien and Sean Flanagan, yep. Both as American as could be imagined, but both with names from the depths of the Emerald Isle. Both brought to Noah a challenge even he had not imagined, but he also found to be an attraction, for their rejection of almost every rule Galt had been taught to respect. Noah could also guide Galt into these dark places, hoping maybe he could help stop the journey for both, as they ascended into the darkness of youth. Both Pat and Sean were built and looked like they were eighteen, with facial hair, deep voices, and origins not known. For if they had been raised in the Village by the Bluff, they would not have acquired the unique sets of skills that should not be tested unless you are ready for the Consequences.

The nectar was made up of a recipe for the last month of junior high, with elements of beer, guns, skipping class, girls that were advanced beyond Galt and Noah, and of course Chief Frankie Knight. These next few pages are not to be considered more of that emerging teens, hormone-driven wildness only, as they serve as the last dance with the devil for a number of years. So no fear, as Galt will grow to what most would define as a good young man, for a while.

What were these adventures with the Irish twins? Well, two will be shared here and how Galt played into them with Noah, as they blend together. The Advanced Girls part we shall leave for the imagination, but in summary it was all new and shocking to Galt how aggressive they were with all of their and his parts. But now Noah was always ahead of him on these first steps into the physical world. Clearly he knew of these desires, as his own body suddenly changed rapidly, and the demands that go with that were becoming almost overwhelming to deal with—a problem Galt would have for most, if not all of his life. Shit, who knows why, be it a blessing or a curse. He did know this; love was not part of these meetings behind an abandoned garage or in the park woods by the creek.

Adventure One and Two, Irish Twins

Having skills that Galt and Noah did not, these two almost took over their operation of wild and wooly adventures. Noah had no more new ideas, as the Twins brought it all. First it was the guns.

BB rifles were quite popular in those days and as such, target practice in the woods against an old oak or at cans was the norm for Galt and Noah, until the twins said one sunny day, just before eighth-grade graduation, "Let's go hunting. Shoot something that moves, not just a stand-alone target." Noah said, "Cool," and, "Let's meet them after school and see what they are talking about, Galt."

The rendezvous was in a ditch not far from home, along the railroad tracks that carried commuters and freight through their little community from Wisconsin to the north to Chicago. It was about four o'clock on a weekday that the four of them settled down into their "blind" and began to wait patiently for the command from Flanagan. Even O'Brien followed Sean in these moments of truth. Fear gripped Galt, as he just wanted to run, and all Noah could say was, "Let's hang in there, we won't do anything to hurt anybody, just BB guns and some new fun."

Along came the freight train, almost a hundred cars long. The Twins took aim with their Crossman air-powered BB pellet combos, much more powerful than Galt and Noah's pump BB Winchester lookalike. POP POP POP POP, BING BING BING BING—the triggers were pulled and the amazing sound of the pellets hitting the sides of boxcars rang out. Wow, moving targets, and no harm, no foul!

So all four then proceeded to pick a car coming at fast speeds and attempted to nail the doors, cheering and commending each other as their marksmanship improved. Galt and Noah had unloaded all their ammo, as had Patrick O'Brien. But Sean Flanagan had not. In retrospect, he clearly knew what he was to achieve on this day, which Patrick, and for sure the virgin riflemen Galt and Noah, had not anticipated.

The caboose came tumbling down the track, and out the back steps a gentle railroad man waved at the boys, even after he saw our BB rifles, clearly not upset with what he may have seen before on his boxcars. But Flanagan, of loose screws, and who knows why to this day, unloaded his BB rifle at the windows on the caboose. The caboose man quickly ran inside, as Flanagan let another round of BBs go at the back steps and rail where he had stood. Then there was only the sound of the distant rattle of wheels on tracks as it disappeared southbound. O'Brien swore at Flanagan, calling him a "stupid son of bitch," saying, "You went too far this time, a-hole!" Words Galt had not heard. Maybe from his grandfather as he would yell at bad drivers on the road. They two yelled back and forth as Flanagan was pumped up and proud of his new level of man-child terrorism, filling his system with adrenaline. These guys should have been a linebacker or in a juvenile home, thought Galt.

Galt was terrified, and almost in tears; this one guy had turned a new risky adventure into a very bad act of one human on another. Be it BB guns or not, glass was shattered and who knows what else had happened. Noah, always knowing when even madness had passed the line or limit, screamed, "Let's get out of here!" O'Brien just saw them run for the woods away from the tracks and the highway not far on the other side of the rail. He and Kelly were not to be seen, ever again.

Noah knew they must get home and hide their rifles. They stayed in a safe place in the woods, sneaking through ditches and along a road to be able to cross to their street.

Noah shouted to Galt, "Get down! It's a police car!" Both had spotted it cruising up the road from the viaduct below the rail and up the hill. Both crouched silently for what seemed to be an hour (most likely five minutes), and then surfaced to spring across the state highway, thinking of home and dinner and shelter from the madness. They knew, though, this bad act would stay with them in the center of guilt.

As they stepped out of the ditch hideout to cross the street, there he was: Chief Knight (one of three officers for the sleepy, leafy hamlet), waiting next to his squad car. "Hello, boys, what have we been up to?" It didn't take long, as they sat in the back of his cruiser and were taken home to their folks, to admit to him in that short two-block drive that they had been there, and did partake in boxcar pinging, but not in the final act of destruction. They had no value at this moment of being identified as a squealer or the implication of Flanagan's wrath as they did tell all, which they did in a two-part harmony. Noah was as forthcoming, if not more so, than Galt, with details on who, what, where, when, and how many shots were fired at the caboose. The chief knew of all of it, and was very appreciative of our candor on the way home to a very bad meal that evening. They were to catch hell from their old-school, WWII-vet fathers, which both had become used to, but never in a violent way. Instead it was through some very loud lectures laced with profanity and shame for us, as well as a complete lock-down on our free time until and after graduation; until they felt it was time to let us become outlaws again.

The penalty was reduced due to the boys' confessions. Their confirmed Methodist values held no limits to how far Galt and Noah were to tell of all the details to get the minimum we could. They were escorted to the police station right after school the next day with their mothers. Both of them feared the handcuffs and juvenile pen with Flanagan and O'Brien. Oddly, it was that moment, for a flash, that Galt could only think of Patrick O'Brien. A good soul, but with some very bad intentions, led by his nose by Flanagan. He had no such feelings for the wild and crazy Flanagan, but would always wonder why he was so extreme in his desire for fun and destruction being laced together.

The penalty was to write a 500-page paper on the importance of railroads in America. There were no spelling errors, and it was neatly typed up and delivered to the chief in three days.

The summer was chewing its way through their souls and their fellow students in those last two weeks of glory in the Village by the Bluff.

Flanagan did wind up in juvenile jail and never returned. His folks moved away again; this was his fifth home in the last seven years. O'Brien was suspended, and had to attend a summer program for juvenile behavior, and ultimately was accepted as a junior high graduate, one year after his former classmates graduated, with the humiliation of having to maybe go back again for eighth grade. He also was able to attend high school, and was a changed Man-child after that. A relationship we were able to have was of friendship, though distant, but his good would come forth and he was respected by many, the guy you didn't mess with in high school, and a champion wrestler!

This was to be part A of the last great madness and darkness of man-child growth in eighth grade.

As Galt came back to school from lunch at home, just a few days later from the great train shooting, one of the peripheral players in the Twins' former gang, a tall, lanky new man moved into the Village, named Johnny Van Wagner. Six feet, deep voice, and long-armed, but damn skinny, but always pushing and trying to make an impression to learn the inside membership to the Twins crew of terror. It was on his way back to school around 12:45 that last week of junior high that Galt saw a large group of both friends, and some of the Twins' remnant crew. It was on the football field/baseball outfield/track/all-purpose lawn, across the street from the school that this very large group of man-child boys and young women were gathered. Talking and pointing as Galt approached, Noah ran up to Galt and gave him a warning.

"Johnny Van is looking for you, Galt! He wants to teach you a lesson for being a snitch. He has also said after he finishes with you, he is coming after me, for a beat-down as well." Galt, who stood about 5'6' at this stage, and about six inches short of where he would grow to next year, with about 140 pounds packed on him—some muscle, but mostly Mom's great cooking. Noah was of the same height, but was closer to 115, and thus of no similar girth. Noah said he would help and we would take them on together, "John Van or any other comers." , as Noah was loyal to the end.

Galt suddenly felt himself growing up with a massive injection of adult wisdom, courage, and clarity. Never having been in anything other than a pushing match at Boy Scouts or in a football game against St. Mary's eight-man team, he never had leveled a punch. The only exception for those many times with his little brother Ben, trying to stop him from attacking him on so many fronts. But with Ben, all it took was a couple of punches to the body, and he would stop, and cry to Mom, despite being the root cause for the attack. More often than not Galt became good at holding his little brother, less than fourteen months younger, but as tall, with his mighty girth in those days. (Note: In case we forget, Galt will grow to six feet and weigh exactly the same when he reaches summer camp for football his sophomore year.) But this day, it was this ball of red and freckled dough on that field, as he faced that army of both friends, neutrals, and enemies.

The clarity he felt was to be a trait he would find under extreme threat and stress many, many more times over his life on earth. Somehow through death of loved ones, major car accidents, work crises, or just sports-intensive situations, he saw all for what it was and became calm. This would manifest itself in the workplace when the BS began to fly, and/or under stress and the potential for two parties to play hardball. He would use this to become a master facilitator in those later years, but also for calm and help to family and friends in their times of major trauma and life stress. It was a skill meant for others, as he rarely called upon it, until he found his spirit many years later.

So he walked, like many of his western movie heroes, into the center of what was becoming a circle of two dozen people, all of his eighth-grade class, ten yards in diameter. There was Johnny Van Wagner standing in the middle. All six feet of stick as he stood and began to challenge Galt with words of "Mother F-ing snitch," "Teach you a lesson as I kick your ass all over this field!"

Some cheered, others looked on in horror. His two pals Anthony and William also looked on, and could only stare at Galt, and were speechless. William, however, had a look; *I am here to help when you need it, Galt.* Noah took one last look at Galt as he entered the circle, and Galt gave him a pat on the back, and just said, "Noah, he is wrong, and we will make this right today," and walked up to the taunts of Johnny.

Galt told him to back down, or he would come out with whatever he had learned from his dad's punching lessons. Much of it from the Marine grandpa's training, or the new rush he now felt building inside his puberty, exploding body and soul. Clearly this was an energy and force he had never felt. Johnny wouldn't back down and let him go. He began to shove Galt, then take a cut at him that Galt had the sense to duck. Then Van Wagner made a big mistake. He took a second follow up, as Galt stared at him in disbelief, and landed one on Galt's nose. A nose that would become a push button to a fury, to be experienced a few more times in life, and yet impossible to describe as to how or why it is connected to strength and adrenaline. It ignited Galt, and then it rained punches from him all over Johnny's body and face. Johnny had no idea what was coming at him with all that speed and flaying. Galt was relentless in his attack. Head, body, shoulders, but never below the belt.

Johnny was staggering and bleeding in a few places as he landed a few on Galt's back and ears, as Galt just kept low and inside, pounding in a sequence of body and then jaw.

It was then that the other fully physically mature man-child who had been to this point part of the collapsing gang of the Irish Twins stepped in and grabbed Galt off him as he collapsed to the ground, and Galt just jumped and kept coming at him. Both were pulled apart, and Noah stepped in to grab Galt and the other bums who were saving Johnny. Noah said, "Let's get the F out of here, we are done here," dusted Galt off and began to walk with him, Anthony, and William (a gang of friends unto themselves) to the bell ringing for afternoon classes in those closing days of junior high. Van didn't make it to those last days of school, but did go to graduation, and never spoke to Galt again. Even the girls that Galt enjoyed dancing with at the mixers were in his corner, commending him for how he took it to the bully crew, in these last days before breaking up into other peer groups. The fact that they would now talk to him would remain a mystery.

Galt never felt better, even though his head was killing him, and despite his even greater surprise at how his knuckle hurt. He had no idea how much of a toll head-pounding took on your hands. Sweaty, shirt buttons ripped, he marched into Mrs. Harper's eighth-grade English class, and received from the grand dame of the school teachers a wink, smile, and a pat on the back, and the instruction to go to the bathroom and get cleaned up. It became known that more than one teacher watched from their widows across the field that early afternoon at 12:45 on an early June day. She was to be the last in a long line of amazing female teachers in nine years in the Village by the Bluff elementary school. Each unique, but each sharing also in that passion and joy of helping young minds to shape their own futures with the tools of knowledge. To them he owed much. Galt had not realized the view the school staff had from across the street.

It was a grand moment and beyond his later reflections in his experiences of those amazing transition years to puberty; he now became focused on a mission to be as Galahad had been in *Once and Future King*, a freshman book in high school, that Galt would find to be amazing in its character and the value of great human effort and faults, but also in its amazing symbolism for the war in Europe when it was written. Those others we will read about in the next chapter are to have huge influences in these next two years, as our Galt grew into a very focused student athlete, and celebrates youth, until we return to that day we began with, at the dinner table that evening in April of his sixteenth year on the planet, when he learned the land to the north with Native American names was to be his new home. When he learned he was to be torn from the place he had paid amazing dues and gained friendship, love and lessons, and plunged into a whole new world. But for now, the best possible summation of the two years in the best high school in the state for a random soul to become perfect.

Lessons Every Time with the Prayer!

More on Friendship
1. There are friends who decide to go where you both want to go, and provide kindness and comfort;
2. Friends are those who take you to places you would never have ventured without their "help;"
3. Friends are *and/also*; they do both, Wild and Refined, and often you cannot find them or appreciate them till later in life. But that can be cool, too;
4. Someone who wants the best for you, is best for your commitment, is a friend.
5. Virgin voyages launched under full moons will repeat themselves in a graduated style over their lifetime.

CHAPTER 5:

A Man Child Begins to Find His Own Galahad

Here comes high school, an awakening, and not an easy one. Puberty blossoms, as does the fire for knowledge, and a taste of actually being an adult, more often than not. Galt crosses over the "Fifty %" line of being a teenager.

Some reflection before we advance into this significant period of transformation of our Galt. This reflection is on the faith-based dimension of life, and how it has set him up for finding his new mission. For it is with his experience of faith, he begins to respect those who came before him, who were driven by singular faith and pureness of heart. It's as T. H. White, who wrote in his famous novel about the tales of King Richard, Lancelot, and Guinevere in the *The Once and Future King*. There is also a knight who is not well liked by many of his knights, as he is truly perfect, to the point of being in-human. This character is Galahad, a character that Galt reads of in his freshman English class at his new high school. He begins to combine these perfect behaviors and his learnings from his faith training to be an imagined role model. It is Galahad who others refer to as "having a strength of ten, because his heart is pure."

A purpose is defined by Galt over that first year, woven with his background as a Lutheran baptized and Methodist confirmed youth. While in his confirmation class, a field trip was taken to a neighboring community to the south. Hyde Park, a beautiful community much like his Village on the Bluff, but a community that was as Jewish as his was Christian, with a tilt to protestant reformation. The bar mitzvah, the coming-of-age ritual for boys, was seen as a celebration worthy of any young man, one that seemed perfect, as it clearly defined a line of demarcation for a thirteen-year-old to manhood. It is a demarcation coupled with his understanding of Christ, and the readings of T.H. White, that has now settled into his spirit. This acceptance creates a harmony of sorts, and a peace that begins to surround his state of confusion and high beta as a man-child. So with this background, we now enter into that time for Galt where he moved from a child being greater than fifty percent of his spirit and behavior to a daily shrinking percentage, as manhood fills the cup with well over fifty percent. This growth of maturity is in perfect harmony with the shrinkage of the boy-child, and its share of his body, mind, and spirit.

That summer before his first day, his mom came to him and didn't ask, she told him. Galt was unclear why, but his mother insisted he attend a summer school program at the new high school, "Forest Prep." He was to take typing that summer at the Big School, a school that had been an image of where the cool older kids go. The ones he had come to admire as a grade schooler, be they neighboring girls who mentored him, or the amazing athletes he watched playing Saturday football games, winning, winning and more winning. Galt began to like this winning thing a lot. It seemed they never lost, nor did the girls who were his babysitters for years, and now to be his ride to Forest Prep every morning. The school had the look of an eastern university, with a front entrance that was all preparatory school, but public, in the neighboring community of Forest on the Bluff, a community that was about three times larger than Village on the Bluff, but also had significant trappings of old and new wealth. His tiny village was not of this nature. Upper income for sure, but not of this wealth on display. In later years, Galt learned that the Village on the Bluff, actually, in their smaller homes and understated lifestyles, had a higher net worth per household than did the community of Forest, with its monster homes, cars, and stores. Perhaps also a Higher Ground to live upon? This public school was one of the best one could attend in his home state, and the nation. So although large and his graduation class was only to make up only twenty-five of the new freshman class, he desperately wanted to explore this world and see what it was, along with the seventy-five percent he had never met before.

It was now twenty-two months away from that dinner table meeting of the family, where his dad had told all about Milwaukee or bust journey. It was to be another brief stay for Galt in academia, a pattern that began with his attendance in four kindergartens almost nine years ago. Other than for a few military brats, this experience of fifteen different schools over his twenty years of formal education was unusual, and would manifest itself again and again in his professional career. The number of buildings, jobs, challenges, and business cards would also cover thirty-six years and twenty-four "jobs" in twenty-eight different buildings and desks. Yep.

Mom felt that this summer-school typing class would have two benefits for him:

1. He would gain a lifetime skill that would serve him well in creating and placing his own words and thoughts on paper, be it for school, work, or the arts.

2. He would have the experience of getting a feel for the big school of Forest Prep, with seven times the number of students his junior high had.

With that many students, all Galt could imagine was that any fisticuffs he might be forced into would draw a crowd as big as the varsity football game. To date, that had been Galt's largest audience. He set his mind to no fights, as the large crowd with eyes glaring at him was not an image he wanted again, although the moment he experienced that day was to never be forgotten, as it was one he felt proud of for his calm and collected nature, as well as for doing or saying what was right for a very mercurial situation.

Summer school passed very fast, and he felt a confidence-building about his short bike commute to the school, and his ability to begin to type fifty-plus words a minute with less than three errors, his first exposure to minimum standards. He also was able to put some money away, as this was to be his second summer of hauling golf bags and guiding very wealthy members over their third-generation membership elite country club course. Two bags on the shoulders for very wealthy people, with names of great Chicago companies. They spoke as if they were from England, but were born of Lake Forest, and in one case, a spouse was Russian and claimed she had been one of the last Romanoff cousins before the great revolution. She couldn't have been kinder, or more on the ball than her much older husband, and the second generation of wealthy third son. This experience of brushing with great names meant very little to Galt. He saw all as just adults, some with kindness and some who were assholes. But all were just people. As they were. The name, title, or wealth certainly didn't seem to differentiate them from other adults he had met. So wealth may not be one of the keys to this puzzle of life and manhood.

There was a short break from golf, and a week or so of vacation with the family at his grandparents' favorite lodge in central Wisconsin. Cabins, dining halls, pools. Ping-pong on concrete tables, shuffleboard, and Native American cultural experiences at night. They grabbed another tendon from Galt, one he didn't quite understand, but later would learn that his genetic code was to be somewhere between five and ten percent Native American. There was the Black Foot or Nez Perce history his Grandmother had told him of. One she was never clear on herself. Just that both might be in her and thus him.

That fuzzy fact, along with his red color, made for an interesting combo in the gene pool of our species.

Upon return from the vacation, the true making of the man-child to a young man began, with the third dimension of intense development of the protestant triangle, the body. HIs first football summer day camp was to start the next day. This day he would venture down into the smell of the locker room, and with those who were beasts of great facial hair, and deep loud voices, from seniors to slow developing freshmen, as he was. Being fitted for mouthpieces, to not lose all that expensive dental work, as well as for those practice pads, jerseys, and pants with slots for pads, all that stuff some other pudgy 5'6" kid had worn many, many more times before Galt was handed his new seat suit. Terror, or fun? Didn't seem like this was going to be fun at all. His father kept saying, "It is one of the greatest moments you will experience in your youth." Sure was a lot different than baseball practice and just getting a hat.

Out we went. A few from the Village, and a lot more from both the public schools and Catholic schools down the road jogged onto the practice field, where 85 degrees was the norm at 9:30 in the morning in August, with humidity close to the same number. RUN, SQUAT, JUMP, HIT, RUN, SQUAT, JUMP, HIT. Over and over. No specifics, just grinding for two hours, people throwing up everywhere, young men crying for their momma, a coach who seemed a nice man, but surrounded himself with some tough old gym teaching birds. The other guys from Forest were also big, some as big as six feet were the quarterbacks and running backs, while Galt became linemen. This position is second or third to being the smallest. Then it was shower, and showing off your stuff or the lack thereof of hair, in a public shower; Wow, Dad was full of crap!. This was no picnic, nor did it appear to have any redeeming qualities to Galt. It was harassment, collisions; bigger people everywhere, and exhaustion unheard or felt ever. None of his inner three pals went out, as they either chose to not play or run cross-country. Galt had to wonder if he might convince Dad that this is a great alternative strategy, but he was not to be convinced. "Stick it out, or you will never be successful in anything in life." "But Dad, what about personal choices, isn't that important too?" "You are not ready for this type of choice. This is one we made for you. So go get 'em, boy!"

It was good to be clean, shorts, t-shirt, and flips on, heading home by himself, for some—a *lot*—of water. There were no electrolytes or Gatorade in those days, so they handed you salt tablets to choke down over the next three hours. Because in just three f-ing hours, you were to be back there for the afternoon session of the same.

So it went, mornings in the heat and afternoons in more heat. Draining the body and hammering the head and fatty tissue like never had been experienced. Small guy, big coaches and competition. Then finally some techniques were introduced: how to hit, how to run, how to play your position, in Galt's case, guard. Guard, what did that mean? Hell, it didn't matter, as survival was all that did matter. Certainly he gathered it meant he wasn't fast enough to play with the ball, but be with the *big* people who hit it more than the people who got to practice with the ball. What kind of damn sport was this football?

It struck him that the specialization was over the top. Position was one thing, but then Defense or Offense specifically, or special teams only, or just back up on the B team. WTH?

These two weeks would pass; Galt would find himself on the B team, dressing for the early morning Saturday games, but never seeing one minute of playtime, much to his father's disappointment. Galt was not being aggressive enough! What did that mean?

B teams did get games, against other schools who were the largest to rally a B team, on an off afternoon during the week, usually with short quarters, and on a practice field. in game uniforms, but borrowed from one of the twenty or so who were starters. The experience was one of humiliation, violence, angst at home, guys who didn't care to know a second stringer, and none of his friends to be found during these insane two weeks. And now school was to begin, too.

School was as football was, without the violence, but with greater chaos—classroom to classroom with so many young people of all types of dress and groups. Rushing, talking, laughing, and all Galt could feel was loneliness, and longing for the crappy grades and unpredictable times back in the Village, and going home for lunch. Homework stacked as the day went on, load after load till his binders and books would be sticking out a foot under his arm, as he finally made it out to a moment of peace in the basement cafeteria with all the other jocks. It was the jock study hall, organized at the end of the day for all to get a start on their homework. Galt quickly began, though Lord knows how, because he had never really done homework, to dig in and do what was asked as much as possible during this hour, the hour before the violent madness was to begin again for five days until game day. So it went for the fall semester. No new friends, classes of size and speed he struggled to keep up with, homework up his ass, and valiant attempts at getting it done at home before collapsing on his books.

Other stuff was also happening inside of Galt at this time. He would see Madison in the halls, and her locker was just three away. She would look at him with the warmest of smiles, and he would shy away, still. He would see her walking the halls and bigger men from the other junior highs walking with her. She was becoming even more beautiful every day. This was to be his way that year with girls.

Of course, having never lived on the earth before, he was unclear about this path. One was the feelings he would get and the physical manifestation there of a hard-on, while at his locker, while in the halls, while in class, while crashing off at night, despite exhaustion. He figured one way only to find some peace and pleasure during this boot camp of sorts, and that was to pleasure himself. Where were those playboys Noah and he had read? Buried somewhere in a box in the woods. Would have to take a Sunday morning and go find them. Over and over again. Maybe once in the morning in the shower, and once before a deep sleep. Then like a machine on the weekends, which held no social life whatsoever.

His old friends had also faded into their own private places, as all were struggling to make it, even an amazing adopted baby sitting with older twins across the street, who were like cheerleaders to Galt, to not give up, and it will get easier…

His folks were not sure how to handle this monastic version of the Galt, for this was their first time. They would use it over and over with his four other siblings. Being first was groundbreaking in many ways. He didn't care, he just kept showing up and plugging away. Slowly, day by day, getting what it took, both for afternoons of terror on the football field, school work, and his quiet times on the weekends. He was becoming comfortable.

First came warnings to his parents of his poor performance in English, French and social studies, the first semester mid-point. As he had somehow remembered his favorite teacher in math, and what she had taught him, he had the math thing down. But the rest wasn't that he couldn't, he just didn't seem to have enough time to keep up.

Then, as his perseverance did not waver, he found that calm and rhythm. He found how to prioritize his work, and how to get the easy stuff out of the way first, during his study halls, saving one or two tough ones for the evening after dinner, and falling into a very deep sleep. Second semester, four notes came home to his parents, *all stating he had raised his grades exponentially*; and, of course, football had ended. He went to his second favorite element, water, that winter, and swam and swam, doing well enough to compete, despite most of the guys having been on private club swim teams while Galt was building castles in the sand, picking up baseball, and also trouble, back in the Village on the Bluff. It was a coach he admired, too, one who encouraged, and somehow let Galt know he had it in him. His mother and father had said this, too, but he now understood what it meant, and Coach Barron was perfect timing for our growing child to man. He was the head varsity coach for football, and a task master, but fair. He admired Galt and saw how he would swim through whistles and gradually improve his times. It was Coach Baron who told him to come back for the sophomore team if that was what he wanted, but to seriously consider the wrestling team to grow strength for football next winter. He finished the swim team, and now had two freshman awards for sports, but was cut from the baseball team, when his arm went bad that cold spring, and didn't find a ball to hit during the early spring practices. The same coach who ran fresh football was the fresh baseball team coach, a man who wasn't as nice as he put on, nor was he much of a fan of Galt. What goes around comes around . . . and it would, soon.

WIth no sport in the spring, Galt now could walk home from school, study before dinner, study after dinner, and by the end of his freshman year, all grades were at honors levels. He had also decided to no longer play in the band, and his trumpet was to be put away for the rest of his adult life. He loved playing, but the completion of the band, the practice times required, and the humiliation of dressing up after Fresh football games in a uniform and marching on the varsity field and playing was too much. His sort-of peers were in the stands cheering and hanging out with the other kids and girls. He was soon to approach the level of straight As in his sophomore year. As well, his body was changing rapidly, too.

GIVE ME A BODY WITH HAIR, LONG RED HAIR.... FINALLY WHERE IT SHOULD BE!

That spring Galt grows six inches and gains five pounds. Height of six feet tall, and weighs 150 pounds. He is one lean dude.

Now as Coach Vukovich and the "Glory Road" in sports begins. Society still does not exist in his sphere, as his venture into monastic behavior and pursuit of Galahad virtues continues. Feeding his development were the more spiritual books in his Dr. Linden's English honors class. Expanding his spirit and mind with *Catcher in the Rye, A Separate Peace, Once and Future King*, on and on into the modern classics. Yet women still don't seem to matter.

HE HAD FOUND HIGHER GROUND? Or was it to be his highest altitude in life's journey to enlightenment?

A Supplemental Insert

Not much mention has been made of Galt's four younger siblings. The youngest, Dirk, was almost fourteen years younger than Galt, and thus was fun to hold, but also at this time, he spent very little time with him, as Mom was very occupied with this new baby in the house. Years later, we will learn how this relationship matures, as well as the challenge it presents to Galt in his journey to Higher Ground.

Ada, his only sister, is twelve years younger, and through his life, he had little to do with her. She was fun to play with from time to time, but when she was three years old, they had little interaction as siblings, but would become closer in age.

Wes, the third child, ten at the time of our story, was a quiet kid, who Galt enjoyed quiet time with. He seemed to have more in common with Galt and his interests. Galt shared his baseball card collection, his military war games, and how to play chess with Wes. He truly enjoyed this common ground shared with his biggest brother, and together on weekends, primarily Sundays, they shared games together. Galt took on the role of teacher to Wes, and they bonded very closely. It was a role Galt truly valued.

Ben, the closest in age, perhaps the one who would be most impacted by this big move to the land up north, is only fourteen months younger, and was just finishing eighth grade when he was told of this move. Ben had always aspired for whatever Galt had or appeared to have. They were close, but clearly there was a competitive spirit in Ben that Galt would never understand. It seemed he must be involved with Galt and his friends, who enjoyed Ben, but also found the little brother tagalong to be a bit much. Galt, in maybe his meanest character, rejected Ben and his constant desire to be with his older brother. Ben was no weak one, though, and quickly learned how to cut his own path, often bringing much terror and amusement to their parents. Ben at this stage was also known as the inflictor of three major scars on Galt. One was on his forehead from a nasty swing Ben took at him with a steel vacuum cleaner tube when they were much younger. One was an issue with weakness in Galt's right eye, primarily due to Ben spraying Mennen deodorant in his eyes when they were little, when sharing a bathtub, long before the other three were born. So many pranks Been executed that Galt could never be sure what Ben was going to bring next. Again, they were spiritually close, but Galt saw his brother as a wild cat, partner in multiple fists-fights that played to Ben's satisfaction and usually not Galt's. He was also the one Galt would miss the most when he wandered off to the great West after high school.

So it was with Galt: his siblings were siblings, and due to his birth role of number one, along with the expectations his successful mother and father put on him, he very rarely looked back at the younger clan. For he was told over and over again by his father that he was to be the role model. Later in life he would very much appreciate all of them for what they became and how they found a way to reunite as a family from time to time, usually due to Galt's family events, but also when their parents' passing drew them back.

CHAPTER 6:

"There is always a way."

Galt walked into the summer camp for sophomore football, the locker room for mouthpiece fitting, gear pick up, locker assignment, meeting the coaches, getting the schedule—what was last year the first round of humiliation. This environment seems to have remained the same, but changed so very much. He began to understand that physical places are only just that, it is how you are and how you have become that is what matters in a physical place. First of all, by being as tall or taller than ninety percent of the guys in the locker room, including the varsity players, he felt pretty confident. His trumpet was put away for good. His final grades freshman year had put him into honors classes in the upcoming semester. His body had begun to shape up. He had left his Beatles albums, games, lonely moments, and continuous introspection behind. He was ready.

There he was, that freshman football coach, the same guy who cut him from the baseball team. The nice man, who did nothing but shove Galt to the back of the line and roster. He shouted out Galt's full name, and he was standing next to Galt. Galt looked down at him, and said in a bass tone, "Coach, I am right here."

Coach looked up, and said "No way. Look at what has happened to you in just a few months." Galt just smiled down at him, and decided best to not say anything else, and move ahead in line to get his mouthpiece fitted. A choice he makes again and again.

It was true. Galt had grown this sprint in just five months, three pairs of shoe sizes and much longer jeans to fit that longer inseam. So much had changed. His shoulders were getting bigger too, as he trained for this season, running and lifting all summer, and working his tush off at the golf course carrying two bags a day, as many "loops" as he could get. He made good coin, but also his physical strength grew, as did his spirit. His soul was put to the back of the bus for this time in his life, as the body and mind seemed to be the way to Galahad Ground. Two out of three ain't bad, but he would realize a few years later that trading soul for dominance of the other two was hardly a win, but the way of youth growing and striving to expand all three wasn't perfect harmony.

The triangle may appear to be a balanced interdependent and equilateral, but in growth it is very lopsided and always shifting. As we age we begin to value how we take the richness of our experiences and believe life has given us into a balance of all three. As Spirit feeds Body, Body feeds Spirit back. Body also feeds Mind. Mind feeds the Body back, and Mind also feeds Spirit, as Spirit also feeds the Mind. All three are constantly feeding upon each other.

That morning in the high school gym, Galt was only concerned with two, and it was these two that were firing on all cylinders.

That sophomore summer football began with Coach Vuckovich running the show.

Coach Vuck was a tough old dude (old meaning probably in his late forties), who walked with a hint of hip and knee injuries from past experiences. He wore the white sweat socks with loafers and khakis, white shirt, and only three different ties every damn day. He was big in stance, and had a voice to go with it, with just enough profanity to make his point. He taught geometry, and had the skills to run the whole athletic complex at this elite Forest Prep. But there were others ahead, and it was to Galt's benefit that those days for Vuck had not come yet, as the relationship these two were to have was like Lancelot and Arthur, Lance being the soul who forgot his, and leveraged his mind and body to achieve glory. Galahad knew all three mattered. Galt was aspiring to be mirror Lance at this stage. Vuck only knew he had a kid on fire for football and aspirations to just get better every minute on the field. One who could do a lot of different things on the field he needed to repeat as the conference champions.

So after the usual first week of two days from hell, and yet to Galt, this time it didn't seem like hell. It seemed like training, and it actually felt good to max out on every sprint, drill, and exercise. Hot as it was that summer, the end of the first week usually meant that it was time to put on all those pads of ignorance and go to full contact, and hitting drills, one after another. So it was. They hit and hit and hit. Galt, due to his new physical posture, speed, and embrace of training rigor, was set into the crowd with the lineman and defensive linebackers, a step up on defense for him. But he never thought of himself as any more than a lineman. Though when playing touch in the hood, he had a great feel for the ball and his old catcher's arm delivered a good spiral. That seemed irrelevant, as Galt didn't know where he would land, he just knew he was ready to play this very violent game, and get back to class, too! These two objectives, along with an uncontrollable sex drive, occupied his mind. From time to time he would ask himself, "Why does a fifteen-year-old have this sex drive, demonstrated by a continuous hard-on?" Being the early developer philosopher he would be, he concluded it must be a practical human survival instinct. Cavemen must have had to breed early, as life span was short, and the species' desire to survive was dependent on his erection at this point when cave women were able and ready to bring the next generation of humans onto a very rough earth. More is better, as survival is difficult at best. He had perspective, but that was all, as it was his soul mate when not studying or footballing.

So it began, that hot August, about a week before school started. Time to find out who goes where, and what is to be this fall for Galt in this after school pursuit.

Coach Vuck called out eleven names for the offense's starting positions, and each was to quickly lock on his helmet and run to the position before the QB would make the snap.

As he called out the linemen from left to right, it seemed the odds might be tipping back against Galt again. By the time he had announced the left tight end, left guard, center, and right guard, in this unbalanced line offense, Galt doubted. Only two positions remained open to him. One was the outside tackle, usually reserved for the biggest guy on the team, and the most reliable stand up blocker to protect the QB. The other was a rare odd job, called the inside pulling tackle, a position that rarely stood still, Galt would learn in this offense; rarely blocked straight ahead. The inside slot tackle was to be a position where you were always either cross-blocked with the other guard, or the big tackle to your right. Or you pulled left or right very quickly. Running like the wind to trap a defender with basically a blind-side hit, or get ahead of the back carrying the ball around the corner. Objective to to take out downfield defensive players and provide an open freeway for the running back carrying the ball.

What Vuck had done was wait for the last position in the line to yell,

"Galt, get into the inside slot in the line. And you had better never let a back get ahead of you!"

So, at 150 pounds, on a big school program, where the tackles to his right were 6 '3 and 250, and the guard to his left was as tall, but weighed 200 pounds, Galt became a blocking back of sorts. Criss-crossing the line taking his violent hits on defenders as best he could. This was a grand moment for him, and yet he felt the other much larger fellow students in full gear giving burning stares into his back. There were two who both thought a tackle job should be theirs. What they didn't understand is what Vuck had done, and it was a great lesson in life. He took what folks thought and had practiced as standard, and modified the standards to fit the people he had, to best achieve an optimum result. Vuck had demonstrated that it wasn't an either/or in football, but an and/also. You can have an unbalanced line with two tackles but they need not be either big or not; rather, they can be fast and aggressive and fill this odd role Galt had been given. It is understandable for many that this nuance to football seems way over the top, but it is also important to understand that shaping the future is all about effort and preparation. It may not go as you thought, but the road will lay out for you, if you do. Galt did not become the Dick Butkus linebacker this year, as he had hoped, but he was cemented with consistent performance and many great games, a starting role on the team.

But there was more to come that morning from Vuck, as the coach called all the team had expected. For Galt this was a good day, but he didn't realize that Vuck was about to unleash more that fed off Galt being put in the small tackle pulling slot.

The given was that the freshman QB, nicknamed RG, a top big-time leader and the one all looked up to as the ultimate football player, would be the starting QB again this year. Likely destined to succeed the all state QB on varsity who was to graduate next year.

But Vuck knew what he was doing with his talent, and that others did not see. Like an artist with paint and canvas, here did what most thought should be. He yelled, "Milton, get over and take the QB slot behind the center, now!"

RG just turned, as did all of us, in complete disbelief. Had Vuck suddenly demoted RG to the bench?

It was not to be. Milton took the QB spot with some trepidation and head down, unable to look RG in the eye. Milton was to be an accomplished QB for this monster crew of footballers, who didn't know how to lose. When they did, they suffered immeasurably, and the world turned that loss into smashing victories the next Saturday on the varsity field. No more band for Galt, just football.

This was one of those moments in life he would see plenty of, but didn't quite get that the moments of truth were to be plenty at this time. It may have been his second after the fight and the calm he felt before the fight that morning in the spring of eighth grade.

Next, Coach Vuck took the three back, or the runner who was to carry the ball the most as a halfback of sorts in this option offense, and removed the fastest guy on the team from that job. Larry B. was a jet, but never was comfortable taking on those tacklers. He was a good-looking guy, and always put that first, through the rest of his life. Today he would also be put into the position to succeed as well by Vuck. Vuck called out for another three back. It was RG. RG as the big running back carrying the mail? WTH, Coach? RG felt like he had been removed from the driver's seat and put in the back seat. A QB all your life, with destiny, now a three back who would run the ball in this offense thirty-plus times a game? Fast as hell Larry B., well he had found a new home too. They moved him to flanker back, a pass catching and wide-ranging runner from time to time where his amazing speed would pay off in spades for the next three years. Then Kurt, the big back who had a take it or leave it about the game, was strong and with good speed, and had been a flanker of sorts, was thrown into a full back position, or the two back. Kurt knew this would mean lots of blocking, but what he didn't know was that his vicious ability to want to hit people versus being hit as a back would make him the starting line-backer. The guy who would command the defense to a one-loss season, with little or no scoring in all the games, including the one loss.

All four moves proved to be moves that lasted all the way to their senior year and third conference championship, with RG going onto to college and running like a deer into the NFL tryouts. Galt, however, was left out of this future; the family dinner talk would spoil that vision.

None of that mattered that day and that fall, as the putting of people in position to succeed, and aligning the play book around their talent, had been executed in a form of beauty by coach Vuck. A vision with action that any manager or CEO could learn from. Galt had a season, and even got to rest Kurt at linebacker in the hot, tougher games. It was like being a blocking back who never got the ball on offense, but boy, did he love laying it out in a cross-body block, or a straight-on hit, helmet to helmet on a defender, then falling to the ground and lifting his head up in a pile of young men, just high enough to see the dust coming off RG's hells down field to the end zone. It was a feeling he would never forget. RG was the guy, and the rest of the team still followed him, but in a different role. He became a back who was your teammate, not one who felt you were a pawn in their scheme. Thus we all launched into that beautiful fall. When there is perseverance for something you know is right for you, you will always find there is a way to succeed.

Note: Body and spirit in competition dominate all.

CHAPTER 7:

Finding the Interdependence of Three.. "The Triangle is rarely in balance"

G alt was truly wired into the mind and body path to perfection, but also had a strange emptiness; no matter how excellent the grade or the sports result, there was a nagging in balance in his pursuit of Galahad. It was earlier in the spring of that sophomore year, before that family dinner, when he began to have flashes of not only the cracks in his model, but also the missing fulfillment of the heart to others beyond his family. The word SHE came in his sleep, but he never could figure out what it meant. But every few weeks it would call out to him, a feeling as much as an image in his dreams that spoke to him differently than a parent, friend or teacher. Rather as a spiritual twin, but very feminine in her outlines, beautiful, beloved, and tender. Her unfocused image stood in hills of green and never demanded, but only made him feel so very comfortable. Each evening as SHE came to him, he would sleep after as never before. Then in the morning had very little recall of what or where, just an amazing feeling of bliss and to some extent a horny condition unlike other mornings would also rise to the surface in the shower before setting out for school. Galt was only fifteen, but he was sure he had found something few do, a spiritual and also physical partner, unobtainable in this time and place, but assuredly would come to visit him again and again as he journeyed to adulthood and even through his last third of life. Yet, the inability to connect past the dream awakened in him an awareness and deep desire to better understand the spiritual and soul in us, including his own. It became a muscle in understanding and early climb to Higher Ground.

Many experiences in life help shape us and also push us to hierarchy measurement versus that of our actual self or territory. Sports and academics are focused only on themselves. Beauty, as was shared earlier in the interdependence of mind, body, and soul, provides discovery to all. In this case, Galt found the keys and the paths to many spiritual journeys through his mind and the fortune of having Jonathan Laughlin for his sophomore honors class in English. Mr. L. was desired by many students for his progressive teachings and introductions to a syllabus that broke many barriers at Forest Prep. His ability to speak to and listen to the students, along with allowing them the spiritual exploration of themselves in papers and discussion through literature, was a privilege.

Galt dove into the reading list, often finishing ahead of schedule, reading ahead into another book on the semester and year's list. Steinbeck's *Tortilla Flats* and *Wayward Bus*, Ken Kesey's *Sometimes a Great Notion*, Herman Hesse's *Siddhartha*, Jerzy Kosinski's *Being There*, Orwell's *Animal Farm*, Burgess's *Clockwork Orange*, Knowles' *A Separate Peace*, Antoine de Saint Exupery's *The Little Prince*, Thoreau's *On Walden Pond*, and finally, Ayn Rand's *Fountainhead*. They were even handed various photocopies of eastern philosophy teachings. These students were asked to join a round table and present as a group their various impressions and impact on their own filters and perspectives of life. One example that stuck with Galt was only a small excerpt from *The Teaching of Buddha*, from chapter four, "Defilements or Human Defilements."

The following is the introduction to this profound insight, as well as the most powerful image tattooed on Galt's soul; three pieces of a puzzle that allow the light to shine through. As shared by in The Teachings of Buddha:

> There are two kinds of worldly passions that defile and cover the purity of a Buddha-nature. The first is the passion of analysis and discussion by which people become confused in judgment. The second is the passion for emotional experience by which people's values become confused. Both delusion of reasoning and delusion of practice can be thought of as a classification of all human defilement, but really there are two original predicaments in theirs.
> The first is ignorance and the second is desire.
> The delusions of reasoning are based upon ignorance and the delusions of practice are based upon desire, so that the two sets are really one set after all, and together they are the source of all unhappiness.

Galt and his colleagues were really stumped by this, until they were handed the second piece of paper on which was written the following:

> If people are ignorant they cannot reason correctly, and safely. As they yield to a desire for existence, grasping, clinging, and attachments, to everything inevitable will follow. It is this constant hunger for every pleasant thing seen and heard that leads people to the delusions of habit. Some people yearn to yield to the desire for the death of the body.
> From their primary sources all greed, anger, foolishness, misunderstanding, resentment, jealousy, flattery, deceit, pride, contempt, selfishness, have their generations and appearances.

Mr. L. asked the students to reflect upon these teachings and interpret them for themselves in real life examples. Was this not a far-out teacher and class for sophomore English? But he knew that if the students could see from their own eyes, they would also be able to see from the author's eyes the meaning and purpose of the words, and their drama and/or truth that helps feed the soul and mind simultaneously.

FINALLY, they were asked to read:

> It is easy to shield the outer body from poisoned arrows, but it is impossible to shield the mind from poison darts that originate with itself. Greed, hierarchy, anger, foolishness, and the infatuation of egoism . . . These four poisoned arts originate with the mind and infect it with deadly poison. We can be our own inoculation, and/or our own test lab, who in turn can be seduced by it or not...

Said Mr. L., "How do you feel about that?"

Holy shit, Galt was finding, despite not raising his hand, that this was truly a place of thought, soul, and even some body rushes; he truly desired for more understanding. Had the wall between body and mind, that had been built to keep the soul asleep, began to be taken down one brick at a time through these great books?

The last Buddha teaching they read that day, that Galt used his adult life in organizations as his goal, will shed light on our Galt's journey back to balance in the triangle or power of the three in balance:

> There are three kinds of people in the world. They first are those who are like letters carved in rock, they easily give way to anger and retain their angry thoughts for a long time. The second are those that are like letters written in the sand. They find a way to anger also but their thoughts quickly pass away. The third are those who are like letters written in running water. They do not retain their passing thoughts, they let abuse end, dumbfounded gossip pass by unnoticed, their minds are always pure and undisturbed.

As these three types find themselves in organization structures, they can only find common ground through the perfect organization, something Galt was fascinated by, including sports teams, class structure, and his family hierarchy. All seemed to him to be organizations of some type. As he spoke to Mr. L. about this curiosity, he was handed *the* book, and with a silk marker on the pages was sent to the copier to make his own copy, and then consider what it might mean to help him get perspective on the organizations and organisms of our world. Mr. L. was always happy to discuss after class if time permitted, but he always demanded that students read, absorb, think, introspect, then come prepared to be honest, speak up, and learn from each other, feeding their territory. Here is what Galt was to keep with him for all his life in organizations. It would surface again when business conditions were mercurial, and he was being pushed to levels of altitude he was unsure of, and ultimately drive his commitment to sharing the path to Higher Ground with others. :

Of organizations, there are three kinds. First, there are those that are organized on the basis of the power and wealth or authority of great leaders. Second, there are those that are organized because of the convenience of the members, which will continue to exist as long as the members satisfy their conveniences and do not quarrel.

Then there are those that are organized with some good teaching at its center and harmony at its very life.

Of course, the third or last of these is the only true organization, for in it the members live in one spirit, from which the unity of spirit and various kinds of virtue will arise. In such an organization there will prevail harmony, satisfaction and happiness. This is how the many types of people find a noble calling for themselves, and move beyond their own petty weaknesses, through that connection to a noble organization or belief, from which their true heart and self can grow, and achieve a higher awareness.

Or, as Galt thought, a Higher Ground. This was to be *alignment*, from which came the third major teaching that connected the whole of the individual, the organization, and their part of our world. It began:

> Enlightenment is like rain that falls on a mountain and gathers in rivulets that run into brooks, and then into rivers, which finally flow in the ocean.
>
> The rain of sacred teachings falls on all people alike without regard to their conditions or circumstances. Those who accept gather into small groups, then into organization, then communities, and finally, find themselves in the great ocean of enlightenment. The minds of these people mix like milk and water and finally organization of a harmonious brotherhood.
>
> This is the organization that is formed on the perfect teaching of Buddha, only it can be called a brotherhood.
>
> They should observe these teachings, remember them in their minds accordingly. Thus the Buddha's brotherhood will theoretically include not everyone, but in fact, only those who have the same religious faith can or are members...

Take that, Harvard Business School!

So the vision, acumen, and trust triangle now had found its way into Galt's tool kit. He was unsure how it would apply at fifteen, but it was clear this was the holy trinity, a triangular interdependence that could serve to help him and others achieve a Higher Ground.

Galt did not know during that moment of despair and sadness in his frontal awareness, when his parents informed him of the move they were planning, that this move was to be his journey to Lhasa or, as his yet-unknown Blackfoot roots would indicate, his Vision Quest; that this move he could not be better prepared for, and that it seemed almost unfair in the universe that a change such as this was to happen for him at exactly the right time and right place.

CHAPTER 8:

The Journey to Lhasa Waukee

(...and the two become three, and again he finds the balance impossible to sustain.)

D ad finished the conversation that April evening of Galt's sophomore year, with all of his four siblings still unclear why Galt was so upset. The three younger ones just didn't understand the hot knife that had just cut through their butter-warm lifestyle. Ben, who was in eighth grade, got it. He saw nothing but a bad deal as well, as he was ready for Forest Prep and had yet to step foot there, other than to join Mom and Dad in attending band concerts and Galt's sports events at the school. But he knew he was ready to be a Forest Warrior.

"We will be fine, as we are a family, and we will have a grand experience in our move to Milwaukee. It is not our first move, nor will it be our last, I believe."

The subtlety of this comment didn't stick with Galt or his younger siblings. But it was true. Dad knew this was a turnaround of a division for his corporate HQ, and that if he pulled it off, it meant a big new assignment back in Chicago. But he also was unsure of the total time frame beyond what his boss, the president of the division, had said, "Five years at most." But Dad knew better than to put this into our heads, and so did Mom. They understood that some of this knowledge would be just a whipsaw of experience. Focus on what is ahead, make that grand, and the rest will fall into place. It wasn't to be easy on them by any means, with the distance between our grandparents and them lengthening, and also their health beginning to waver. But it was a done deal, and *done* Dad did, as he pulled the division up by its bootstraps by empowering good people who were there. Bringing his own flair to the party, and he was awarded with the big returning assignment in three years instead of five. He had done what he was asked in less time, and with greater results, a lesson for all Galt's siblings and especially for him. No matter how hard, how it had the appearance of an undoable assignment, that was what made it worthwhile. Get it done right, faster, and with an eye to the next project always. That is how life in corporate America can actually be interesting and not only pay bills, maybe build wealth, but also feed the trifecta of Mind, Body and Soul. But it was to be a perfect four years in Lhaskawaukee before returning to the Village on the Bluff.

That evening at the dinner table Galt recalled Mom adding, "Life can shift on all of us very fast, and we will always have what we gained and learned here in the Village. It will never leave us. But what we will gain is even more friends, and experiences, that will make our lives even richer. So fear not, all of you, for as Dad said, we will always be a family. One who loves and supports each of us for who we are, and together can do anything that comes our way. Together we can also reach a Higher Ground as people, too."

All had no more to say. It was a done deal, and Galt slouched down, and then excused himself as he went down to the basement-converted bedroom he shared with Ben. He didn't feel much like doing homework on this Thursday evening, despite his chance to have straight A's for the first time in his academic career. He sat at his desk, staring at his honors geometry book where a critical test was to be the next day. He could only see images of friends, places, and those he had not had in his head. His doubt about this having any good outcomes was truly growing within him. He had it made, he had it figured out, he even was about to ask a longtime friend and beautiful fellow alum of his grade school, Janine, to spring prom. But, he didn't do it. In fact, he didn't get his straight A's, either. Four A's and one B+ in honors geometry didn't seem to matter.

He spent the last weeks of school saying goodbyes, and "We'll be back," and telling of his dad's opportunity to take on a great new corporate role, as well as a lake, his own bedroom etc., when his friends asked, "Why?"

Most peers couldn't believe it, and didn't quite understand. Wasn't this place that combined the best of Village on the Bluff and Forest Bluff to make for a perfect world at Forest Prep? All knew that their dress, school, mighty oak-lined winding streets, along with never-lose sports teams and beautiful homes made up for heaven on earth for a fifteen going on sixteen-year-old.

CHAPTER 9:

The Summer from Hell

Summer from hell, but the angels were there to help him find his way back.

The move for Galt was a non-event. Physical packing and loading into the Lincoln town car and mom's station wagon didn't matter, but what did add a twist to the story was the health of the brother in the middle, Wes, and his health deterioration.

Wes had been not recovering from various bugs or colds as he should have. He had always been the small one of the family. Galt's parents, grandparents, aunt, and folks were all tall people. Galt's new height of six feet just put him at the minimum of what the family ruler was. The kids, all but Wes, were headed in that direction even as little ones, with big shoes and way above average heights at their annual physical. Except Wes, whom Galt was to learn may not have been growing physically, but in his soul and heart he was expanding bigger than life would allow.

Once the family had arrived at the beautiful new home on the hill, overlooking the new, much smaller lake, life began to settle in. The goodbyes had been said to all back home, and no visits back were planned for the foreseeable future. Galt went back to his room and closed the door, unable to get into those games, records, and collections that had been his passion before the variances set in at twelve. He had lived life to its fullest, and yet, here he was in a new place with the worst feeling of the possibilities he could imagine. He was fifteen years old, without a driver's license, no friends, but in a new beautiful environment and with a younger brother, Ben, who, along with Galt, never stopped complaining about what had happened to them, long in accepting this new world and embracing it for the wonder it was to become, both crying at the dinner table. Yep; crying. But this phase took a shock when it was diagnosed that the middle, blond, blue-eyed brother Wes had leukemia. It was the opinion of a Milwaukee doctor, and then also of a second, trusted doc back in Chicago. No longer did the move and the cultural shock serve as the excuse for not living life and embracing this new place. Suddenly the potential of their quiet brother passing into death was upon the whole family. It was a tough case of the disease, and one that with all the treatments could not be stopped. Wes went in just four months. His funeral was held in their new hometown of Manitoka. Home was where he needed to be laid, and Mom was adamant about it.

Home was Manitoka, and nowhere else.

Galt spent more hours with his second youngest brother that summer than he had his entire life. He realized that this was a special kid, who looked up to Galt, who desired to be just as his oldest brother was, and more importantly asked to play some of Galt's games with him, and share in his Beatles music. Wes was only ten, but was as smart as any Galt had known in his short life. Wes picked up on his adult war board games, and played Galt into a corner in *Avalon Hills*, *Stalingrad* and *Battle of the Bulge*. They would also go for sails on the new smaller lake with the Sunfish Grandma and Grandpa had bought for them as a house-warming gift. Wes loved to sit with his brother Galt and duck under the sail when they came about, shouting in his wavering voice, "Coming about, Galt, look out!" He would smile back at Galt who would duck, and Galt would look away to the water, as tears fell from his cheeks. He did not want this beautiful child to know how sad and how regretful Galt was for being so focused on his own agenda, and not getting to know or spend the time with his sibling.

Wes was remarkable in so many ways, and it made no sense to Galt that finding his brother meant that he would now lose him.

Mom and Dad carried this huge burden with great quiet and strength, but also talked to the children about every step of Wes' technical medical process. They wanted the siblings to know what they knew. There was to be no secrets. But despite this awful situation, and death of a sibling, there was a beautiful embrace that was to come from the neighbors of Manitoka and Lake La Belle development. New people who had no idea who the new family was quickly learned across the neighborhood of a hundred homes, and came knocking and offering their condolences, food, and support to the family, as Mom chased everywhere with Wes for his treatments and hospice, and Dad held it together as best he could in his new huge job as well.

Galt did sign up for varsity football that late summer, but it seemed more routine than passionate, as it had been in the past at Forest Prep. The new high school was called Braveheart, with a mascot that was a tall, tall Highlander. School colors were red and white, and the sprawling campus was to be the largest on one floor in the state of Wisconsin. Even the community was the second largest in area, owing to its large footprint as a township around a little village smack in the middle, called Centerville. It was ten-by-ten miles of new subdivisions, with a sprawling and twisting Wisconsin River, shoreline on lake Michigan, and Galt's 'hood, that also wrapped itself around a forty-acre lake where he and Wes sailed that summer in the evenings.

Wes passed that Labor Day, and with his death came many families from all over the U.S., to be with the family in their new home for this time. The house was packed, Mom and Dad cried a lot, as did all, but they remained strong. The neighbors the family had not known well yet, other than next-door hellos, came to the service and reception by the hundreds. It was here that Galt began to learn of the amazing heart and soul of these people of Wisconsin. Many had farming roots, or industrial roots from the early factories, but there were also those of highly educated, white-collar backgrounds. All were one, people who knew how to be great neighbors, trusting friends, and giving beyond belief. They also knew how to eat and drink. Galt had not touched a drop since that evening in Noah's trailer in eighth grade, but this day at the reception he was to dive into the culture of Wisconsin full blast—eat, drink, cry, hug, and meet so many people, including one who was to be one of his greatest pals over his lifetime. Tall, quiet, from a family of nine, his name was Peter. He was the oldest as well. He had not gone out for football, as Galt had, but was still pretty good at the toss and catch of the football out back. For it was ok in Wisconsin to have a beer in your hand at this sad time, and be out back tossing footballs with new friends who had come to the home that afternoon.

That Pabst Blue Ribbon brought calm and warmth, as well as the realization that Wes's passing was a catalyst for how they had truly arrived in this special place. His family of Bears who invaded Packerland, along with every family of the new hood, and all the siblings. Many best-friends-to-be. It was as Wes would have wanted it to be: Love all, embrace change, and be strong when you need to be to those who you love. Stop and get to know those who are different from you, and don't let life's tragedy stop you from striving for the Higher Ground. Galt at that moment knew that the three elements of Body, Mind and Soul, when in harmony, even under the most stressful of times, would lift you up and provide for you the shoes to move on and continue life's journey.

Galt had never felt so many ranges of emotion in his sixteen years on earth, from the lows of loss to the pure amazement of how people can come together when a tragedy happens and recognize the human condition is meant to be shared as much as it is an individual thing. Galt's team members from football showed up as well, guys he'd had some pretty rough shoving and pushing matches with just a few weeks earlier on the summer practice field. They'd been testing him, or attempting to prove to their coach that they were not going to give up their position to Galt, this new guy, this damn *Bear fan* from Chicago. As a Bear fan was a hated fan. The passion in a cheese head (a Wisconsin term of endearment) never recedes. The Green Bay Packers NFL franchise represented as much pride in their state as any of the rich dimensions of Wisconsin. Theirs was a championship legacy set by Vince Lombardi and his band that exceeded even the great Bear history of championships in the last decade. But Galt was a third-generation Bears fan, worshiper of Dick Butkus and Gale Sayers, along with the likes of Doug Buffone and Ed O'Bradovich; these were his heroes. The Pack had enjoyed some glorious years up to 1968, but was on the downhill track. The Bears had already reached the bottom of the pit, and would remain there as long as Galt would live on the soil of Wisconsin. The folks up here had lost their baseball team, had an NHL hockey team, and just started an NBA franchise, but the Pack ruled all on Sundays in the fall, heroes and role models. Galt would adopt Jerry Kramer and his wonderful book *Instant Replay* as his guiding light on football in Wisconsin, and the value all put on the culture around it as much as on the game. But Galt never gave up his Bears loyalties, even on Sundays when he would be invited to fellow football teammates' homes for *big* sausages, big hard buns, and kraut (sour cooked cabbage his grandfather had cooked his pork with), and this hot (?) mustard, as the '68 Bears and Packers went at it with the vengeance that their rivalry demanded.

"Now, you must be a Packers fan, Galt?" would be the repeated question asked by his expanding circle of friends. Again he would answer, "No, always a Bears Fan. My grandfather played football with George Halas."

Oddly, the ties between the two storied franchises went far back into their origins. Many Pack fans had no idea that it was George Halas, the founder of the Bears and the NFL, who fought for and helped finance the Packers when it looked like they would fold. As well, the greatest Packers linebacker of those times (and maybe the second greatest to Dick Butkus of the Bears), was from Proviso, Galt's parents' high school on the west side of Chicago (as was Ed O'Bradovich, the tenacious and giant of a defensive end on the Bears). With no Chicago there would be no Notre Dame, and of course the star back and playboy of the Pack in that decade, Paul Horning, was from Notre Dame. As was the case with economics, leisure, and sports, these two states had a marriage that neither would admit to in public. Galt, who was about to become a half-breed of sorts, understood this bond and how important it was to both. Not many would ever understand that bond, but he embraced the joy and intellectual pursuit it provided to him.

Wes, and his death, did eventually move into memory and away from everyday mourning. Galt never missed a practice, school day, or football game that junior year. He had won a spot at pulling guard, and as a rotating linebacker, two positions he truly enjoyed. It took some very difficult fights on the practice field, brought on by hard-ass Highlanders, but it never stopped our Galt. The spirit of Wes stayed with him throughout that year, and though extreme sadness and loss was poured over all of his family, he was inspired by his little brother's last words to him:

> *"Big brother Galt, promise me you will always chase your dreams. Don't let others and their view of the world stop your pursuits. You have a unique intuition that will only get more powerful for you as you age. It will serve you well. So, promise me you will always do it like I am watching. For I will be. I love you, Galt."*

It was this ten year old with the spirit of a wise old man, brother Wes who spoke those soft words to him. What Galt didn't know was that Wes, who had begun to visit the angels in those last days, was also sharing thoughts and words with them. It was their words, and the guidance of his mystery mate from his dreams, that was actually speaking to him through Wes. Galt had intense, very intense dreams those next months of the fall of '68, speaking with a spirit and maybe his lost brother, too. SHE was there, and with Wes, which made Galt very happy in his heart. SHE came many more times than had been the past experience in his dreams, and SHE would also go away for long periods again. All he knew was that when he awoke those mornings after her visits, he never felt so damn alive. Every pore, extension of his body, and his smile were as big as they could be to absorb what was to come that day. He had found a deeper meaning in his soul, than his own personal alignments with body and mind. He had learned that the spirits we share this life with, be they with us now, or in another way, are the key to joy. We can strive to align and grow our trifecta of life, but only through achievement with others can it truly be utilized as well as optimized for all, in our collective spirits and collective pursuit of finding *"Higher Ground." Those were the words SHE always left him with in those early days.*

CHAPTER 10:

Lessons in Love, Lancers Wine, Death, and Wild Cheddar

So many other unplanned or predicted experiences.

As '68 became '69 and '70, Galt was expanding his social circle exponentially, dating and getting serious with two women, one younger and one of his class. These two were to be his first serious heartbeats since he walked away from the powerful magnetism at age thirteen with Madison back in the Village on the Bluff. It had been three years, finally a driver's license; and new pals, and beautiful, kind, and free spirited Wisconsin women, surrounded his emotions. Yes, sports mattered, but as the football team his junior year was a 500 team and his senior year they lost all but one game. Galt tried one year of wrestling and some golf, he quickly got used to losing on the sports field, not in a quiet or depressed way, but rather, in the way that you give it all you have, and it still doesn't become victory, then you learn that some systems don't mean victory for you only.

Academics were at the same pace of earned grades, and he sustained his National Honors Society GPA, but it had become easier. He had figured out how to master the study, score well, and play high school academics. There were moments where he felt challenged, but they were fewer than those where he felt he was just playing a grade-point game, and playing it quite well. Girls as friends and interests, with good friendships building, easy school points scored, and lousy at sports, became his new mantra, as he experienced the richness of life that Wisconsin folks seemed to have a handle on. Something his old environment to the south did not. Things began to feel like seventh and eighth grade again, where hedonism and exploration of the body and related thrills became the new mission; the balance again was to go out of synchronization. Again, he felt it was ok. His family did not begin to see this shift, as he was very good at keeping his crazy weekend events and romances to himself. As well, his brother Ben had now established himself as a true Highlander, doing every wild thing a student could to break the mold of what was expected by this traditional crowd of the late 60s: wearing his mother's big fur coat to school, with white Alaskan boots the size of Li'l Abner, cutting his hair to a Mohawk multiple times, and finally just raising hell with his new-found crew.

Galt learned in those days how to have fun Wisconsin-style, with great aplomb.

Their town was so large beyond the new subdivisions that had been built over the last ten years, and the country clubs, that farmland and backcountry roads ran deep into its northern border. On these roads, one could literally park in the north farm country on a Saturday night, under a full moon, break out the beer, grape juice, and vodka, and drink and laugh to the heart's content with friends and date. There was no fear of another car coming, or even a policeman, for that matter. Swimming at midnight nude, co-rec became a wonderful experience he had never even considered back in Illinois. Sex, with *other people*, suddenly became a reality, touching, kissing with a depth into the back of the mouth, and finally, time after time, one hopes of climax. God, it was wondrous, this next level of body research. The first of his girlfriends, the youngest by a year, was a beautiful girl. Her ability to kiss sent Galt to his knees. She, a fourteen-year-old, taught him as a fifteen and a half, "how-to". She was fearless, and literally attacked Galt, but never did he feel like it was wrong. He just realized he should sit back and enjoy this ride, as short as it was the spring of his junior year.

His growing friendship with Peter, who had a serious on-again, off-again girlfriend, was a slow deliberate development. They shared music, stories, motorcycle details (both owned one), and eventually double dated with Galt's next high-school girlfriend. Peter and he would slowly, over many years, share in many experiences, and also learn to grow in their own lives. These early years the foundation of sharing philosophy, life experiences, risks, transitions, career, and family was established on those double dates, and on the adventures they would take throughout the state.

The one who was to become his "high-school sweetheart" of his same class, and the warmest and kindest woman he had ever met, was named Mesa, and she was smitten with Galt the moment they first spoke in the halls between classes. He didn't see her as sex partner, at first, nor a lover. More like a good person he was fascinated by, and wanted to become good friends with, and see what happened after that. It was to be the way for Galt with women in his life. There were those who between the two of them had one common objective, and that would be wild and rapidly executed sex, with little knowledge of who they were as people. Then there were the others who he knew he wanted to befriend; get to know her, and as the friendship grew, so did the physical traits that drive sixteen- to eighteen-year-olds. It was different than with his first love Madison, because it involved two consenting adults. But friendship, knowing the family, knowing their love, fears, joys, goals, and interests—that was as much romance in early stages as Galt felt was best. It was a joy to get to know each other, and then let the physical growth as a catalyst for more depth of knowing each other. He came to think of true love with women as true friendship first. If that were magical, the best lovemaking and/or sex would follow. Galt followed it with great abundance and joy, only making for better friends who also were lovers. He remained unclear as to the roots of this way of seeing women, and the early days of meeting, and growing or blowing up a relationship, but it was to become clear in later years that this aura or spirit that visited him during times of need was at the root of this value and belief system with those of the opposite sex. She had shown him that friendship and insight into others was at the foundation of all rich human experiences. She had also always left him with a strong physical hangover, where his horns would be very big and ridged. So it was for Galt, either horns found horns and locked up for a short share and match of sexual experiences, or friendship met friendship and it grew and became a very powerful influence for him, and catalyst for a deeper friendship, a way to break on through to the other side of rich love with another, to stand together on the Higher Ground.

ADDENDUM TO CHAPTER 10:

Top Ten Adventures of the Soul, Body, and Death

G alt had in his own mind that his mind had come far enough, and that it was about as well-tuned as any could be. After all, how much more could one even consider learning about math, reading, retention, history, and science? He had taken chemistry, biology, ancient, modern, and U.S. history; he had kicked the challenges of dy/dx in calculus down the hall and back into the syllabus. No need for much of that anymore. Braveheart High School did provide some intro to business inside of their intro to economics class. Insight to the world of making money only seemed relevant to him insofar as he had enough in his pocket to enjoy the weekends, beer, movies and dates. Most of this cash he had saved from his summer jobs, and from taking on extra work for his father on holidays in the city. So why learn more, when you also know how to beat the grade game? After all, this college thing seemed miles away, even though the sword of its intense edge hung only eleven months in his future, as Galt began his senior year.

His little brother Ben was coming into his own as a wild and often expelled student and sophomore at BHS. He was making himself known, not only as a good athlete, but also as a fellow who would cut his hair to a Mohawk, and wear coveralls to class with flip flops, long before the straight-laced dress codes had been crushed by the current Gen X and Millennial children of the Boomers. So as he was breaking ground and also diverting attention from Galt's future by their folks, the other two smaller siblings, Ada and Dirk, were growing up into figures of people that Galt could now remember himself as. Remarkable that these two little kids, babies born only a few years apart after Wes, were now in grade school and kindergarten, respectively. Despite their growth as young children, they were still just that to Galt. He was so irritated by his brother making a noise and issues in his high school playground, and it was getting harder to get money out of Mom and Dad, much less the car, as Ben became sixteen. Undeterred, Galt in his clever way would point out all the errors in judgment by Ben to Mom and Dad, and thus would also plan ahead for car usage, often grabbing the keys hours before Ben would even consider needing them. After all, Galt was a senior and he thought he had life by the balls. So wrong…so wrong…So very wrong….

1. Death in the Eye

It was a fall warm Indian Summer night, as the Midwest often has, that Galt and his girlfriend and sweet high school lover Mesa were hanging on the beach and dock at Lac LaBelle, in their hood on a Friday night, awaiting being picked up by Peter and his high school gal Terri. Suddenly, shirtless guys and bikini-clad, tough-looking kids came running out of the woods path around the lake from the clubhouse. Many an evening the police would be called down, as kids from other towns would find this lake much to their skinny-dipping amusement. But as it was a private lake, and had been a deep quarry at one time, they were unfamiliar with its deep cold holes that had been the death grip on more than one teenager in this lake.

Out of the woods they came screaming this evening: "Come help, our friend has drowned and we can't find him!"

They were out of control and sweating, as they had just run about a mile around the shoreline in the woods, on no path. The small bay we called Death Hole, as others had drowned there in the past, was where they had snuck in and lost their fourth on this double date for these kids from the farm town to the north, Augsburg, Wisconsin, a farm hamlet that had the reputation of dominating as much as they lost with Highlanders.

Galt and the on-duty pool guard, along with the tennis instructor, who had been holding classes at the courts next to the beach, quickly followed the kids, as others went sprinting to the phones to call the fire and police in their homes down the road. As they approached the shoreline, which was all bushes and no beach of any kind, the tennis instructor and a history teacher at the high school yelled for all of us to get into a line and wade into the water. The others admitted to not being strong swimmers, but Galt had been taught years ago by Mom and Dad. So Galt, the tennis teacher, and one other dad who had been in lessons waded in with a back-and-forth motion, scanning the bottom. As it got deeper and colder, as the September evening set in, the trio began surface dives, going deeper and deeper on each dive, kids screaming on the shoreline, pointing and screaming, but lost in our ears, as the cold and deep water left no room for their sounds. They were scanning back and forth, in a very methodical way, as Mr. Dietrich had instructed the three of them, which seemed a futile attempt to find this poor soul before it was too late. As they approached fifty yards off shore, Galt took what he had thought ten minutes ago would be his last dive, and went as deep as he could into that evening light's rays penetrating down into the foggy tannins of the various fall deterioration of life in their leaves. He took a stare into that darkness and suddenly, he saw a hand reaching up to him!

Was it moving or not didn't matter, as he knew at this moment a face also stood behind it deeper in the darkness with eyes wide open. *Shit.* He rocketed to the surface and screamed with no breath, *"He is here! He is right here!"*

He dove down, back to the very same spot he had just climbed up through fifteen feet of ice-cold lake water, and found his hand again. It was a grab he never thought twice to make; in fact, his calmness to get help was the right thing, and wasting only seconds went back to bring him up as help from the other swimmers arrived on site. As he surfaced with the weight of three teen-age men, others helped Galt pull him to the shoreline as the joy and then hysteria began all over again from his three friends, for all the pumping by Mr. Dietrich and Mr. Echelman would never help his breathing, heart, or mind come back to this world. Paramedics arrived, and quickly moved him to the shoreline of their ambulance. It was just one year after Galt had seen his little brother Wes close his eyes, only a few hundred yards up the road from that beach, for the last time, too. My God, this was not right. As they pulled the sheet over his head and rolled the cart off the sand into the van, tears and shock were on the faces of all. The kids who had been his good friends couldn't stop saying how they had warned him to not go out so far, and to drink so much schnapps and PBRs, as kids in Wisconsin were often conditioned to do at age sixteen and above, but it was all too late. Death had come again, and would forever leave this image of his hand and eyes staring up at Galt, as life had left his body. Forever.

Galt had seen enough of death for one year, or so it seemed. This and Wes's passing were not to be the last, as death comes for all we love sooner or later.

2. Up North There:

He and Peter had become better and better friends, as it was that summer between junior and senior year where Peter invited Galt with him, as his buddy, up north to the lakes, tall pines, water skiing, fishing with his dad, and staying in a small cabin with his eight siblings. Galt and Peter were of much the same make-up at this early age, as they both were the oldest, bright, good athletes, dating great women, and all for the debauchery and wild experiences a great senior year would bring. Peter had decided to return to football with Galt that fall, and both had but only a few days before that August's summer camp was to begin. They went on the vacation with Peter's folks and sibs. It was a grand time, with water in the day, and drinking outrageous amounts of .50 cent PBRs at the broken-down shell of a building on US 51, that only served beer and had a loud jukebox; an underage drinking shelter of sorts, where the cars from all the cabins along those many lakes would line up from 8:30 PM on, and in those days, also drive back to their squeaky beds, maybe a grocery bag next to it. So many drunks, so much testosterone, so many beautiful girls, and only one song that kept playing over and over again, this summer of love in 1969, The Youngblood's "Get Together." Over and over it would play, as the young Badgers would sing every word, with the amazing and low-grade buzz of PBR deep into their blood streams. It was their last night there, just a few weeks after the drowning on Lac LaBelle, that Peter and Galt went for it. Peter's dad was a hot car buff, as were many in this state. Galt, having been raised in the leafy suburbs of Village on the Bluff and Cliff on the Lake, knew only of foreign sports cars. Here in 1969, while Haight-Ashbury was expanding minds, it was all about muscle cars, all kinds, from 440-magnum various Chrysler products, to Ford Mustangs from the movie *Bullet*, to Peter's dad's car, a '67 Pontiac GTO, with dual pipes and an engine you could hear for blocks. Quite a commuter vehicle for a top investment banker in Milwaukee, but Galt's dad also had his own with his 65 Pony. Both cars were fast, and both Galt and Peter had dragged them, and pushed them to their limits on those Manitoka backcountry roads. Rolling and flat too, *hot, fast, and loud*. The smoke of peace and love had not quite reached this center of the heart-land. Maybe it penetrated culture and many young minds in the East and the West Coast, but not yet. Girls, alcohol, fast cars, and water with fast boats all seemed perfect to them.

But that night it all was put into risk, as the deviation of their adventures every night went to the zenith of consumption, as it was the last before football camp and those hellish two-a-days. Peter had something to prove that night, as the music was loud and the beer poured out of its long necks down both their throats. But as Galt had always found, almost always, that he had a knack for knowing when to quit and not lose his wits, he did this night, too. Drunk as a rat in a vat (a Wisconsin expression), he was still light-years ahead of what his tall lanky pal was doing, downing those bottles for .50 cents apiece. As Galt said to Peter, "It is time to go," Peter just looked at him and said, "We have done this much and more before with our girls, let's just do one or two more." Galt just said "No! Time to go, pal." Peter calmly sensed for the first time that night (which for Peter was odd, as he rarely lost his composure), handed the keys to the GOAT over to Galt, and said, "Ok, partner, get us back to the barn."

Galt turned it over, and felt the power in a different way than one would in the passenger seat, and certainly felt the power when he burned dirt, rocks and blacktop pulling out of that old shell of a bar that evening, dust covering up their tail lights. He kept the powerful engine just on the speed limit, fearing for the bust, as he and Peter had avoided busts, or getting caught in high school, and weren't about to let this night break that awesome record. The ten miles back to the cabin complex seemed like a three-day drive to Galt. But quietly he shut off the engine, as there were only the overhead lights on the dock shining, and all of Peter's big clan was sound asleep.

Peter was alert enough to realize he wasn't ready to lay down and just puke, so he felt a good shot of the northern lake water would do them both good that evening. Being lake rats as they had become, they both agreed, and with t-shirts and shorts laying on the beach dove in nude and went kicking and sinking into the dark night waters of the north. It felt great to Galt, so good he wasn't paying any attention to Peter, and he dove over and over, getting what he foolishly thought was his sobriety and sanity back. But after his third dive, he found some soft sand about five feet deep just past the pier, and the lights reflected on the lake, and he said to Peter, "Wow, this is just what the doctor ordered." Probably too loud, but it was for sure, until he realized there was no Peter anywhere to be seen. Galt had not yet found our drowned teen, but saw that fear that Death brings when it climbs up inside of us; he didn't panic and he was to learn that was his way, and never could figure out why he got calm in tragic or traumatic moments. He realized Peter had not come up. So he began his swimming recall from class in the summers back in the Village on the Bluff, where, if you didn't know how to swim on Lake Michigan, or rescue others, you had no business on that beach, in that water or even on those little skinny sailfish they loved to rip across that big wild Lake Michigan.

Back and forth he dove, then kicking water in front of him as he got closer to the shore. Panic did begin to set in when it seemed like more than twenty or so seconds that he had not seen Peter's head, that this was a horrific ending to a very big epic night for them, when BAM!... Peter's head jumped above the water as Galt kicked him square in the ribs. Peter had been on the bottom in three feet of water, and came up yelling at him, "What the fuck, Galt!" Then he sank back below the water. To this day Peter probably didn't know if he was just holding his breath, enjoying the pier's light reflection on the bottom of the sandy floor of the lake, but clearly he had no idea to come up for air, as Galt grabbed him by the shoulders and neck and pulled him to shore. It was to be one of the few, if not the only, night of Peter's life where he truly lost control. But as he climbed on the shore, and they slowly crawled back to their room, both only knew this was a night neither would ever forget. Peter spent all night waking up his mom, we are told later, vomiting into a grocery bag Galt found in the kitchen and put next to Peter's cot. Next day, they did 'fess up to Peter's ma and pa, and with great hugs and sadness. They piled into the hot car and headed back home for football summer camp. Stopping at Paul Bunyan's Buffet and eating their way through the five buck all you can eat breakfast. Most likely owing closer to twenty-five bucks, with hangovers and Paul Bunyan staring down at them from above. It was time to get back to being seniors and discovering where that next adventure would be, that amazing year of '69-'70.

3. From One Extreme to the Other

Returning the night before practice started, Galt sat with Mesa on her porch and sipped her mom's Lancers Red and smoked a cigarette (she and her mom were good with this). He could only recall that night and how lucky he and his good pal had been too. It seemed right it was to be that night, with Mesa, his first true girlfriend and female friend, that they found that bond that two young lovers can. They were so close in their shared stories, common interests, varied opinions on hippies, rock-and-roll, school, life, etc., and so much shared in terms of trust and friendship, that they took it to the next step that night, becoming closer than Galt had ever felt to a girl, and with an electricity that first-time true love-making can bring, combined with the wild emotions of seeing death just a few hours before. They both had a feel for each other as two first-time lovers, and it would be that memory that would drive this act of passion and love that fall and spring. They would share many over their senior year, sometimes drunk as skunks, sometimes in the front of her Mom's in his dad's red '65 mustang convertible, at drive-ins, on her mom's couch, or in her bed. Her mother, a peaceful soul of the beat generation, was very comfortable if they smoked cigs, pot, drank beer or wine, and made love in her apartment in Centerville. Dances, movies, hanging with friends, long talks of life, it was a love Galt would never forget, and also compared to all others to come. It wasn't the hard physical wildness, but rather the knowing, feeling each other, and coming together as two lovers can in a magical moment, one after another, that made it so mind-blowing for this young man.

4. Losing Fuel for Higher Ground

Senior year was to be full of new groundbreakings for Galt, but also it was to be full of disappointment, just flat-out depression and feelings of helplessness, much like the poor bastard who had decided to take his poor swimming skills deep into the quarry. Galt was unable to find time, so his pursuit of football excellence was also flat. As there had been a fire inside of him just two short years before in his last year at Forest Prep, he now was realizing that this could be the last year he was to play this violent game, one he had come to love, fought for his fan loyalty, and actually began to enjoy just a few years ago. The fall season of junior year was an unusual season. Galt had won his role on the team, and they had a decent season, playing with some good Wisconsin boys, but he had gone out of wrestling that winter on his coach's recommendation, and had gotten his ass kicked. Weighing in at 158 pounds and wrestling in the 165 classes hardly seemed like a leap of great risk. But that class was referred to as the "Muscle Class" by his fellow wrestlers, the Knaack brothers, of which there were four on the squad. This was only four of the nine that were born of Mrs. Knaack, but these middle four were tough cats. As well, the team was anchored by a small but very tough and living demonstration of will power, Rod McNulty, who was to become a lifetime friend of both Peter and Galt, but also the state wrestling champion two years running, at first 107, then 118? Between the Knaacks and McNulty, they had a strong team at the lower weights. But for some reason, this high school of Highlanders, with over 1,300 students, didn't have any truly big guys. Football had graduated many of them from the prior year, and in Galt's class he stood out as a *big* guy, at 6 feet, 158-pound (going to 180 later his senior year). Hardly powerful, 165-180, and heavyweight talent. As well, at that weight, Galt may have had wide shoulders, but his arm strength, past laying a great head-first tackle on somebody, or a clever block, was not a match for the farm boys, who mostly stood 5'8 to 5'9 and worked like hell to get down to 165 every week. The Muscle Class, every match, would bring to Galt a guy who the Knaack brothers were quick to demonstrate, in the full spirit of team support, before the match across the gym—"There's your guy, the hairy, eighteen-inch neck, bald guy who looks like the wrestling coach. Jesus look at his forearms and biceps!"

Wrong. Every damn time, with some variances for three-day-beard darkness, they were always his next opponents. So Galt made his junior year a mission to not quit, and to take one for the team. He never did learn wrestling, and after thinking he had mastered the art and science of winning at sports, he now found himself eleven defeats at the end of his junior year. A total loss, or a gift of lessons?

5. The Losses and Lessons Keep Stacking Up

For football, he and Peter scrambled back home for the first practice senior year. The team was to be manned by two tackles on offense that stood at 5 '10 and about 220 pounds, square and stocky for sure, but no match for the NFL-sized cats they were to face in competition in their rapidly growing Milwaukee suburb. So it went with football that year, with a similar beat-down and a season of one win and eight losses; hardly anything to write home about, and a lesson in perseverance and finding the way every week to give it all you had, despite knowing it was going to not go your way. Yes, there were a few very close games, where this team actually thought they could be the 500 team their predecessors were the prior year, before graduating all the big guys. But they always came up short. Losses began to pile up, and the cheerleaders seemed to never lose faith. Remember, this is in the land of the Green Bay Packers, world champions like thirty times, where the great coach Lombardi would say, "We don't lose games, we just run out of time." If you listened to Wisconsin folks enough after four brandy Manhattans at the Friday fish fry at the VFW, it was a sport that was life.

But this team was not to be completely denied. Keeping in the spirit of this pursuit of as much debauchery and adventure, without getting caught, as could possibly be accomplished by the class leaders, the Highlanders were to win their homecoming game by a small margin. They took the lead from the beginning and never relinquished it. It was a remarkable Saturday, where all in the stands, as well as on the field, felt a magic that was being brewed in between the white lines. Every phase of the game was working. The look in the eyes of Galt's teammates was different that day as well. These Highlanders knew how to pull their shit together when they needed to. The season had run to 0-7, so that goose egg was removed that day against Minnetonka North, a team who had a better record than their own last-place team, but a team the Highlanders were to have their way with that day. Galt felt the power of purpose and teamwork linking up that day, but also he felt the power of ability. It was for him a day where the three-pointed interdependent triangle came to life for him again. This time it was around organization and success, how ability fed purpose, fed trust and vice versa. Why the coach chose to put people in different roles, and give the team the opportunity to finally win, versus what he had been forcing as player roles prior, one will never understand. But that day was to be their day. It had been a while since Galt had seen a leader on the field like RG back in Forest on the Bluff, but that leader emerged. He was a smaller player with a great heart, but not as much ability to match. But on that day he stopped all of us and the coach from running out on the field through the homecoming ring, to the band playing with the bagpipes, and the cheering crowd of red fans, cheerleaders, and opposition awaiting. Coach said, "Move aside, Van Volker!" Van would not budge: He just took all of his 5'6" frame and stood there blocking the door to the field from the locker room. He stood face to face with our 6'4" losing head coach, and denied him the field…along with the team who didn't believe in itself.

He said to all in that line that day, for this 0-7 team, "I am not going out on that field unless everybody here has one thing they want and is willing to give all they have to get it done. That's a WIN today, and nothing else will do." He finished by saying, "Anybody else wants to not go on the field with me, until you are ready to come back a winner, then I will stay here with you until we all are ready." It was a strike for an emotional commitment by every damn member of that losing bunch to demand victory at all costs for their pride and more importantly for their team and school. But let us also not forget, it would also provide fuel for a great night at homecoming!

All went silent, even the coach, as Van went on to say, "This is our day, nobody else, It is ours to do, and we don't do it unless all in these jerseys are ready"

Nobody knew what came over Van that day; it had not been his style, and usually he was being run over at cornerback by freight trains of big pulling guards and blocking fullbacks bigger than our tackles. But clearly he was done with this losing bullshit, and somehow let his Highlander pride rise to a boiling point. One by one, everybody on the team stepped on his side of the ball and behind him, facing the others and the losing *big* coach, banging helmets with him as they walked with determination not seen to the other side of the locker room runway. Soon, all stood behind Van Volker, son of one of the last dairy farmers in this fast-growing suburban rolling hills. This guy milked cows seven days a week, twice a day, went to school, and also had football practice. But today he was our Highlander with his pipes, and all stood facing the coach across from the thirty-six footballers in Highlander red. The coach stood with a stare at Van and all of his team. He then gently smiled a *big* smile, and said to all of them,

"You guys lead out there, I am going to follow you today to victory."

So it was that day, for four quarters. Coach made a few decisions, but what he did was make the changes his assistants and players with enough balls had been asking to do over his stubborn Vince Lombardi attempts. There was only one Vince Lombardi, and certainly that model didn't apply to this undermanned group of kids. But on this day, it was their day, with all working in harmony. Ability, purpose, and trust of each other, interdependence and success in getting that one day, on this team, to Higher Ground.

6. The Homecoming Dance That Night

Wow.

7. Winter of No Sports

When football season (as Galt thought his last) was coming to an end with a one-point loss to the top team in the conference the week after homecoming, they all walked off that field feeling perhaps even better than they did that day they won homecoming and broke the losing streak. Yes, it left them one and eight and the second-worst record in school history, but the state champions victors that final game had the fear of God put in them, as the boys just wouldn't give an inch, despite the inability to score more than six points, losing seven to six in a first-quarter kick return by the Monsters from Brookfield. It felt good, and the lessons had been learned, but our Galt had enough of sports at this point. He had been playing organized baseball, football, swimming, golf, and wrestling since he could put on a jock, if not before, but now he was done. Losing had taken its toll, but the spirit of how to pull together and always *find a way* was to stay with him for life. That winter proved to be a great time to return to that which he truly loved, and that was those wonderful outdoor winter sports of skiing and pick-up hockey.

8. Skiing and Skating into Spring, with No Winners or Losers

While also being in love, Galt felt this winter term and Christmas break was the best he had ever had, with girlfriend, local ski trips to the north, and pick-up hockey with dads and kids in the hood, and any other takers on the lake ice. Sundays couldn't have gotten any sweeter. Grades continued to slip slowly, but in a very unnoticeable way to all but Galt. A managed decline of sorts. His honors status was being pushed, and thus his National Honor society membership, and cords at the upcoming graduation were also at risk. Galt would put in as much as was needed to keep the numbers where they needed to be. But to what end is it any better? There was no reason he could see. Drinking, dating, and winter sports made for a great winter, and escape from life defined as winning or losing was peace. The pending major transformation was about to come. . .

9. Quitting Golf, Playing Golf, Eating like Two Men, and

Spring of senior year came rolling out of the northern Wisconsin winter winds. A beautiful and yet sometimes bittersweet time it was. The pending end of this two-year run for our wander master was about to come to an end. He knew it, and it made him sad if he let it get inside the frontal lobes, those lobes that he was truly enjoying operating at full capacity.

Frontal lobes per Wikipedia: "The frontal lobes are involved in motor function, problem solving, spontaneity, memory, language, initiation, judgment, impulse control, social and sexual behavior."

The knowledge to "have the end in mind', as yet to be put into Galt's head. One that is becoming good at understanding to observe, analyze, and remember to act as needed. But the "why and to what" end remains a very dark hole, he has yet to shine a light of understanding on

The Wisconsin folks, as Galt had learned just a year before upon his brother Wes's death, truly embraced transition with all feet in. Some decided to go to Viet Nam as Marine volunteers, many to college, some back to finish the apprenticeship of their family dairy farm, and some to just take off for the West and never come back. Either way, spring prom was clearly the best party of the year, staying out till the next day's afternoon sunlight, with all night bonfires on the beaches of Lake Michigan north to Oostburg, with beer, smokes, and your best gal and pals all with you for the entire event. There was something else Galt was to learn, that his buddies, guys and gals, were also becoming his best friends during this time of great emotion. Their steady hand, calmness, and openness to a male friend was a step in Galt's growth, but would also require him to continue to build on that spring's new friends. Realizing he now had twice as many pals as he thought, after all the schools and homes he had seen since birth, was a joyful moment for him. But the one thing that was not clear to Galt, and would become even muddier as the next six years were to pass quickly, was that he was about to enter another period of great variability, as he had in junior high, and in his four kindergartens, a time when up and down was constant, and sideways seemed the best step, darkness again before the light... Was he to be a college boy?

Certainly not as one would think.

10. Who Actually Picks the College? Or, "Any Place but There

With honor cords around his neck, National Honor Society recognition, and coaches at Colorado College, Colby College, Colgate, and Cornell asking him to come play football and get an Ivy-ike education, Galt was ready for the East, or so he thought. Colorado College just seemed to not meet his prep expectations. His dad, who was quite proud of his "number one son," also (Galt believed) harbored a hope that going away would end his high school romance, despite the fact this was his parents' love roots and served them very well in their adventure in life together. Despite the beauty of Mesa and her family, along with the pot, the beatnik amazing mom, taking Galt to see Woodstock at the premiere in hippie town (by University of Wisconsin Milwaukee, old Downer Theater) . . . Galt would talk about the wonderful family experiences he shared with Mesa and hers. He would also share with his parents the details of the film Woodstock, including all the naked people, awesome music, and the thick smell of pot in the theater that evening . . . So a break-up was their hope, and one would have thought that going to New York state or Maine would help bring an end to this love affair with this "very nice" girl, before the two of them might even make an engagement announcement. Certainly they had talked of marriage in their intimate times. Often she led the conversation, but he never shied away or chose to stop it.

But . . .

Dad decided, with Galt's SAT scores being far and above what was needed for most universities, to help his son with his choice. Budget was not the issue, as his folks worked their asses off to assure all their children would get a post- high-school education at the institution of their choice. Mom had earned her degree while Dad was in the navy, and they were engaged after World War II. Dad was not to earn his degree until Galt's freshman year in high school. He went to seven colleges, accumulating credits as needed while also growing his career and providing for his family over twenty-four years; truly who he was. But in the case of guidance for the firstborn, it was only the following criteria Dad considered:

a.   Closer to home than those East and West "great institutions."
b.   Equivalent education standards.
c.   A smaller school, so Galt could play football, join a frat, get a pre-law degree and go onto a law school and a great career.

His dad had it figured out for him, and with all his love, knew he didn't want number one to go through what he had gone through. This was to be his path to a great life. Mom was too busy to push back, with Ben being his own man, and little sis and baby bro also needing all she had.

So it came down to a bonding event with dad and son. Galt didn't want any part of a small liberal arts college in Minnesota, which is where Mackey College was located, number eight on the list of best colleges by *U. S. News*, and a honey pot for National Merit Scholarships, as well where Galt's 1300 composite SAT would put him in the bottom third of the acceptance levels. But numerous grads went onto law school, etc. Galt never saw the campus, but in a last-ditch effort, attempted to get his dad to agree to staying close to home, at a great school, the University of Wisconsin (where "liberal radicals" had just blown up the Math Research Center, and Jane Fonda made an annual spring trip to the May Day rally on the street the SDS and Weather Underground called home). But Galt knew little of this, he only knew the U in Madtown was a cool place with a business school and lots of options, lots of them. Dad won, Galt lost. Seems an odd way to put it, but that is how it felt to him. Never having stepped foot on campus, Galt was to find himself that September of 1970 in a dorm with some truly interesting characters His old friend and fellow Highlander, national honors-winner, and state wrestling champion Rod McNulty. Did all of that make it ok? Doubt began to weave its way into his confidence, sense of value, and finally, reason. Why am I here? To what end or objective am I striving for?

CHAPTER 11:

How Many Colleges Can One Go To?

B rains and Curds.

Seventeen, with a chest full of all the medals and recognition any senior in high school could ever expect, Galt suddenly didn't feel like his last two years of accomplishments and mastery of the game in high school was going to matter soon. This concept of going to the best college one could was branded on him, and how fortunate he was to have the choice as well. But suddenly, this didn't seem like a choice, or even the right step for him. He didn't realize it that August, as his many friends began to disappear to state schools, but he wasn't prepared at all. Grades, sports, social events, great family, something had gone out of balance, and suddenly his triangle was back and reminded him that his soul and spirit weren't in sync with the body and mind he now developed. Maturing didn't even cross his mind, for he knew he could go it on his own if he had to, but he also had no clue where he was supposed to be. Stand up, be accountable but to what end? Make enough money to move out, join the VietNam war, be a bum, or go to college and see if he could figure it out there?

With the late start at Mackey, the third week of September, all his friends had left town, and there he was hanging, no summer job anymore, and a new place to live and learn, one he had never even been to or even close to it, was to be his new home.

The drive to the small town and the campus setting dead-center on main street , a week before classes, couldn't have been any prettier. The fall colors were in full exposure over the beautiful landscapes of the Wisconsin Driftless region as they approached the Mississippi River. They crossed into Minnesota, and to the remote area made famous by the attempted robbery of the First National Bank of Northfield by the James Younger Gang in 1876; 106 years ago almost to the day that Galt arrived with his folks in their Ford Country Squire wagon. Twenty thousand people and about forty-five miles from the Twin Cities, it was truly a country town, supported by this institution of extremely higher learning. Calvanist in its origins from 1866, it was a place for the best of liberal arts education.

Academic standards for admissions were almost equivalent to the small Ivy League, but also attracted a very different crowd. Seventy percent of the students were from out of state, with half of that number being from East Coast prep schools. Mackey had achieved an exceptional reputation for the kid who didn't quite fit the Ivy League mold, but who was almost too smart for even that level of undergraduate education. Its liberal arts focus and pristine campus of two hundred students, supported by a full athletic program and Greek life, was a perfect place for the parents of East Coast and Chicago kids' parents, who had sent their child away when very young to a prep school for reasons tough to grasp beyond abdication. At Mackey these parents could "drop" their children off for another four years, and fly back home feeling their child, now seventeen or eighteen, was to get the ultimate liberal arts education at its best, with exceptional faculty in a value system of old fashion Midwest roots. Little did they know that removing a young adult with a great mind to another remote location, and no outlets to speak of beyond more academic independence, with a peer group of the same framework, meant that some very deep, dark, and wildly interesting explorations would take place. These explorations went way past academia, and the rational education their folks held hopes for.

Galt's folks said goodbye with a hug and kiss, and words of "Do well," "We love you," and "Call us."

Galt then proceeded to set his trunk in his seventy-year-old dorm room, and pick a bed of the two, as his roommate was not there yet during orientation week. He then walked the halls to the door, went outside, took a deep breath, and explored his new home for the next four years.

His roommate did show up, but a few days after the expedited deadline. That meant he missed his chance to participate in the blind date the school had set up for a getto-know, based on some questions the students answered about three months ago on a computer punch card. Their point was that the cards were then entered into their new computer on campus, and you were matched to your most likely date for the first mixer. WTH?

Galt, still polite and a bit naïve on the ways of the world beyond his suburban enclaves he was raised in, was still in a bit of shock, but trying like hell to be cool as new faces and very long-haired people walked by, none of them smiling. The odor he had last smelt in his girlfriend Mesa's apartment with her mom, and at the theater during the premier of "Woodstock," was permeating the halls during this sunny afternoon, day two, as most of the students had arrived. Galt made ready, now feeling anxious for this "blind date."

He was dressed in his best preppy outfit, while others wore scarfs, shirts un-tucked, sandals, weird shirts with paisley patterns, and ponytails, and some had beards even. Galt found his way to the dorm to meet his blind date, Margaret Olsen. He knew very little about her, other than the time and place he was to pick her up, and walk over to the student union for the "party." She was a pretty girl, but she also had a very serious look about her, with her very blond hair and deep blue eyes. For Margaret (not Maggie Galt please!) was a girl of deep Scandinavian roots, as most of the instate kids were. She had attended a very large, three-thousand-student school in the 'burbs of Minnesota. As they walked and did the very few pleasantries about hometowns and schools, she opened things up for Galt by asking (the first, but not the last time he would hear this question at CC):

"So, Galt, where did you graduate in your senior class?"

Galt: "Thirty-nine out of four hundred and twelve; top ten percent, I think."

Maggie didn't even wait for his question. She said she graduated *summa cum laude* or was number one in her class. She then said, "My school was three thousand students."

Galt was feeling a movement in his whole body of discomfort. More than the anxious feelings of an unknown first date…."What is this all about?"

She then asked the other Mackey question that was always number two in that first semester of getting to know people: "What was your SAT score, Galt?"

He repeated this one with great pride, because he knew it had been good enough for the small Ivy League schools back east, with a resounding 1310 composite! She smiled and turned away, as she said "mine was 1430".

Needless to say, the date did not go well. Maggie, believing she had actually turned off Galt, as she may have before and after to other eligible bachelors and breeding stock for her fine brilliant Scandinavian lines. She then tried to pivot the conversation over a beer. Yes, a beer in the union, as Minnesota allowed 3.2 percent in those days for eighteen-year-olds. Galt felt older, despite being only seventeen, when he was able to fill two cups of Minnesota North Stars lager for his date.

She said to Galt, "Did you look at other schools?" and he of course laid out his entire manifest of options he had, and that his dad had cast aside. She warmed up a bit after that list was promoted, but her smile was never warm, and he knew this must be a freak on campus, as all of them can't be like this? New people, unknown people were everywhere, odd short conversations with other new freshmen and all about status and standing from their past. He just wanted to get her back to the dorm and crawl into bed, hoping the MIA roommate had not yet shown up. He did, and about two hours later walked her back, and she suddenly got warm, maybe in a last-ditch attempt to get this Galt to ask her out again. It was as if she had transformed on those dorm steps. He just turned as she went for the lips, as did Jordan many years ago, but he turned because this was no Jordan, and clearly not something he was ever hoping to experience again: a freaking blind date with a genius.

As he opened his dorm door, thinking he might put his Crosby Stills and Nash album on his small turntable and stereo speakers, he lay down to contemplate what was going on here to "Wooden Ships." Suddenly he heard the floor creak next to his bed. Opening his eyes, Koss headphones on, he saw this 6 '5," 300-pound man staring at him from the other bed by the window. The man lay there, with blond hair in a ponytail, and a pack of Winston Golds by his side, and an ashtray, too, as he was pulling on that Gold as hard as anybody could. His name, and this is not shit, was Roger Superior, and he looked like a gigantic Cheshire cat from *Alice in Wonderland* on that bed, a position Galt would get used to seeing him in over and over again. He had the courtesy to open the window behind him to a beautiful fall evening, in the northland, but the smoke just blew back in.

Of course, after a hello and name share, and Roger not sharing his academic prowess, Galt then thought he must conform and ask the questions Maggie had just put him through, hoping to break the ice of this big man of little words.

Roger said: "I am from a prep school in the Chicago area called Lake Forest Academy."

Ok, that was all he had to say, so Galt pried again: "Why are you late getting here?"

"Oh, yeah, that; I didn't want to do the date shit, and I had to fly back from Boston yesterday to get a ride up here with my folks."

Galt: "Why Boston?" as Roger had not added a damn thing to that sentence either, as he continued to pull big on a second Winston Gold.

"Oh, yeah, that. Well. . ." Moments that seemed to be hours passed . . . "I was at MIT, in their accelerated math program. Place was a bunch of freaks, and competitive as hell. So I dropped out and folks scrambled to get me in here."

"Why freaks?"

"They were all serious, you know man, like not into the Doors, Rare Earth, Blues Image, or Black Sabbath, much less just hanging out."

Galt then did the other routine Mackey freshman orientation question that was mandatory: "What was your SAT score, if I could ask?"

"Who gives a shit? But if you must know, I had 430 on my verbal"—almost 250 points below Galt's score—"and I had an 800 on my math score."

Galt was stunned, as these numbers actually meant something to him. "800...Isn't that perfect?"

Roger: "Yes, man, but 800 really isn't perfect on SATS."

Galt: "Why not?"

"The exam developers, being the math geeks they are, calculated a risk and failure factor into their scoring methods, which also aligns with the potential for an error in their own plethora of questions and problems they ask. So it is actually a perfect *plus or minus* three answers."

So it went that evening, as the two got to know each other, with Roger saying, "You are the all-American boy!" and Galt saying he had no idea what Roger meant.

Then Roger left him this one to sleep and dream on, as the next day was the last of two before his classes would begin. "Hey, man," said Rog. "Do you smoke?"

Galt said no.

"Don't you smoke pot?"

Galt said, "No; why, do you?"

Roger: "Yes, man, I find if I get a little lit, I can solve my advanced calculus better, as they put me in junior level math and physics, so I am hoping to be able to smoke a lot of marijuana here in our room. I hope the school is cool with that, as are you?"

Shit, Galt was in trouble, or he was about to venture down one weird hole. The *Alice in Wonderland* analogy would come to apply at every turn here at Mackey, as would a new definition of The Trinity.

Galt Continues his Peel Back of Odd Carl

Galt was uneasy in the dorms during orientation week. He knew this place never felt comfortable, and the fellow students had continued to surprise and also freak him out at every introduction.

He was trying, and so he had accepted ANOTHER blinder set up by his pal Rod, who had hit it off with his computer date. She had a roommate, and Rod had, in his way, talked Galt into not giving up, though he still had feelings for Mesa, and was now beginning to long for her and her touch.

He cleaned up with a shower and came back to his room wishing he still had the song he thought he had. But Roger was lost among those Winston Gold cigs and noodling math formulas, so he decided to get dressed early and took a long walk out of the dorm to pick up his blind date.

She came down the stairs looking pretty nice, with a big smile and a pantsuit. Very avant garde for Minnesota in 1970. But he wore his khakis, Bass Weejun loafers with pennies, his blue crew sweater, and navy button-down shirt, and thus felt every bit the part of a preppy in the making who was headed to Northfield Minnesota and not New York state.

Her name was Allison, and he quickly found her to be a huge bore. Not less than five minutes into the walk to the student union, the patterned Mackey Q & A began. "What HS did you go to? Where did you graduate in rank, and what were your SAT scores?" Rod kept nudging Galt to listen, hissing, "Get into it," in his ear.

Allison got it all from Galt in five to ten seconds, but it became clear she would need ten minutes to articulate her status as a just-about-perfect SAT tester, number one at her high school in Green Bay, in a class of 500 (aka valedictorian. Two valedictorians in two nights. What was this place?)

Galt was on his way back to his room and the giant Cheshire cat after about ninety minutes and one lousy light beer. (Beer was perhaps Minnesota's gift to all the kids going and coming back from Nam.)

Either way, the brat was good (his first of many in his life of a remarkable thing called a Johnsonville Bratwurst, with kraut on a hard roll).

Her articulation of her personal genius was only interrupted by her fellow dormer and Rod's date, who sat down with what Galt thought was a cult of valedictorians. He was quickly growing tired of these academic measures of who you were, as he had his senior spring. He had already lost his interest in school, which didn't bode well for his future in this period of three-term, ten-week, three classes of rapid speed learning with a pack of valedictorians and as many near-valedictorians.

As he dropped her back home and the awkward moment of the goodnight, eyes and maybe lips meeting, he suddenly felt she may have mellowed a bit and may have realized she had bored him to death. So she got warm and tousled his hair, gave him a very different look, and began to bring her mouth to his. Galt wasn't to be fooled; he took it in as a bad situation not getting better, and gave her a kiss on her cheek and a nice, firm goodbye hug, and said, "See you around campus," and trotted back quickly to hide from this, and join more Wonderland in his dorm room.

Three a.m. that night, after two nights of valedictorian nightmares, there was Galt in his boxers and t-shirts, rising out of bed, hearing Rachmaninoff's second piano concerto rising up from the first-floor living room grand piano down the hall. He always had liked it, as it was part of his dad's eclectic record collection, and remembered the story of Rachmaninoff's fingers being twice the size of an average man, enabling him to play spans on the keys never before seen by Chopin or others who could not reach his written chords.

He stumbled down the hall and saw a long greasy ponytail, black tattered blazer with the collar turned up, an ascot tied around the neck like an urban version of Roy Rogers. He was Alex Lowenstein from New York City, playing it like he was born too. Alex was as tall as Roger, but couldn't have weighed more than 150 pounds on his 6' 5" frame. Next to him on a couch, with long strawberry hair, was what Galt concluded in his short tenure to be one of the prettiest girls on campus. Her name was Alice Mahoney, and she was also a Manhattan-raised child, and also attended, with Alex, a prep music school in Connecticut. They found the conservatory at Mackey to be their choice for their continued pursuit of music. He played the piano and she played the violin. Both were just pals, but both had some other twisted chemistry Galt was to find out about shortly.

She motioned with her eyes and flipped her hair, for him to sit next to her. Without hesitation, he joined her on the couch, about three feet away from where she was patting the pillow for his ass and boxers to rest upon.

He was quiet and awed by Alex playing, but also staring at her hair and green eyes, as she would turn to see if he was listening. She was in a baggie pair of khakis and an irish wool sweater turtleneck, that as baggie as they were, were made for her. Suddenly Alex turned around while spanning multiple keys and said, "This four-way orange sunshine is amazing." She smiled and acknowledged the same bliss, and as he finished his last chord she recommended they move to his single room in the roof apartments of the dorm, for "some mellowing out." She asked Galt to join them. No names or any other words had been shared up to that point, despite a good twenty minutes passing of some of the greatest classic piano rendition Galt had ever heard. He also made note of the "4 way orange sunshine" comment, but figured he would let that lie, because he really didn't know what it was.

He followed despite being very unsure, but his spirit of adventure and need for friendship drew him in. His words, in a quiet way he didn't even think were his voice, said, "Cool, let me go put on some clothes and join you on the fourth floor."

They both said, "No need, it's cool, man, come as you are."

Before he knew it, he was in the single bedroom sitting on the window sill, as Alice put on the soundtrack to Fantasia. Alex lit up a small pipe of what seemed to be pot—it had a pot smell—but the product inside was a sticky herb cube. She said, "Sunday brunch would be awesome after all this? I think it's at 10:30. Just four hours, we can work up a bigger appetite, and Galt, you can join us for that, too."

Galt became a bit paranoid as he refused the pipe, despite her beautiful red hair, those green eyes, and perfect freckles. She had removed that sweater, and was wearing that army green t-shirt, no bra, and had what seemed to be remarkable breasts. He was occupied by this beauty with his body, and his intake of the mind for any comparison to anything he had ever seen, but yet his soul was pushing back.

They both now had two pulls of the blond Lebanese hash, as Tchaikovsky's "Sugar Plum Fairies" played. He knew the conditions were out there, but the conditions were also brand new, and so he motioned to her, after Alex had done his pull again for a hit. Hot it was, but also very smooth. A small cough came after he followed her instructions of holding for a count of thirty. Thus it entered his clean, drug-free body, with no point of reference beyond the beer and infrequent purple passion punch from his senior year in high school. Suddenly images from an album he had liked when drinking beer in Rod's basement last summer. She had changed up the vinyl, and now it seemed it was an album Rod's older brother had left behind last summer, but it wasn't. It was the same voice, but he was singing, "I'm waiting for my man." Then it was onto a long, strange song about heroin, with the same chords over and over, but it seemed to be speeding up, then slowing down, then speeding up. So with his brain now going soft, he was able to build a comparison to these too being a red haired version of Nico, and a tall version of Andy Warhol with black long hair. Alice motioned for him to move to the bed with both of them. She had left a narrow space between her and Alex, and motioned for him to get off the window sill and get over t h e r e, with that same pat-pat from the couch, now on the mattress.

WTH, his boxers suddenly were no longer able to hide his personal stuff, as the tension between the fly and the band began to get tighter. It had been weeks since he and Mesa had sex, and so even with that greasy tall version of Andy Warhol watching or as the other book end, he began to calculate why not?

He struggled to just lay down his developing intuition, a power he was to develop unconsciously, that somehow tied with the voice of that spirit who came in his dreams, the one who always brought him a smile at dawn's early light when waking up. SHE, the spirited one, was waving at him from the window sill, now an image of her, for the first time. He found himself staring at her with another blast of emotion more powerful than the seduction and hashish of this room was bringing him. This wasn't a pagan urge, but rather a beautiful thing. Her hair lay over her shoulder, her beautiful hips and short waist, neck smooth, long and tender, along with those eyes and smile had him paralyzed.

So why had this spirit chosen to come visit him now at this moment? SHE was a visitor to him only a few times a year, and usually in his sleep when puberty began.

SHE then whispered to him, "Go now Galt, Go Now!"

So as his body weight and momentum rolled him to his side on the bed between Alex and Alice, with his head in his hand on his side, he found he was staring at Alex, and not Alice, Alex then took a bit of his now-growing long hair, and pushed it away from his forehead, and said: "How beautiful you are, your strawberry blonde hair and freckles remind me of Alice." Alice then whispered in his ear, "Don't be afraid, go ahead, I will take my clothes off while you two get to know each other! The three of us will work up quite an appetite."

Lou Reed was now singing "I don't know where I'm going, but I'm going to try, because it makes me feel like a man, as I feel like Jesus' son. . .wish I was born a thousand years ago, so I could sail the darkest seas. . . when I'm closing in on death...You all can go take a walk...I just don't know, I guess I just don't know."

Galt was suddenly without any tension between his legs, despite all the carnal foreplay going on with both sexes, and could only come up with one thought: Escape Now, or become something you are not destined to be.

He rolled off the small single bed onto the wooden floor and banged his knees hard, but indifferent to pain. His best sense of politeness surfaced—completely out of context, with four eyes with no spirit behind them and their two naked bodies—in his awkward way.

He thanked them, but said he needed to get some pre-work done this Sunday before classes began on Monday. He said, "I hope to see you at brunch," wishing it to not be true, and that it was likely only intended for her, not Alex. He didn't look back as he ran down the four flights to his

Roger Cheshire roommate snoring across the stinky room of tobacco. He pulled his comforter over his head and could only think one thought: "I wish my dad had been more flexible with *his* college choices."

Then as he laid his tired and very confused head down on that dorm room pillow, as his Cheshire cat roommate snored across the room, he realized why SHE had come in this most sensuous of images. It was how she had pulled his curiosity away from the other two, giving him the sense to get the hell out of there.

As orientation week went on, Galt grew more uneasy. That discomfort, fear, or just a feeling of not liking where he was, cascaded into his school work. Work he had been so good at. Escape became his answer to the situation. He knew this place never felt comfortable, that he never belonged. The fellow students had continued to surprise and also freak him out at every introduction, with their drill of the same academic rank questions from the past. The Cheshire Cat Roger, the smoke, the MIT dropout, the very aggressive computer date, the two refugees from New York City, intense academics, a very long winter, and of course the fact he never wanted to be here...all of it was too much.

CHAPTER 11.5:

How Many Colleges Can One Attend?

T he fall wore on, the pot became more important to him, and the hope that maybe joining the football team would save his ass from this darkness seemed to be slipping too. He made a few friends, good friends. But in general, that was not to be the prep he should have or needed, because he was truly lost and didn't know it. He ran from the truth, that at seventeen going on eighteen he had no purpose, no sense of soul. So he worked his brain, joined the football team, hoping to achieve some kind of high school balance. But putting all your resources into those two of the three was never a winning formula anyway, was it?

He ran from his soul, deeper and deeper into the darkness he slipped. Girls didn't even seem important. He was so far afield from this desire he had so strongly in high school. When he got home for Christmas vacation, he arranged for he and Mesa to be together for their final date. They were to double date with old high school pals Peter and Terri. Peter had let his hair grow and was expanding his soul and life in Missoula, and Terri was on course to be the amazing doctor she was destined to be with her care and great mind.

They were to meet at Terri's north side apartment, and it was there that they would then venture for a retro double date to one of the old Milwaukee pizza and beer halls near University of Wisconsin-Milwaukee. As Galt and Mesa pulled up to the apartment, he saw Peter's dad's Bullet '68 fastback red Mustang parked. Galt pulled up behind it in his dad's new '70 Black convertible Mustang. Both the pops loved speed and their ponies as means to commute. He put the car in park, turned off the radio playing "American Women," by the Guess Who. The lyrics were too coarse for this moment but he knew he couldn't let it go any further. It wasn't for another woman, or for her intent. He just needed to be alone and as deep inside his own thoughts as he could possibly be these days.

He turned to her and said, "Mesa, you know I love you, but I don't love in the way we have in the past. You are an amazing and beautiful woman, and what we had will always be with me." Of course, that was his true feeling, but it rang to disguise as it so often does with break-ups. Galt had barely kept his ass off probation, despite studying at a level he had never done before, and he had been stoned a bit too much, had won six football games for the fresh Vikings of Mackey, and traveled to other small Midwest colleges. Yet his soul was lost. She need not come with him down this dark path he was headed.

She did not of course expect this at all, as she was deeply in love with him. It was not easy in the next few minutes to respond to the "Why, why, why?" It seemed there was no rational way to explain this place he was, and he only wanted to make sure she would stop crying, and they could get out of the car for some air. She did finally turn to him and say, "What are we going to do? Go up to Terri's and explain to them it is over, and I am a disaster, and we go out to dinner? Galt, what do you want?"

That was the worst she could have said to him at that moment, as she always was there for him, and had always asked him that question whatever the circumstances in their deep relationship. He could only say, "Let's get out, take a walk and decide if we want to do this or not with them. We do have to let them know." He did know this, and it was a lesson he would have to relearn again and again, as life brings with it these awful twists and then regeneration.

Love, Loss and Renewal and More Love

Galt and Mesa walked hand in hand, with tears; and then some calm began with the fresh air. Mesa said, "Let's go up there and tell them where we are and see what we do next? Are you ok with that?"

Was that asked again? He did love that, but he would learn that the woman that challenged him kept him on his toes with his emotions and experiences, and needed yet did not need him at any time, but trusted that when together there was no more powerful couple on earth. Women who stood and taught him, as well as wanting to learn from him would become the way to finding the one with whom never ending love would be shared. He was to learn one more time of the pain of a broken heart, from one born under the sign of Scorpio. He would have to go through a much more painful experience, but also the most powerful renewal he would have. That renewal was to come years after that rainy December evening in Milwaukee, and it was to bring he and SHE together someday, to a place of Higher Ground, that Galt would learn as the pinnacle of life on earth.

They went to the fourth floor of the building and knocked. Terri answered the door, tears in her eyes. Galt could only try to imagine how she may have known of the messy stuff that had just taken place on Oakland Avenue in his dad's car. He would learn that there was no connection, other than there was!

Peter had come back from Montana with another love, one he had fallen for pretty hard. He had no choice, as both of them were men of honor in this regard. There was to be no dual dealing with women they loved and were loved back by. He had just told Terri the basic same speech as had Galt. For that matter, it could have been at the same damn moment. Mesa then explained to Terri what Galt had just "done" down on the street. They both in tears went into a huge, girl-best-pals hug. Galt felt even worse, with sadness, yet had no regret for what had happened.

Over the girls' shoulders was Peter sitting on the couch looking in shock back at Galt. His face then went to a look of, "Are you kidding, we both did this on the same night and the same place before a double date?"

It was true, and they knew that this was to be a long night. But these Wisconsin women were much more mature and stronger than these Highlander boys home from college, a lesson Galt was to learn about as he grew into a good man, a lesson that would, however, take a long time. He never did connect the fact that his mom, who was to him the strongest person in the world, and that these women were of the same strength. It would be some time still before that he as a growing man, lost as he was, should know of the power of a strong woman. How they can make a man's life so much fuller when you understand that.

Pizza and beer was a good final date. The two women went and talked in Terri's bedroom. Galt and Peter then had a short, quiet chat about what the hell had just happened, more awed by the coincidence, than by emotion, but both in a bit of shock, and unsure as to what would happen next when the two amazing women would emerge from that bedroom.

Both Mesa and Terri were now calm and pretty collected. They looked at the two dumb asses on the couch and said: "We need to go out and make this the best double date we have ever had. We also know this will be the last one, but we ask both of you to be as good as we know you to be, and let all of us enjoy these final moments as the four of us in the best way we possibly can."

They did. It was as strange and as wonderful as an evening with great women could be. But it was the end for sure. Some follow-ups with Mesa and long letters would follow as she tried to understand, but Galt was to go deeper and deeper into that dark state of a lost eighteen-year-old, who had now begun to ask:

CHAPTER 11.5(B)

Why am I, and why am I doing what I am doing?

He had no idea why college mattered, what he should be if not a college student, and what he then should do next, but escape, and he did that the next semester, to the point where his efforts to even attend classes were irrelevant to him. He would tell his folks on the phone he didn't want to be there, and then they would ask where, and he could only say: "Not here, as I am truly lost." National Honors, multiple letters, never a police record, respected by teachers and friends from childhood on, no family issues, but boy, was he lost. Hockey for the Vikings, football, even trips to the library to study where he knew the environment was conducive, didn't help; even his good few friends at Mackey who didn't want to lose this good pal from college tried to get him straight. Nobody was going to.

Galt did have an escape that he thought might be the hole in the darkness that led to the light for him. That spring, as he was failing classes in all kinds of advanced philosophy and mathematics, he was invited by Peter to come out to Montana to visit for spring break. He also knew Galt was slipping. Not serious drugs, but really dark and deep introspection. So the invite came. Off Galt went all the way to the beautiful Bitterroot valley, a place that had the feel of the land he should be in. He and Peter had a good first few days. Then Peter mentioned the second morning as they were getting breakfast at a local greasy spoon, with magnificent hangovers, that he had met a girl in a class that said she was from Forest Bluff. He then went on to ask her if she knew Galt. She just stared at Peter and said, "Are you kidding?" in that beautiful, still-New England accent she had in sixth grade when Galt first put eyes on this steady first love. Peter then told Galt, as his eyes began opening with some life that probably had not been seen in a few months, that he had her address and she wanted Galt to call her if he did come out for spring break.

"Have you told her I'm coming out?"

"Yep."

"And she said that?"

"Yep again."

Peter knew Galt's eyes, for these two guys knew each other and were long kindred pals. Both would joke in later life how they knew enough about each other to ruin careers, marriages, and reputations. But it would never happen.

Peter pushed his 400 Suzuki keys across the table to Galt, wrote down on the napkin the address and said, "Go for it, Dancing Bear," a nickname Galt was to hold for many years, as his beard, long hair and growing girth would demonstrate.

Galt said, "You ok with this?

"Galt, man, *go for it*. Get out of that shell, and see if this is a path to some joy and light to Higher Ground. The higher the road you follow here, you will find that there can always be even higher ground. Physically and spiritually."

Galt turned and smiled at Peter, walked out not even thinking about paying the bill. He went out to Peter's big dirt bike, parked out in front of the diner. He turned it on, and as he had learned in high school with his own motorcycle, felt that being on the back of one of these things was true freedom. But freedom and a goal that was a winning combination. He followed the instructions from Peter, and pulled up in front of a very old dorm, in the pines, near the beautiful Clarks Fork River roaring through Missoula that spring. The sun was out, it was ten a.m., and the odds of her being there on a Monday were most likely small. He still jumped off, and walked into the lobby, and asked at the desk for her.

The security guy handed him a phone and said, "Dial 333 and she may answer; if not, you can leave a message on her room phone at that extension."

She picked up, and there was that sweet voice, and it wasn't but a minute she emerged in Levi jeans, pink button-down shirt, wrinkled, hair pulled back in a ponytail, and those big, blue eyes. It had been four years since they last saw each other at their sophomore high school lockers, and five since that first and only kiss.

Galt just stared into the blue eyes, and she also smiled. A very big grin settled in. No words yet, just a shared gaze.

It was 1,600 miles until they came to this moment. Not sure, but they both look like two lost souls who had just found their light together in a better place. Madison had also lost herself at the University of Montana. She and Galt were on exactly the same paths. He got a hug that created a warm glow through his very cold body, and then a kiss that was as warm and inviting as he could even remember. She said, "Galt, let's go for a walk, and we can catch up." Galt asked if she had class, and she said, "Don't worry about that, you are here and so am I, so let's get outside and see where it leads us."

Get to know each other. Galt mentioned he had used the motorcycle parked under the pine tree. She smiled and pointed at it. In a few seconds, he had Madison on the back of the seat, and they had her dorm room in the rearview mirror. He didn't see Peter till the morning he was to leave to head back to the tundra of central Minnesota six days later.

11. 5(C) CONT.:

G alt had his first time in the warm waters of Ataraxis, just when he needed that tranquility.

As he aimed the bike's front forks up the dirt road out of town, Galt felt Madison's arms and hands reach around his waist and squeeze his belly with the touch he had not felt. Perhaps it was the mile high or more air as they sped up and over the Bitterroots to a small mining town at the end of the road. Sitting on the edge of a deep chasm, and a mighty-roaring river, bordered by beautiful cliffs, there it was, a small house of sorts, with a porch and double bar room doors. Parked around the front were 4 x 4 vehicles of all kinds, many that had been modified, and none with roofs. There were also a few dirt bikes like Galt's transportation, and a couple of bikes lying against the old tie-up for horses. The music coming out was familiar to Galt.

Galt and Madison were destined to spend afternoons and evenings in her room, forgetting to eat and where they had even put their clothes. They would learn during those beautiful hours that they both had similar interests in music. So as they walked the stairs and through those old bar room swinging doors, they both knew this music coming from the stage. It was the album she had played on a few occasions along with Cat Stevens' *Tea for the Tillerman* and Traffic's *John Barleycorn Must Die*. Innocent lovers, both trying to figure it out, for it was familiar to both.

121

There he was behind some old wooden tables and chairs, packed with young peers from Missoula on this beautiful spring morning. It was none other than Steven Stills, playing solo, and singing his heart out in between sips of beer. It was magical the way folks smiled, the music was perfect, and Madison held his hand and he gripped back. It was as if being wise or confident came roaring back. It was to be a survival and also a common-sense asset he would have as part of his growing intuition toolbox. This was clearly a spiritual and body experience, and some mind, as they stumbled over the words, but the buzz and altitude were untradeable. Pitcher of beer and a few songs, and Galt knew it was time to get this beautiful woman down to town safely. He knew her well enough to know she would go with the flow and him no matter what was ahead, maybe even sleeping up there in the tiny town of Lolo, in the Jack Saloon, on a grassy field on Graves Creek, Montana. Galt knew better. Galt knew it was time to move to more stable ground.

This amazing tour of the high country was also surfacing the pretty messed up Minnesota life. He had almost forgotten Mackey, and the almost 1600 SAT composite colleagues, but it was Friday, and his plane back to Minneapolis was scheduled tomorrow afternoon. Both had consumed as much Great Falls Select as the other. She drank beer like a man, but moved with such grace and serenity. Her New England accent got richer as they sang, laughed, kissed and listened to the best concert of both their lives. But as the sun began to get lower, and the shadows covered the canyon walls below, Galt's sense of caution awoke.

They only ran into one problem on their way down, full of beer and the need to piss. As he stopped and both of them walked into the pines to relieve themselves, he came back first, but not after a not-so-gentleman-like peek at her behind pulling up those red-tag Levis. He turned the key, and it would not start. She came up and wondered why. He was unsure, but confident as he could be. He knew his motorcycles. He kept trying, and thinking it might be flooded. Then Madison, ever the pragmatist, said, "Galt, look at the fuel gauge. We are out, honey."

Shit.

He looked at her and she at him, they hugged. Fear was not in the cards that day, and both stepped back, as Madison said to him, "It's all downhill from here, Galt. Just throw it into neutral, hold the brakes, and we should be able glide into town and a station."

He smiled, grabbed her again, and both held tight to each other as she pressed her body into him, and their pelvis found each other. She felt him, and he held her tight as their lips now went very long and wet, and their tongues were dancing as two dance partners who had done this a thousand times, but always with passion.

He was shaking as they pulled apart to get on. She could feel him, and then wrapped her arms around his stomach and rubbed his belly as much for gentle passion but also to calm him down and help him stay focused. "Push off, Galt, I am so ready for this."

Those six days were magical. So magical that she left Missoula with all her grades in the fail mode and quickly drove her mom's Volkswagen up to Northfield and visited Galt on campus during the last few weeks of the trimester. During what was to be his term of final probation. Needless to say, this was passion and two lost souls who grabbed onto each other like there was no tomorrow, and of course they both failed their college opportunity, but they had magic together despite this, saving each other from the darkness for just a bit.

As he stood at the window of his gate of the Missoula airport, looking out at the Bitterroots and maybe even that dirt road up to that bar, he heard a voice his foggy mind had not heard in many, many moons. It was SHE, the sweet siren, who had come to him so many times in his dreams during his times of most stress and life's challenges. The spring air, the slight breeze, the sun in his face and the warmth of Madison holding onto his hips and up at his face, he didn't even sense for that moment that SHE, that special soul who was his greatest love, deep inside his heart, where no other could go.

He thought, why now? When I am full of such warmth?

Galt would find love just a few more times in his life, but none would even compare to this warmth and swell brought into his heart. She would whisper to him in his sleep, "Galt, my heart grows when you love, and mine does as well. Yet when we meet, you grow me and I grow you...*I-we-us* is how we grow, how we climb, how we aspire for the place where both can fly as one, or dovetailed together. We are two souls who, when added together, are more than three." She then said to him, "I must go now, but you should be careful, and love Madison for as long as you two must, and never give up over the next few years, because your education as a young adult will not end with Mackey or any of the other four colleges you will attend. Your education is your stained-glass window to build. Both academically, physically and spiritually. Just keep learning, I will, and we shall visit again someday soon, but next time on a bit Higher Ground."

He felt very awkward when SHE did come visit, as SHE seemed so much more powerful and it was like SHE had been alive for many more years than he, but also that SHE so desired his feelings and thoughts to be melded with hers. He became very humbled. Somewhere in that future he just sensed that this spiritual relationship would become reality. That a life together would be as to mortals. It just seemed right.

As he stared at the airport, His mind went back to Madison's hand creeping around his waist, and down the back of his jeans. She was squeezing his ass and whispering in his ear, for they had not eaten for a day or so, and a pitcher of Great Falls Select was starting to make them both light-headed at six thousand feet above sea level. "Galt, let's take a walk, babe, and I will buy you pizza at Grizzly Pub, like you have never had. Then we'll head back to my place and we won't let each other go till you have to head to the airport. OK?"

He had an image of them embracing as he left for the airport from her dorm, the smile and those beautiful eyes, and the confidence they both had on the bright beach, that life was full and life was good. Her words on that mountain forest road, her confidence in the two of them together regardless of the circumstances—it was burned deep.

It was a full adventure by most comparisons to date, this week and last day with Madison so far from Village on the Bluff, and sixth grade when he asked her to go steady. Which, she reminded him that night, they still were. But one more twist was to be written in his deep friendship for Madison. He knew deep that his mind was on a very low idle, when compared to how deep the exchange was between soul and body.

She was not heard from again for a long while. Yet he knew that some man would be very fortunate to find her as his true love. Galt felt fortunate to have shared life lessons with her. and yet now he was beginning to believe he had a renewed desire to chase his education, be it formal or informal. This love that was all encompassing, this spirit, he was ready to learn and anticipate when SHE would come in her next visit. If this was love, it sure was a strange road to travel, but with no regrets.

He also was coming to understand that despite the weirdness of Mackey and his desire to get out of there, that he could find that mosaic for his mind, body. That this spirit was his and his only. Perhaps not as most had imagined or painted his path to be, but to be his. It was not to be always easy, nor was it to be very joyous in these days of young manhood, but he got the vision, and stuck with it. He was to be a philosopher, not in the academic sense of a masters or phd, but as a student of life, with a desire to try as much as the world had, and to use his awareness of the virtue of selfishness as a way to help others. He was not denied the pursuit SHE had wanted from him, even with massive changes coming. There would be a bundle of physical and mind games he would endure, all designed to help him to be as strong and as balanced as SHE was to desire from him and him back to her. All for that day that he prayed would come for both, a time, place and challenge for both to share in a permanent exchange of their mind, body and soul.

Patience, young man, patience. .

Galt was alive, and didn't let this academic trap he was in be that. He told his father over the phone he was done at Mackey, despite the Dean telling him they would take him back after a semester away, but that his grades would also tell this story as well. Despite his father's expectations, he never would. His mom, on the other hand, only wanted to see her firstborn smile again. When he came back from the third semester and his last, he didn't have a warm smile, but he did have a look of relief. It had been a long thirty weeks, three terms, where his confidence and soul got lost. But he did have hope, as the high country of Montana and the deep passion two people could share awoke him to the possibilities of life. Now how to move forward, and not overthink was to be his next opportunity.

CHAPTER 12:

Four More and Beyond; or, the Trinity Makes a Comeback

It would be unfair to our readers to outline all Galt's repeats and rebounds from the bodily experiences he had fallen into. But to summarize, Galt was to attend four more colleges before finally calling it quits. Each, however, left him with important pieces of his legacy and thus his mosaic, the beautiful assembly of the experiences and lessons that fed his body, mind and soul, as well as a lot more mistakes to learn from. He was able to make High Ground on a more frequent basis over those four more years, but never able to sustain firm footing, as the balance of his body, mind and soul would tilt one way or the other. This High Ground was tough to sustain, for sure. Much less consider how to share it with others or show others the way.

Whe he did arrive home after Mackey, he quickly took refuge in his old bedroom. At this point his brother had moved on to school in Arizona, his sister had grown a bit, and his smallest brother was still just that. Milwaukee had been good to Mom and Dad, and it wouldn't be long until the corporate titans would reward them with a bigger assignment back in Chicago, and thus a new beautiful home in Forest Bluff. But for Galt it meant getting a job, and with his mother's encouragement, he would also sign up for two classes at a Catholic women's college near their home. He had to take the New Testament as part of the requirements, taught by a nun and PhD, at night. So it was that the return to feeding his soul and spirit was to be. Through an academic pursuit of the new testament, that part of him awakened that had been asleep since seventh grade. Understanding this faith basis as taught by Sister/Dr. Hoolihan, professor of religious studies at Cardinal Stritch, was a grand opening for light to come into his soul. She saw him to be a lost soul, and it was she who actually requested he be in her class. Seeing his SAT scores and high school record, tarnished by three Fs, three D's, two C's and one B+ at Mackey, she knew her class was where he belonged.

She was to be what Galt thought of as an angel of life on earth, akin to SHE, but he had begun to imagine that these angels were manifestations of SHE, and therefore for him, if he kept his mind and heart open.

They had an amazing relationship as he grew to study again, achieve academic performance, and also gain deep insights into faith. She was not only an academic, but also a mentor. As the semester ended, and he had achieved two As while working full-time in an office as a clerk in the city, she said to him, "I see the light in your eyes again, Galt. You are in touch with the holy trinities. Your desire to find the balance is a noble cause, and one I know you will achieve. Listen to your heart over your amazing objective brain. It serves you well, but it should not lead your direction. You have begun to forgive yourself, now begin to forgive others, and embrace the peace of what your world will be. Go Galt, chase it, chase it and embrace it. It will not always still be easy for you, and I predict there will be more traditional canyons and summits in your climb to the Higher Ground. But now you have what is needed to achieve it. May this love and enthusiasm for life you are blessed with always be there for you."

"Last, Galt, say prayers and allow the spirit to come to you. SHE is your angel before you arrived here, and will be again after. SHE will be there for you when your physical and rational pursuits bring change that seems best, but may very well bury your spirit. She will remind you to not let your spirit be buried by these, but be with them in the shape of three, the triangle, Galt. The strongest shape in the universe. Now go forth and know that someday you and another will do good things for this world of ours, at a time we will most need it"

(reference book II and III in the trilogy)

Galt was a bit overwhelmed by this, but he understood much of what the sister said and its meaning to him. That was the semester they had. He could only think of her as a beautiful person, a person so intent on helping others, with all she could give. This role model was enlightening to him. She was a person who existed to help others find the Higher Ground. She provided Galt so very much, that it wouldn't be until later life that this White Anglo-Saxon Protestant would appreciate the purity of those who facilitate the Holy Catholic Church, as special. Sister/Dr. Hoolihan was to be seen in the same place as the historical read he had on Father Lamy, the first archbishop of Santa Fe. Willa Cather's novel was to reveal in a classic way the spirit, determination of these people who were the essence of Galahad, whose strengths were as that of ten because their hearts were pure. Not a physical strength, but rather a spiritual strength, the top of the triangle that pulled all, and allowed for the balance he so desired, but would not be able to hold onto again.

Same Old Wine in a Brand-New Bottle

So with a clear head, no pot for six months, and very little alcohol, confidence in his academic skills, and a sense of balance, Galt would then move to another venue locally for further full-time pursuits of an academic degree. His dad picked his alma mater for this third adventure of the five to come. It was to be a Lutheran college located in Sheboygan Wisconsin, a bit further south of Mackey, but another northern, small, well-respected liberal arts school. Academics were good, but no 1600s were there. He pleaded with his dad, in his new clarity of world experience and inner peace, to allow him to attend a larger college. He had now migrated his thinking away from Cornell and Colgate, as he knew they would have no part of this damaged goods, and football had no place for his physical being. So it was the University of Wisconsin, or Montana, where he still believed Madison would be back, as she had promised she would if he was to attend there. They had kept their long-distance relationship alive, with Galt's visits to her home back in Village on the Bluff, and every time it got just a bit weirder. She was still in the moment with any fun they could have, and our Galt was finding this to be neither as enticing nor as healthy as he now found himself. He did not judge, as he also saw she was struggling, as he was. But she had not found Sister Hoolihan. She was still the beautiful soul he would always hold dear, but as the last visit was coming to an end in the garage apartment she had at her parents', in bed, both in a state of nineteen-year-old readiness, he suddenly pulled back. Just as it was the time. He lifted himself up off of her smile, now a look of confusion, and said, "I can't do this, Madison. I am not sure why, and I do want you, but I can't do this with us. I have no other explanation."

She was then a bit shocked for sure, but she being ever the amazing soul she was, looked at him and said, "I sense you have found love some-place else? If you have, I can understand. For that love must be powerful for you to pull away from what we have that is so special."

He said he knew of a love, but what he did not know was that he had begun to forgive himself, feed his soul, and the love he had shared with her remained, but that this higher spirit (and was it SHE?) was asking him not to commit if he did not believe in the two of them. For sex for sex was not good enough for Galt, and SHE had come again as Sister Hoolihan had predicted.

Madison did not appear to be sad. She had tried to get him to smoke a joint. He chose to not smoke with her, yet she went ahead anyway. He tried to explain, she said it didn't matter, but it did. He did have a few beers with her at the local pizza place in Forest, but he was very much in touch with his senses. They were both pretty emotional. As they walked to the car, she gave him a big hug, and whispered in his ear, as she pulled him in for what would be the last time, "Galt, you are special, but we are on different paths. You have found a peace and love that I cannot compete with, and for that I will be sad for a time. But I also love you enough to know this love for Her you feel, and now it makes me feel good about us moving in our own paths again."

Shit, he thought, she was one beautiful, smart, and amazing person. But as they hugged the last time, one of courtesy, he left her porch above the garage behind her folks' place, he looked back in those big blue eyes and knew he would always love her and remember her forever, but that there were no regrets. She had pulled him back, but Madison had made it a beautiful moment versus one of sadness. He had hoped he had done the same for her.

So it was this time when Galt was on his way to college number three, and the memory of the mountain girl in Montana from Chicago's North Shore, and his nightmare at Mackey was to end. Onward to another outpost of his father's choosing, with Lutherans and a lot of nice Wisconsin people.

Luther College was a beautiful setting on the bluffs over Galt's favorite body of freshwater, Lake Michigan. People had smiles, people were well dressed, and they all attended class. The smell of cannabis was not there.

There was a chapel requirement every morning, so he went. He had a roommate again; this time they all lived in dorms for all four academic years. He found himself with Zakia Zakia Zaria, an Egyptian student from Chicago, whose mother was Lutheran and father a Muslim. So here was Galt, in the learning mode, and willing to give it another college try for Dad and Mom, but also maybe a bit for himself this time. He still depended on Ma and Pa maybe a bit too much at this stage, as he approached his twentieth birthday, and his third year past high school.

Enter Dr. Reverend Hans Drucker

With sixteen hours of credits, a full load; with a kind, but very perfumed roommate, who had a girlfriend he brought in too many times; and with chapel every morning on the lake, Galt felt he had escaped the snake pit for geniuses and arrived in a padded room of kind and gentle souls, almost too kind. It was to be the last time he was to play that crazy, head-banging game of football by the coach at Lutheran. It was also the last time he would take sixteen credits and get three As and a B+. Best of all at this outpost, besides making his dad very happy, was the engagement he had with Dr. Drucker. He taught the Old Testament class, and was one of the most popular in the university, and a requirement for Galt to attend that first term. His ability to share the facts behind all the Hebrew authors and books written to create the potential for the assembly of the Torah and Christian Bible was very powerful medicine for Galt's soul and brain's interaction. The knowledge that all of what was an imagery of miracles from the beginning, and the realization it was symbolism for lessons in the power of the spirit and the belief in the infiniteness of the creator, was exactly what Galt needed. He now had a deep Catholic and Protestant insight to both sides of the Christian book. But to this he also added insight into the Hebrew origins and the wonder of writings that help teach the ways to live a full life. For whether there was a great flood, or the waters parted, was not as important as was the spiritual, human story, the honor given to those who believed and were challenged in their beliefs, be they Jews of Egypt or Christ and his followers; from the seminal moment that a Jewish man stood tall for the Sermon on the Mount and broke from tradition, to the challenge of Genesis 22, and God's command to Abraham to kill his son.

All pieces of the great stories of religion he would begin to assemble into his belief system over the next few years.

Lutheran gave him some more credits and his high school level grades, but it was to be one and done after a summer school and one semester. Galt's dad *finally* said to him, upon his declaration of interest of next steps in this wondrous journey, "What do you want for yourself now? Because son, I have no clue."

Galt went with his gut, as naive and underdeveloped as it was. It was to be his primary tool over his powerful logic skills. "Dad, I am headed to Montana this summer. I have called the university, and shared my three A's and B+, along with those aging high school transcripts. They also looked at my small pile of credits and three prior experiences. They are prepared to let me in for summer school on probation. I plan to take eight hours, and then stay there."

Although Madison was gone, and his good pal Peter was back home this coming summer to work, he would adventure out to Missoula, Montana and see if he could catch fire there. This made for a bit of an emotional situation for his dad. First, Galt's little brother was interested in Montana, and second, Grandma, Dad's mom, lived down the road about thirty miles from his hometown, the same Grandma who left his dad and his aunt alone with Grandpa (whom his deceased little brother was named after) when they were small children. She was a child raised by her adopted aunt and uncle in Darby, Montana. Both had taken her in as a favor to a friend, Galt's great-grandmother. He was thought to be a descendant of the great tribe of Chief Joseph, leader of the Wallowa band of the Nez Perce, or maybe even the Black Feet to the north. It was all a true mystery. It was told by Dad, but never Grandpa, that his great-grandmother was a carnival and western show gal by trade, who made her way riding, shooting and basically entertaining in small towns throughout the west as an Annie Oakley character of sorts. Her lover, Galt's great-grandfather, was also a western carney, one who also had been a miner, a cowboy, a railroad gandy dancer, and, some thought, a thief, too. They were never married, so that made Grandma a bastard. This meant nothing to Galt, but surely the history of their roots to these ancient people was of great interest. It was as Dad explained all of this again to him during their fourth college talk, again, that Galt had to know and understand more. So Montana was to be the place that summer. Dad nodded in approval, but was still not a believer or confident that was best for Galt. Mom, in her infinite wisdom and love, just said to Galt: "Go there, honey, give it your best, but trust your heart always." So he went back to work during the time off to earn some good money working as an industrial painter, then off to Montana.

As he arrived via Amtrak from Milwaukee, a long, but beautiful journey sleeping in a chair and awaking in the sky car seeing the sun and the rising of the prairies across North Dakota and the splendor of the distant snow peaks of Glacier Park, he knew he belonged here in the West. This was in his blood, but was this school really the answer? He had no idea that question should even be considered, as it was where he needed to be, and if school was how, then so be it.

He arrived, and based on a recommendation from Peter, he hiked up the side of the campus to a beautiful side street, lined with big western odd leafy trees, and frat and sorority houses. He admired all of these grand buildings, and thought this might be a good place to settle in and study, and voiced the madness of the dorms and then the shared sleeping dorm the last term at Mackey.

There it was, an old sorority with the Greek letters engraved in granite above a beautiful entrance, a tired, huge wooden door. He stepped up the stairs, opened the door, and inside was a spacious living room. But as he looked closer the furniture was tired at best. There were folks with very long hair, somewhat dressed in homemade clothing, babies crying and animals crawling all over. The once proud Alpha Phi sorority had fallen on the fate of so many Greek houses in those days of the early 70's at "progressive" campuses. It had become a co-op living space, something Galt did not recall hearing from Peter, not that it would have mattered. Galt asked around and found the co-op volunteer facilitators, there was not to be a manager or supervisor in this culture hive.

She directed him to a room, and asked for a one-month deposit, saying that it was month-by-month; and, after a quick tour of the facilities, he opened his door into the typical dorm room. But there was only a very dirty mattress on the floor. She said he could head to the basement and gather anything he needed, as many of the members didn't think furniture was relevant to living a complete life, but Galt was welcome to whatever he found.

He unpacked his trunk, and realized there was no key or lock on the doors. So he stuck his head out the door and asked, "Keys?"

Her answer was as expected. "We trust each other, as brothers would trust sisters and lovers."

WTH?

He decided to go with it, but his vibe wasn't as it was being defined by the words and policies. He thought a good hot shower might be the answer, then a walk to some of his and Madison's old hangouts during those seven days over a year ago. He laid his sleeping bag over the mattress under his camping pad. He then stripped down to his boxers and grabbed a small towel and some toiletries, and headed down the hall to the public bathrooms. He saw one marked with both a male and female sign on it. That was odd.

He stepped in, found a shower stall with no curtain, and hung his trunks, shirt and towel over the rail. He turned on the water and began to relax. He turned and looked across the shower aisle, and in the other two showers across from him were three women. One had a baby in her arms as she showered both of them. Two were together in the other shower, enjoying the soap they shared. In addition to noticing all the female parts and their long, wet hair, and the baby smiling back at him, he also saw that all three had long hair under their arms and on their legs. The mom looked over at Galt, all but covering himself with his hands, and said, "Welcome to the Titanic Co-op," with a big smile. Galt would meet this mom later in the kitchen, and the story would evolve there, too.

He just said, "Thank you," and as fast as he could, he dried off, threw on his blue boxers, and headed down the hall back to his room, shaking his head and again wondering why this had happened, and how many more of these strange situations would take place in the Titanic?

He knew there was a pattern to his life in some way, as these odd situations came to him so many times; it couldn't be just random. There had to be a reason, or was SHE sending him into these situations to help him find his way to Higher Ground?

He got dressed in his mountain boy best, with a very tired red-tag Levis, a black t-shirt that had CTA silk-screened across the front, and Summerfest 70 across the back. He slipped on his big Vasque climbing and hiking boots, and hoped his hiding place for his wallet had protected it. It had. He remembered the facilitator saying food was shared, as was meal prep. Give what you can, take what you need, she said. So he needed it, and headed to the monstrous kitchen on the first floor, taking one last look at his stuff, hoping it would all be there when he came back.

The kitchen had a cutting table in the center that was large enough for four cooks to prepare meals for a house of sorority sisters. But this time, this day it was to be a room of very long-haired men, women, children, babies, dogs and cats. Cats of course felt they had the right to walk on the counters and the refrigerators.

They all said hello to him with grand smiles, and warm, "Welcome, brother, help yourself." The options were not even of interest to Galt. As he said thank you, he turned and walked out of the house and down the street, headed downtown.

His mind wandered to what he had a vision for and what was happening. Nothing seemed the same, not even the Grizzly Pizza, where he and Madison had spent a memorable evening not too long ago. He walked past where Peter said he would have a room in the fall in a house with him and his Grizzly pals. It was a grand old house, and it gave Galt some hope that maybe surviving this summer would lead to the ground he desired. As he walked downtown, he began to see the army of street people that these college mountain towns attracted in the summers of the early 70's. Some smiled, but most asked for money from him. Others, and the most shocking, were squatting in alleys and, with a dirty sock in one hand and spray paint in the other, would eject paint into the sock, then gently put it to their nose and inhale with all they could, coughing and whispering to those awaiting their turn. Wow man, am I in a dream?

Galt went to Grizzly for that memory pizza and Great Falls Select Lager. He just turned around and headed back to Titanic and quietly climbed up the three flights to his temporary room and his sleeping bag. Despite the bright light of the northwest in June as the solstice approached at ten p.m., he took his bag and closed it over his head and hoped sleep would provide peace and some clarity to his situation.

He did sleep deeply into the middle of the night, when SHE came to him, again.

SHE spoke to him, but not in the physical way that he often felt from her. SHE spoke to him about where he was and challenged him to what was to be next for him.

"Galt, you should first follow your heart, but also know that your strategic alignment for the next lap of this gauntlet does not include this place. It is of your past, not of your future. Your little brother will be grand here, and so will Peter. But for you, know this: *You have wings on your feet, and today, you begin to fly even higher in life.* Have the courage then to take the steps your heart tells you to, not what others may want."

He awoke, and one thing was clear: this was not firm ground and the path up was not to be seen. He had only been there twenty-four hours, and on the first day of classes our Galt did not go to class. Not for the reasons he had at Mackey, but rather with a determination that SHE would smile upon, he headed to the registrar, and said "Good morning; I would like to drop out and get all my money back, please."

They of course asked the normal why, and quickly he was given a receipt and confirmation of his choice, and a commitment to have the check ready for him over at the admin building after the registrar made a quick call. He felt very relieved, but also knew he should also let his dad know of this strategic realignment, and not to include SHE in the why.

The pay phone in the Titanic was a fitting place to call Pop and walk him through the conditions, the sock incident, and the choice he made to not let this place be his. It was to be good for others, he told his dad, but for him it would be a very dark ending. Here his intuition was spot on, and it now was to be a more reliable tool in his life for setting the next steps—not yet a consistent decision method, but better than facts and his immature sense of trying to be part of a group of his peers. He was to be his own and find his own, no matter where it took him.

Dad was also relieved, and he said, "I am proud of you, Galt. I will get you a plane ticket back, and get you home as soon as we can. Head to the airport and we will see you soon."

So he went home. His transformation into a man was not as anybody would have planned or thought for this "all-American boy," but it sure had its share of adventures. Galt knew work was to be his answer for the near term, as work, hard work, was what his heart told him would be next.

Grandma, the lost soul of his dad's lineage, was the most disappointed when he also called her before heading to the airport, but she also was very forgiving. She had been alone from the family, but also knew that Galt's visits there to her land could lead to others coming, as his little brother and sister were, too.

CHAPTER 13:

The Call of the Badger #5

"The meanest animal pound for pound."

So it was that Galt finally found his way to the enrollment line in August, three and a half years out of high school, on the isthmus they call Madison, Wisconsin, home to the Wisconsin Badger Pride, liberal values galore, education everywhere you turned, and 40,000-plus students, who still thought the '60s were not over.

Dad was the first to ask him if he really wanted to keep trying. Galt said, "What are my options?" Dad said he could work, and take night school for a few years where they were living. For his folks had now moved back to the Bluff in Illinois, and found themselves a beautiful home close to the lake, that his three younger siblings could also make the re-entry back in style. Galt only knew that going home meant that he would have to tuck his pride in his back pocket, and be a Forest on the Bluff drop out, like others who had a golden path for them to college and then returned hat in hand to this leafy suburb, and their parents' basements. He had good friends from childhood who also had already reached this point of bewilderment and had begun that buckling down to a hard job and building a future a different way. . But he didn't think himself ready yet for that place, and reflected on what was to be next. It was a bit of relief that the school of his good friend and soon his little brother would be a place he could not go to—a relief from that pressure. He also knew this: If he did choose more college life at twenty years old, it would be his fifth shot at this dream that all in his high school thought he would be glory-bound for.

Galt did what he always did as a younger man, when these difficult transitions faced him, without a strategy or goal. He went to the water. Big Lake Michigan had always provided for him in that way, as had the copper colored tamarac waters of the Wisconsin River as a kid. He jogged to the beach, breathing hard, as his exercise regimen had gone to shit a year or two ago, and found the run to the bluff and down the old road to the sand to be an amazing rush of endorphins. He felt his triangle of balance was not there any longer. His spirit, mind and now even his body were all on low charge. Could the waters of the great lake bring him back, as it had as a child, from darkness? He stripped down, as the sun had already set behind the gigantic oaks on the bluff, and in the full body his mother had delivered him to the earth, ran into the waves and crashed in, surfacing with a powerful pull of the Australian crawl, headed for Michigan. He swam and kicked with no consideration of the June temperatures in the water, sixty-two degrees, but felt an energy that was boundless. As he awoke from his crawl and kicking he stopped and treaded water, turning to the beach and beautiful bluff of his youth. Remembering all the amazing transitions he had experienced on that beach and in that water, he realized that the beach was now very far away. He had swam a good half mile out naked, and knew he would have to find his way back soon, but as always in the great lake, there was no fear. He felt absolutely nothing but energy and clarity of nothingness. This nothing was clear and blank, but it welcomed what was to come next. SHE had not been gone long since the kick in the ass to get out of Missoula before he killed himself in that culture, and yet here SHE was with him again. But this time it was very different.

It wasn't just a voice, or a feeling in a dream, She was there with him, a half mile out off the beach at twilight, naked with her legs wrapped around him, arms holding tight to his shoulders and a smile he had not had much clarity on in all her visits. She was not just holding him with affection, but also holding him up from sinking. This was the most physical he had experienced with her. Could it be real?

SHE whispered into his ear before giving him the kiss he was not to forget, and said: "Go to the isthmus, go to the place the Maharishi Mahesh Yogi called one of three places in America where the karma was in balance. Go there and try again. Do not worry about school, grades, and the typical academic experiences your family may expect and your old self, too. Go there as a student, but go there as a student of life, world, beliefs, faith, sexuality, physical development, and intellectual pursuit. Some of it will be in the classroom, but the final stage of your education will be in the people you meet and learn from. All of your three elements will come back to life in such an expanded way that it will drive you through the second third of your adult life. Make this the final stage of childhood to full adult being." SHE then kissed him again, but this time with all of her mouth. They shared that deep wet richness of tongues and lips in perfect harmony. Then unwrapped her legs, whispered goodbye to Galt in his ear, and said, "I shall be there again for you as needed, but not in this way until you are ready for the true final third. Then I shall be of mortal spirit, and we shall share in 'starter kits' that will light fires across the universe, as we become not just souls who share, but also lovers and best friends as you approach that time, years from now. It will be above a river in red rocks in a place not even you could imagine"

Galt suddenly realized he was treading water again, and not just floating in the lake. His whole body was slowly coming back to the reality of what he was doing. But his feelings of what had just happened and the mission he was about to take on were as clear as the morning daylight. He knew this was to be his greatest education, and he had his mission. He also knew that this physical joy he just had known would not be back for a long time. But it was not to bother him. He just knew it *would* be back that life was about to get a lot better, and that he must now begin to grow, heart first, logic second, and expand every moment he could through the decades of his life, bringing joy to as many as he could, but also building an intuition and love for life that would allow him to meet his mate for eternity and accomplish that which will be of benefit to others. All was somewhere in the distant light, and so it was to be.

He was no longer exhausted, and swam back in what seemed a matter of minutes, and pulled back on his clothes and shoes, wet as he was, but not cold in the early evening light. He ran home faster than he had to the beach just an hour before, and asked for a moment with his folks. It was here the twenty-year-old laid out his next, and final, college plans—the fifth time. He explained how he recognized the academic experience was important but that the whole cultural and spiritual experience was, too, for this the first school he had asked his father to support him in. It had been the days of rage at the University of Wisconsin in Galt's senior year in high school, with bombings; National Guard engagements with students during riots; drugs; rock and roll, and rebellion deep into Madison's culture, brought by the many out-of-state and in-staters who found their way to this, one of three places the yogi had proclaimed experienced perfect karma.

Galt was about to adventure again into a wild and wooly few years of learning, but this time it was to be very different, and a capstone to his youth, a graduation ceremony of sorts after twenty-two years on earth to manhood, with lots of new fuel for his body, mind and spirit.

At this stage, Dad was just happy he could find the juice to stand up and ask, and with such energy and passion to attend this fifth college. Dad and Mom both easily gave him their blessings, as now much of the money he had made would pay for the living, and they the tuition only. He also committed to finding a job and to reduce their demands even more. So began the prep to get to Mad-town and the birth of another UW Badger.

Music Club concerts, films of mind expansion and European origins, Jane Fonda block parties celebrating May Day, sexual liberation and hurt feelings, Burning Down the House, swim your way out. Art, jazz, blues, harmonicas, philosopher Ayn Rand, old reunions from the Bluff of soul mates, swims in another lake of sorts, rediscovery of the Wisconsin River. The Bike culture, Big Ten football, rugby manhood, the Villa Maria, and the lost souls of it ... SHE was to not appear for three years. SHE had given him enough to help him find his own way for the next three. But the big question for Galt was when would he be able to provide her what she needed, beyond that embrace, and support deep into the cold waters of Lake Michigan? He knew that giving was perhaps what was to come, but the four decade marathon of mid-life must first be lived, chasing the right brain of life, but giving all he had to others, becoming very successful by modern logical and deductive standards, but also losing his art for a while during those years.

Galt prepared for this next adventure, and as such he would walk on the Bluff many mornings and evenings looking down at the spot where he and SHE swam together, treading water in that embrace. He was giving thanks in a religious way of sorts, but also awakening creativity and expansion right out of his heart. For it was now he had learned to honor the past by letting it go.

He sat on the Bluff the last day before he was to leave for Madison, and wrote his first of many poems. This is one of the ways he began to prepare for the most amazing adventure one could ever ask for, albeit of typical Galt contractions, but also of growth on all three interdependent dimensions of this life on earth. Here it is as he sat upon the bench above the bluff, pen and paper in hand:

I can see the sun
Going down.

I can see the strongest
of the strong
Pouring their long shadows
On the Ground

Back to the east
Lies the big lake

Straight down the bluff to the beach
The waves crashing
Always battling the shore
for the sand

It's a funny kind of harmony,
Man and the land.
Not like winning or losing,
Crying or dying, laughing, or smiling
Not often enough does reach out
For his capture and friend.

We belong to it
and I understand it now
In the solitude of this day's sundown
I've known it before,
But every night
This knowledge is renewed.

For in my life I may stray
But I will always know
That is the end,
It's back to the master
I shall go.

—Galt, August of his 20th year

He knew that this place had given him a gift, he wanted to give back to it, and the best way he knew how was through this simple poem, expressing the full extent of the power of this piece of nature that had blessed him with a new start and opportunity to truly expand himself. He was to share this poem with only a few in the years ahead, but the actual only one who would see and have a complete copy would be SHE, years ahead from this summer day.

He was to write many more, as the days in Madison would add up, but it was time to make that run up the highway through the very tall corn fields and winding roads of Highway 12 to the isthmus and his new fertile ground for life expansion.

Traveling Down, or Up, the Badger Tail

An old railroad bed lies unused by the trains that would haul lumber and iron ore from the north to the industrial factories of Milwaukee and Chicago. But it is used today as one of the most beautiful biking and hiking trails in the heartland. It is called the Badger Trail, and flows from Madison all the way to the cheese-and beer-rich county seat of Green. It is there that this beautiful trail cuts its way through the rolling hill country, shaped by the glaciers, past the small towns that support the farm lands, winding its way over the old railroad bed. Many beautiful and challenging moments can be found along this trail, as one journeys to the heart of, or escapes to the isthmus that can lead to adulthood, known as Madison and the University of Wisconsin. Many come and go to this beautiful city and its diverse learning institutions, and achieve a full, normal collegiate experience—football games, a few drunken nights, and exams—to finally cross the stage with a degree from one of the many colleges on campus. But these most basic of college experiences were to be only the smallest of all the many our Galt was to experience here.

As he arrived he was excited, as he would not be there alone, as a credited sophomore with a junior age bracket, on this huge campus. A place he had only visited for entertainment purposes in his life. So the stage was set for another Galt blow-out of college degree attempts. But then he was reminded of what SHE had said to him off the Bluff in the lake that evening, reminding him that his purpose there may be a degree, but then again it most likely wasn't to be just that. Nor was it an immutable criterion for him to expand beyond his childhood to rapid realization of adulthood. He still was bent on being a good student, and was still feeling the obligation and mantel of meeting his folks' expectation, but this was to be the breakout to beginning his own self-discovery and expansion. He would owe much to UW, if not an undergraduate diploma.

It was an even better first day to discover just a few days before he was to leave for Mad-town that Michael Thornton, his old pal from high school, as well as from his short stint at Mackey, was to also try out the U, for his break away from the Minnesota falls and winters. This was only to last a semester, as he desired the smaller community, and the friends, as well as the gal who was to be his wife, were back there in Minnesota. They did get an apartment just off Greek Row, and a half block from an old beatnik and now hipster hangout, a bar called the Oasis. It was to become the clubhouse for Galt, Michael and all their entourage of guy and gal pals. With a bowling alley above the bar, it was a place one could sit drinking two-dollar pitchers of PBR and hear the balls and pins above. The six alleys upstairs were so old, they had a help wanted sign in the window of the bar constantly, looking for human pinsetters, folks who would sit behind the rack in a "safe" place and reset pins for the two-buck-a-game bowlers. These bowlers, as drunk college dumb asses, would more often than not throw a ball down the lane when the pinsetter was trying to set the pins.

The Oasis was more than just a cheap beer. It was to be the center of the east side of campus culture, where the music of the Beatles singing "Revolution" would follow with Tammy Wynette singing "Stand by Your Man." Of course, the beer was cheap and cold, but they also sold the classic Wisconsin drinks, including a brandy Manhattan, as well as the little-known (outside the state) Abergut, a concoction of brandy in a shot glass, almost to the top, with a layer schnapps on top. The ultimate in doing a shot over the most important of toasts, was to put the flame of a lighter onto the top layer of schnapps and, with a blue flame raging out of the shot glass, down the hatch the flaming Abergut, hoping to not miss the hole and pour it down your cheeks or shirt. Burns have been known to take place. But the best they had to offer was the Oasis Burger. An amazing patty, with who knows what pounded into the ground beef, fried on the hot table behind the bar in about two minutes, then served on a dark whole-wheat bun, a popular version of wheat for the healthy crowd. There was some kind of sour cream concoction plopped on top with plenty of salt and briny pickles to load up on the side. No more, no less, all for .90 cents. The Oasis also offered grilled cheese versions with ham, fish, and plain-old for .60 cents, .70 cents, and .50 cents respectively. There was a shake for .40 cents, and a malt version for another nickel. Amazing as it sounds, it served as the perfect "oasis" for the starving student, and as the social club for the hood.

Around 9 p.m. on most nights, but primarily on Thursday and Friday evenings, the Oasis would fill up quickly. With the jukebox blaring and every one of the pinball machines occupied, with Tommy playing and Daltrey singing, "See me, feel me," all other eyes would be on who was showing up, and on the two pool tables that always were deep in quarter games stacked on the side with the next challenger to take on a hot shot on the eight-inch tables.

It became a joy and a place of pride for the Galt. He and Michael met new men and women. He also ran into an old high school pal, Johnny, the youngest of the Knaack brothers, and they found their way into free meals, working at a women's private dorm called the Villa Maria de Anime Perse. Here they either waited tables, cleaned dishes and pots, or left the kitchen late after the dinner bell had passed. The commitment was for one shift a day, and you could get paid one or possibly two meals a day, depending on the work. There were over 150 women who were out of the dorms and, in their mid- to late-undergrad levels, lived in single rooms. It was a classic Italian-looking villa, on a small side street leading down to one of the two lakes that bordered the isthmus and campus. Most were very good students, and most had either chosen to be alone, or their parents found this place for them to be away from the darkness of the U social life, a mistake and foolish thought.

The crew he met was made up of a mix of many kinds of men. All were of the college age, but a few of them were older. Galt had no idea what this was, these guys who were twenty-three to twenty-six, and so much more mature than his peers there. Turns out, as it was 1973, that most of them were Vietnam vets, attending on the GI Bill, teaching Galt a few lessons in discipline and wisdom of life and why college was so damn important. He did listen, but yet still couldn't find the answer to why it was. Either way, he did join in many different events and recreation basketball and softball teams with the vets and his other undergraduate gang at the Villa, and never went hungry. He did lose Michael, as referenced over Christmas, for he wanted back to Mackey. It turned out that was a good thing for him.

The next choice he was to make came when he met with a counselor regarding tuition; in-state or out-of-state? Being a half-breed cheese head, he thought he might have a chance at saving Mom and Dad a few bucks, as they were paying tuition out of state, and he was earning his books and food on his own. Rent was a split deal with pals, and at 125 per month he struggled, but always had some cash at the end of the month for whatever met his fancy. He would sell his amazing record collection, which he had been building for years, to the used record store for .50 cents or a buck, depending on the album. Five albums was often enough for a good night of beer on a TGIT (Thank God It's Thursday).

Sex, yes, it was easily earned and shared if one wanted, and yet he struggled to figure that jump into bed that was so easy to do. Lord knows the opportunities were there. But also, the kindest and most thoughtful of women were there, too, women whom Galt admired and respected, and it seemed they all had men in their lives, always hoping one of them would find him to be the one. He still had that lost look in his eyes, and these women had a purpose in college: career *and* right man. There were a few who were as lost as he was.

He did find his major that day meeting with the advisor, and also filled out the form needed to appeal for in-state tuition, a saving to his folks of $750 dollars a semester. He was to win that savings for his parents, and they were actually beginning to believe Galt was fulfilling their vision.

He even led them down a darker primrose path, when the advisor looked at all his religion and related classes credits from across the Midwest and said, "Galt, you are a philosophy minor at this point. You should consider a major and achievement of the additional thirty hours that would prepare you for our law school, as philosophy is the best pre-law major in the U. "

Well, Galt was excited to share this small assembly of credits and the symbol it made for his father. He still didn't figure it out yet; it would matter to him later. But Dad believed his number one son was on his way. He may even be a lawyer, as was his Dads wish.

So it went for the Galt, class of philosophy or two, some other liberal arts thrown in, and finally Thursday nights. The campus students seemed to live for Thursday nights, including the many female friends he gained by being the night clean-up man at the Villa. As this was the time, the true loaners and those prone to being stoned would wander into the kitchen looking for food or. . .? They, too, were as lost as he was, wondering about college life, living moment to moment. Most had some high expectations from high school, and yet they only wanted his comfort those evenings after the kitchen visit, after hours.

Galt was not supposed to share any food. The head cook, a 200-pound tough but fair German woman, with rosy cheeks, named Ethel came to trust and leave him with all the keys. His role was to mop, clean up the fryer when needed, and finally take out the garbage. However, he would find himself making favors of small stuff opened in the pantry and some leftovers in the fridge. He was covered for by the morning cook, Lois, the nicest woman one could know, who kept from Ethel seeing her tin wraps or plastic over the evening's leftovers opened and resealed. Lois and Galt had a friendship and an understanding that the head dame would never know of. So it was Galt who thought he was being kind, and the residents would come to him, higher than a kite, looking to fill up some very empty spaces. He would oblige sometimes, and others he could only see deeper lost eyes than his own.

He did great with grades that first semester, but the Villa, the plaza and then the rugby team came knocking. Too many extracurriculars could become a problem, but Galt was determined to pursue it if it felt like a learning experience. This included taking the most difficult class in the philosophy program, taught by Dr. Hammerstein. The class was called Man, Religion and Society, with the principle lesson being that religions require belief for their dialectic to bridge to reality, whereas true philosophy only required the dialectic and logic train to prove out their reality to man. As he got into this class and a study group, he met a TA who was a master's student and deeply into Objectivism and the writings of Ayn Rand. Galt had no idea what this stuff of modern fiction was about until he devoured these books almost as fast as he had devoured *Siddhartha*, beginning with *The Fountainhead*, then *Atlas Shrugged*, then *Anthem*, *We the Living*, *The Virtue of Selfishness*, *Capitalism: The Unknown Ideal*, and many white papers.

Their study group was made up of folks who were, on the whole, desirous of becoming modern socialists, much like the tempo the U had felt in the late 60s, but now being transformed into the academic world through the syllabus of the instructors. Galt chose Objectivism to prove as a philosophy versus a religion for a final grade from the good doctor. Much debate and heat was felt from his study group on this, as they couldn't believe he would even try to defend the *Virtue of Selfishness*. But Galt saw this as a very different piece of his learning. It was not to be taken in its entirety, but it was to be taken and fit into his mosaic of beliefs, to be tried and tested in life, as well with the other dimensions he had gained from Buddhism in a eastern religions class, the Lutheran teachings, and the New Testament according to Catholic nuns. Either way, this class, along with his taking 300-level and above classes in politics and logic, was shaping Galt into a different place of understanding. He came to believe at twenty that no religion was perfect, that in fact, Buddha taught of the respect for other faiths on the way to his belief system. Galt would vary here, and take the marvelous perspectives of the teachings of Buddha, Ayn Rand, Christianity, and his academic experience of Muslim faith history, and begin to assemble his own belief system in the power of God or Almighty, Holy spirit, omnipotent, Jehovah, Allah, Numen,

Yahweh, Divine One, or King of Kings. All had meaning, and all could work together. But it would require that the individual have some sense of their own being, strength, weaknesses, as well as a path of confidence and reward in their life work. If one was to achieve these basic tenets, then one could find the combination, mosaic, or the pure faith of one of the traditional religions and be a strong messenger as well as a facilitator of the faith and its benefits to the world. Ayn Rand, when taken for what Galt felt she represented. She has a lesson or lessons on how the individual must take care of themselves if they are to take care of others well, or begin to share in their learning. So he went with it, as he now was truly building his own mosaic and path to enlightenment someday.

Either way, the paper he crafted in this class was awesome in his view, but his TA warned him of the light it would put on the socialism of Dr. Hammerstein's teachings in advanced philosophy; but that it was of sound logic and should be presented without fear of reprisal. So he did.

The Doc, of course completely disagreed with him, but based on his use of the teachings of religion definitions vs philosophy, and the depth of research Galt did, gave Galt an A-, but he marked it down the total grade with red pen to C++ . This was Galt's first taste of what Ayn Rand had been talking about. But it was also his kindle of fire, that someday he would lead and also start from the bottom of the industrial complex as a worker who would feel the sweat and the muscle ache of true industrial labor. That day would come soon back in Chicago, but there were still two more years of deep-shoulder education, body expansion, and mind tuning to adulthood he also had to experience.

He never let go of his copy of *Atlas Shrugged*, or the *Teachings of Buddha*, and kept both in his pack to read and read. He felt they both worked together. As if their sense of individual responsibility was of common ground. He also was introduced to some other very different books by both religion, philosophy, and women from the Villa. Some were further readings from the authors his English teacher 6 years before had introduced him to. Examples of the expanding library and insights that were shaping this crazy triangle of his were as follows:

Edward Abbey, everything he wrote

Kant, Sartre, De Cartes, Locke, Plato, Aristotle, and his distant relative Kierkegaard

Charles Reich, *The Greening of America*

Herman Hesse, going deeper than *Siddhartha* to *Steppenwolf*

All Ken Kesey, and knowledge of never giving an inch, and *Sometimes a Great Notion*

William Burroughs, and not letting yourself get depressed

Richard Brautigan, and the simple life of fishing for trout and Waterman Sugar

On Walden Pond, David Thoreau

The Drifters, by Michener

All of Jack Kerouac, including *Dharma Bums* and *On the Road*

Science and the World by the one and only Buckminster Fuller

Poetry of all sorts by Ginsberg, Gary Snyder, Rod McKuen

Tom Wolfe nonfiction, with *The Electric Kool-Aid Acid Test*

Gestalt Therapy, by Fritz Perls

The Greening of America by Charles Reich

Separate Reality, by Carlos Castaneda

The Velvet Monkey Wrench, by John Muir

The sayings of Baba Hari Dass

Marx and Engels

On Liberty, John Mill

The Devil Tree, Jerzy Kosinski

Future Shock, Alvin Toffler

Marcel Proust, *Cities of the Plain*

Alan Watts, *In My Own Way*

The Little Prince, Antoine De Saint Exupéry

A Sand County Almanac, Aldo Lepold

Even Cowgirls Get the Blues, Tom Robbins

Tortilla Flats, John Steinbeck

In Watermelon Sugar and *Trout Fishing in America*, Richard Brautigan…etc etc etc

Galt could go on forever with the depth of readings he would pick up or go find in the used book store. It became such a passion that he spent less than twenty-five percent of his time, and the readings of his contact with grad students, Villa women, vets from the Villa and just people he would meet in the bar culture of Madison became his passion, as was a continued redesign and reduction of his record collections. His life was full, what with music, the Villa, readings, some class, swimming in the evenings with a Villa woman in the yellow hat (aka the one he would never catch), as well as attending football and hockey, which was becoming a Badger championship path to glory the day he stepped on campus. Coincidence, but a long ten-year drought suddenly struck their sports and he got the fever to participate despite his very long strawberry hair, and growing philosophy girth.

He was beginning to structure the simple trinity of how his Body, Mind, and Spirit were interdependent, and that the ability to recognize this and then strive in one's life to achieve fulfillment of each without compromise to the other was a framework that would serve him for the rest of his life. As he awoke to the early concept of these three in balance providing the path to a place in life that is higher, and a place that one can serve and fulfill themselves; A Path to Higher Ground.

One night he and a fellow Villa worker and newfound pal named Will from Wausau Wis. (who, by the way, was the state track champion in the 440's and related hurdles) were enjoying their first PBR in The Pub, the center of the universe for frat folks and non-frats smack in the middle of State Street, the center of all social events. It was here that two older gentlemen, handlebar mustaches, and some balding long hair, whom Galt thought to be old, offered the two of them a pitcher to share. Now Galt had already become accustomed to the gay community here, some of his co-workers were gay, and frequented the various bars and locations in the old student union where men and few women of that desire would hang and be social. So he had come to understand it a bit, and had no phobia with it, other than what it might be if he got hit on. So Will looked over and whispered in his ear, as he was a bit more obtuse to this interest, and said, "These guys are queer," and, "They are hitting on us." Galt wasn't so sure, so he turned and put out his hand, as his copy of *Atlas Shrugged* sat on the bar. Both of them introduced themselves and said they were curious if the friends were enrolled and were involved in any extracurricular activities at the U. Galt and Will of course said yes, laughing.

They asked, "Ever hear of the game of ruffians played by gentlemen?"

They said, "No, what the hell is that?"

The big handlebar guy with no neck responded, "Union League Rugby, young man."

Galt had no clue what he was talking about, but as this gentleman who played ruffian began to explain the outcomes and philosophy of this amazing game, maybe the greatest game he would play, it became obvious to Galt this might be a soul, mind, and body expander for sure. The simple fact that these guys defined a sport by the beliefs and philosophy of life tied in, the lessons one could gain in life, and how different it was from football was a strong pitch. As Will looked at Galt, they knew it was crazy enough for two now-old jocks to give it a shot. So both agreed with the team captains to come out for practice the next day on the south field to become members of the University of Wisconsin Rugby Club!

CHAPTER 13.2:

Section R for R U G B Y

Will and Galt found their old gym clothes in the backs of both their respective apartment closets. Both had not done anything at a high aerobic level in a number of months...or was it years?

But there they were with sweatpants, old baseball cleats, and sweatshirts standing on the early spring grass of the fields in front of the UW Nielsen Swimming center (aka the Natatorium). Gathering was a group of many shapes of guys, who all looked to be older to both of them. It was clear that this was just not a couple of graduate students that led this team. It was gentlemen of all ages, from twenty to fifty years old. All had played for the team in their youth, and some were profs, some were businessmen who were active alumni, others were who-knows-where-from. There were even a couple who spoke with Irish and British accents.

Memory kicked in and thus they braced themselves for this first gathering of spring UW rugby, assuming it would be as grueling as high school football summer camp had been. But boy, were they wrong. This was to be a different kind of prep or training for a sport. These guys knew what they were doing, and though conditioning was important, the art and science of mastering the skills of the individual and the team adjustments were

155

much more important. As Galt would learn, this was not about taking somebody's head off, but rather the objective was to control the ball, and utilize the team for all efforts whenever possible. Finally, if faced with no alternative, but to make an individual play, that is what one would do. But the similarities with old football principles that were born out of this game of "ruffians, played by gentlemen," would stop at a ball that was larger, profound pride in the drop kick, and all play both ways.

So practice was about rules and weird formations, as well as where Galt and Will would wind up. Teams were set up as A and B sides, meaning first and second string. Both were to start on B. But Galt and Will both knew this was a game that they felt very lucky to have stumbled onto, as it represented all they loved in sports, including contact, but wise contact, no gear, a ball, an all-team unabashed effort, and some very cool older dudes who espoused rugby wisdom. Will said after that first practice as they walked back to campus and their respective apartments, "How did we stumble into this? It is just what I needed and may keep me here for another semester or two. How about you, Galt?"

Galt could only spew a few words, as he was really out of shape, and said, "You bet, Will. It gives me hope."

They received their Union Rugby little history and rules book, published somewhere in England, and were asked to read it and then come back on Tuesday for another practice. which they figured they would do over beer on the Union patio. As they were leaving, after running maybe two miles at most and getting schooled by the vets on formations and their new roles, Will tugged at his sweatshirt and said, "Galt, you have to see this. Look over there." And he pointed to the far end of the field where a football goal post stood. The team captain, who they met in the pub just two days before, had about six balls and some pals back behind the posts. He was literally dropping the nose of the swollen football (they call it the rock), on the dirt in front of him. Then, with a huge kick of his toe, he sent it end over end in what would be considered a perfect football field-goal kick, through the uprights from a good forty yards away. This wasn't enough to impress both the old American football players, but the captain then took off on the run and, as he turned to face the posts at a good clip, he watched these vets do the same beautiful thing over and over.

This was an amazing event of pure football, an event of splendor that only those who have played either football or rugby would appreciate. The final lesson was the history of the game that came from the Irish A-side hooker, Daire Mac Fiachna.

He explained, "Some good ole boys, must have been of Irish blood, in ancient Greece created a game called Episkyros, in which a kick game was replaced by an *and/also* game of both picking up the ball and running, and also kicking."

"So one could say rugby was a game long before soccer began. It was believed modern rugby began either in France in the 1850s or in Edinburgh in the 1870s, when somebody again picked up the ball, as the rules for soccer had not precluded that happening, and suddenly a new game, with very ancient history, began again. The establishment of the Rugby Football Union and its rules was in 1871. From the first match in 1859 to the Union being formed, to the global touring of the 1920s by the All Blacks, to the 60s on British campuses, and finally to the establishment of the Tournament of Roses, where all of continental Europe and the British Isles teams met to determine the champion, the modern game took flight. That was, of course, until the New Zealanders and Aussies found the game and took it to another level with a more open field style of kicking and long runs. They also took some of the original spirit of the plodding of scrums and lineouts with slow progression down the field to a "try" (touchdown for football fans), much like what happened to American football in the '80s with Air Coryell. We play old school here at UW, boys, and that is how we plan to teach you."

Daire's words stuck with Galt, and he couldn't wait to be part of this legacy and the next practice. He quickly picked up on his new assignment as a tight head prop. A position, an aggressor in the scrum over the other front-line mates of the hooker in the middle and the loose head prop., who was more akin to an offensive lineman to help support the scrum and the hooker efforts to toe the ball back, as he hung between Galt and his mate, the loose head. With an arm between the crotch of his trusted second row mate, a very tall guy usually, and back to the eight man or qb, it was a phalanx of effort, uniformed power, with rolls and efforts aimed at that one goal of controlling the ball. Lord, he loved it. As the scrum would break, the pack, or the eight men of the scrum, would run the field in a wolf pack-like formation, and the other seven men of the fleet and drop kick skills would ramble the line on either side adjusting for the ball with the synchronization of the pack. An amazing formation of fifteen men who would move in a second from offense to defense and back, always aware of who their mates were, and the location of the ball. Tackles were not vicious, but they could be very aggressive. All they wore were those heavy red jerseys with the big "W" on them and a white collar, and those short white pants, knee socks of their choosing, and those old baseball cleats, as Galt did not have the money to buy new soccer shoes.

Fun it was as the first match was against the UW Milwaukee teams of A and B side. Galt was exhausted and yet exhilarated, also happy that Will was named his outside wing forward, who would support his hip as he went after the other loose head opposition with that wrestling tie-up, while also mindful of his hooker and the "boys" behind him. All worked in perfect harmony to control the ball until it crossed the goal line for that beautiful try, a moment when one would not just run in and prance around, but just touch it down to pay-dirk gently and run back to his teammates. A score or try had been a subtle thing, but again not the win.

It was on this cold Saturday that he also was introduced to the rugby cultural and immutable standard of hosting the other team to your home pub.

For the Badgers, this was to be a place way out of the campus reach, three to four miles maybe, called Pitchers Pub, an old tavern across from a field that would become their home pitch next season. The UW administration had let the club know that this was their last season on campus due to insurance reasons, although the lack of insight here was that other club sports had much more potential for injury and risk; ruggers just play, and if a new patch is needed they make it happen, for the game and the control and the party after is the objective.

The owner, old man Pitcher, was a classic. Scottish in his accent, and his pipes were his to start all the matches. In the back of his bar, was a cement-block room. A square wooden hand-nailed bar in the center of those rafters with nothing but tappers and room for half barrels was dead in the center of this cement floored room. This was the Badger club house he built just for the boys. Although, as Galt had come to know, most of the boys were not that at all.

This first post-game was a good one, and of course the game heroics were shared by all who played and watched, both players and the female fans that came to be known as rugger huggers.

So it was that Galt had found another expansion of his soul, body, and maybe his mind on leadership and teamwork on the isthmus, but the most memorable of what was to be three seasons of rugby was to come next.

The following Saturday was again an A and B game against Galt's old home state of Illinois, the University of; Blue and Orange.

It was a good day, but it had the makings of being hot, as Galt awoke from his apartment, where his studies were getting further and further behind, but his independent readings and work at the Villa were blooming. He was achieving what SHE had promised him when he began this journey in the chilly fall waters of Lake Michigan. The memory of Madison, and the periodic feeling of the need to travel back to the hometown and knock on her door was still with him. But those feelings were slowly becoming fewer and fewer. SHE had gone deep into his heart, and likely would never leave it, but this was a bridge he found himself on. Was it to real adulthood? Not clear, but he was beginning to explore all three of the elements of life balance, as they came to dominate slowly over the old three of beer, pot, and music.

So it was on this Saturday morning before the big U of Illinois match.

Galt heard Will knock on the door about ten a.m., and stumbled over to let him in. Will said, "Galt, let's get your shit together, game time in two hours!"

Galt was learning to love this guy, a truly good man, who was fast as he was, and quiet as he was, a good friend, and a mate to explore new worlds with. Michael Thornton (DPQ) had decided this big pond was not to his liking and had long returned to Mackey for his life's work, love, and becoming a man in his way. He was a good friend, who had to go back. This meant Galt had his own apartment, a one-room affair with a small kitchen and bathroom down by the lake and only a block from the Villa and, oh yeah, only three blocks from campus.

As both Galt and Will mounted their bikes for the three-mile ride out to the patch, dressed in their red jerseys with the big white W and those short white shorts, they couldn't stop talking about their last game, and what was coming as B-game members, who had dominated UW Milwaukee.

As they arrived at the pitch, the team captains approached both of them and said:

"Galt, Will, we need you boys to step it up today. Our starting right-wing forward is out of town on business, and our reliable for many years, tight head Joe, is out with a neck injury. So you two boys are going *A-side against* the Illini!"

Both looked at each other and then a huge smile came over both their faces. This was a fast-developing sport for these guys, but to be bumped up to play the big boys was both terrifying and also exhilarating. Galt felt the nerves and then the calm that he did so many times in his life when a trauma or game-changing event took place. He knew he didn't have a clue how to be a good rugger yet, but he also knew he had an amazing group of thirteen other guys around him; and Will would be on his right hip. But one other variable began to play in, too. It was a very unusually hot April day, as the temperature at noon on the pitch was in the mid-eighties and humidity was rising on the isthmus, between those four lakes that border this unusual piece of land. It was hot and sticky with those big heavy sweaters. They did have another forty-five minutes to worry about this level of the game of ruffians played by gentlemen, as the U of I women had mustered their female rugby team to play a group of rugger huggers from Wisconsin, who were friends and fans to the UW men's. This was to be the inaugural game of the Wisconsin Women's Rugby team. Here they were; the women of Illinois, tall and powerful, experienced, and had their way with the rookies of the UW first women's game in history. But it was over as soon as it started, and it was match time for Galt and Will.

Whistle went off, and Daire the Irish hooker just said, "Stick with me, Galt, and we will have a hell of a good day."

He tried, but he was not as good at following as would seem a simple assignment. Also, the other prop from Illinois was a tree trunk. So as the first half progressed, the scrum and the pack was not doing as well, due in large part to the missing vets, and the Galt/Will combo struggling with all forms of this much-faster game than the B-side warm-ups had been.

As a short moment of action stopped, Daire came over to Galt and put his arm around his shoulder and said, "Galt, my boy, we are about to go to another level of rugby, both you and me. Are you ready?"

Galt was totally out of breath, but was able to squeeze out, "Sure," faintly.

Daire then took his face with both hands and looked him directly in the eyes, not more than six inches apart, and said, "Here is what we are going to do to that tree trunk across from you with that blue, piece-of-shit jersey, who is putting your nose in the dirt every damn scrum."

Dair then took the back of Galt's neck with both hands and in a very fast and violent way slammed Galt's forehead into his own, being very wise to only hit his left temple with Galts left temple bone. WHAM!!!!

Galt whipped his head back and said, "What the fuck, Daire!"

Daire, in his wisdom and need to get to the next scrum, just said, "Don't hurt, does it, brother?"

It didn't hurt, it was just shock, but the ref and the rest of the pack was now calling for the scrum, and Galt was suddenly getting to square up with Will on his right hip, and Daire being supported as Galt was to again lock up with that fucking Blue Jersey tree trunk, and such as it was meant to be. . . As they scrummed down, Galt let the tree trunk have it across his temple with his hard-ass head bone (as he was to learn later, the hardest bone in the head). The Trunk gave out a howl as would a water buffalo being gored on the Serengeti, as the ball was being tossed into the hookers and center of the two teams scrum down, about twenty yards from pay dirt. Tree Trunk lifted up his head and Galt drove his body through him with his ass and the force of eight men behind and side-by-side, and their whole scrum collapsed like hack architecture or a house of cards. A pile up, but mostly with Red on top of Blue Illinois big-bodies. Galt then looked up to see Will glide into the end zone, and touch the ball down on the grass with the style of a veteran.

What had just happened, he wasn't sure, but it sure felt good. Daire turned him up off the pile and said, "Welcome to the next level, Galt. Now, we are going to treat their scrum to our Badger hospitality, and believe me, the big tree isn't going to want any part of you for the rest of this day."

It was a great moment, to be followed by another, and more, though not as on-the-fly education, but a deeper rugby lesson. He would learn many that would follow him into his professional life and all forms of life, all that would touch his body, mind and soul.

It was half-time now, and the W side was up big, having seen the captain also kick a forty-plus on the run, drop-kick through the uprights to take the gas out of a very good Illinois team, but the game was being won in the pits with the pack. Many good smiles were on the sideline as they took off their jerseys and drank water, in what was an almost 90-degree, freaky late April day. There was no locker room in this club sport but a bunch of amazing men who Galt felt very proud to be with. First Will, who came up as the whistle blew for the half. Galt asked how in the heck Will got the ball first, being a wing forward? Ball progress was usually reserved for back through the scrum to the other wings.

Will just smiled and said, "When the big Tree went down and their whole scrum, the ball leaked out behind the second row, and our eight-man was lost in the mess; I saw the ball and just picked it up and let my track instincts take over to the goal line. This was your and my score, Galt!"

As proud as he was, he was also exhausted. The heat of the jersey and all his running at full speed, along with some strange head-ringing, made him a bit woozy. He wasn't sure how the second half would go for his legs, which didn't want to move.

He then looked over at Frank, the aging, second-row, 6'4' guy whose hand went through Galt's crouch on the scrum down–a true rugger of style and grace. There he sat with his red jersey in his lap and poured water over his head. He suddenly saw Galt's face and expression, about to puke, and said, "Galt, you ok, boy?"

Galt couldn't answer, as his words were held up by suddenly seeing the gigantic vertical, foot-long 3" wide scar across Frank's chest. He stared, and Frank responded when he saw Galt's eyes lower to his chest.

"I took a grenade in my chest while saving a buddy in the Korean war. Had to have one lung removed, but my buddy was saved."

Galt suddenly got his wits back with this amazing sharing of how or why. The Korean war was in 1951, and this was 1974. That would have been twenty-three years ago. This wasn't a Vietnam vet, similar to his pals at the Villa; this was a Korean War Marine at least forty-five to fifty years old.

Galt, again on the rugby pitch, was in awe of his mates, and in reflection years later would be so appreciative of this crew of men he could learn from and emulate in later life.

Frank then said, "Galt, just follow me on the pitch this half. You are running all over hell when the ball is loose and the wings are having their fun. You probably ran four to five miles in this heat in addition to the heavy lifting we do. I may run only two to three miles in an entire match, and can be very effective in my role on this club. Almost easier than walking 18 holes of golf. Just follow me, boy, for it isn't how far or how fast, it is how well you know what to do. Move with the game, and let it come to you, don't try to force twenty-nine men and a goofy oversized football to come to you, because it ain't never going to happen."

These words gave Galt some peace, and suddenly his belly and head didn't hurt as much, as they trotted onto the field for the second half. The captain came up to him and Will and, with two pats on the back, said, "You boys are playing a hell of a match. Let's have some real fun, and take this to *higher ground this half.* What do you say?" With his big handlebar and smile, Galt and Will knew this was a moment unparalleled in sports for them. Hell, this wasn't a sport; this was a holy place of men playing men, with no animosity, where teamwork and ball control were all that mattered. He would retain:.

> *The goal isn't the goal. The goal is the control of the ball and team-work you use to make it happen. For if you focus only on the score, it can happen, but not at the rate or amount that it will if you work on the process and the team effort. Numbers are metrics, not goals. The beauty of the game is the goal that will lead to the numbers.*

Second half was now over, and up to Pitchers Pub club house it was, with both the women's teams and the good men of the Illini, who had just had a thrashing by the UW club of thirty-five to six. But that was rugby, and the bruises and the past game animosity got put in a box, and the drinking of much beer, the songs, and who knew what else was about to begin, as old man Pitcher played the pipes as loud and as powerful as ever, and up we all went to the cement-block room for an afternoon of another new lesson in life.

Rugby, Part C: Women's Rugby Has Arrived

s both Blue Illini and Red Badgers gathered in mass, all sweaty and muddy humanity, the four beer taps began to flow, as well as the pass-around of the Irish Mist whiskey that Daire would always bring to the post-game gathering. For it was a mighty important tradition that a home team must follow to host the visitors from out of town, at their local pub, to as much beer as it would take to provide for a memorable reflection and lubricant for songs and new friendships. It was in the nature of a club sport that this type of ritual could be followed. Better it be off-campus for the UW club, as this type of special adult behavior would hardly be approved, unless it was the U's annual fasching event...more to come on that one for Galt later...or the ever Friday political protest where pot was thick in the air. But here on this beautiful spring afternoon, in the dark windowless hall built by an old Scottish immigrant to honor the great game of rugby, the hat that was passed by the teams to all, where uniform color meant nothing eventually, and comradery was the purpose. Ranging in age from twenty to fifty, this crew of old and new ruggers began to build the event, one that had no script, but rituals would surface as the beer and Irish whiskey would require. The limericks and the dances, as well as the cheers from one team to the other, would all be in good spirits. Bagpipes would cease once all were inside with the doors closed, and a simple juke box with some of the best '60s and '70s rock would begin in the background. The singing of the teams was about to begin, and thus rock was only there as filler.

Galt and Will were on their third cup within a quick ten minutes, and a six-foot-tall, long-haired woman with long braids and beautiful face, wearing a navy-blue jersey with an orange I on the back, approached him. He wasn't the type of guy who would attract women because of his good looks. He was a decent-looking young man, but his red hair and freckles, along with his sometimes-confused look of innocence, could ever be attractive to only the most bold and unusual of women. This was not a Villa situation, this was a celebration, and there she was in his face, clicking her red plastic cup with his, introducing herself as Annie from Springfield, Illinois, a junior at U of I, and majoring in physical therapy.

He choked a bit, but finally got it out, and introduced himself as Galt, a kind of junior in his fourth year, majoring in philosophy and eastern religions. Then he was nervous and his fifth gear kicked in and he began to also bore her, he though, with his private readings he had embarked on, and feelings that the U was an environment for him to find a Higher Ground, and thus, studies on curriculum were only a stepping stone to a deeper education and experience there.

She smiled a big wide smile, and Galt noticed she also had a strawberry blond head of hair, but very large blue eyes. He was staring. She then said, "That's cool, Galt," and complimented him on his game. He nervously did the same of hers, even though he had no idea how she played, as the pregame for him to this first A-side start was spent in the porta toilet. However, he now wished he had seen her play. She had dirt on her forehead, and as he looked above her eyes, she dipped a paper napkin in her beer, and began to brush away the blood on his forehead he had not to this point noticed from the violent head-butts to the Tree Trunk.

She then said: "You know, that the big guy you brought to his knees is a PhD candidate from Liverpool England, and has played for the All-British Black in his younger days. He does have a head problem from too many knocks, so your play to his forehead, though not damaging, freaked him out, for you have found his weaknesses. It was beautiful from that point on."

Galt could only see the blues and hear some of her words...

Here was a six-foot-tall, beautiful female rugger, well educated, with a sense of humor, wiping his blood off, complimenting him on his game level, and also matching him beer for beer. It was not more than fifteen minutes, but seemed timeless, and she brought up her plans to hang out in Madison and enjoy the city before driving back with her teammates on Sunday to Champaign. As Galt stumbled with a quick and suave response of, "I would be happy to be your guide," she was called by her sisters, female rugger-mates, over to a gathered circle dead center on the bar floor. The crowd was thick with guys in both blue and red jerseys. All 15 of the navy blue jersey wearing women then formed a rigid circle, locking arms, and began a very strange Gaelic or old English—shit, Galt didn't know, but it reminded him of a Pentangle song—and chanted words that he could only pick up pieces of. Anie then had an open door into the circle by her teammates, and they relocked arms again. Galt had just gotten her the fourth beer and his fifth, and she then moved to the center of the all-women, navy-blue-sweater circle that was swaying and singing in that chant. Annie then put the full beer cup on the top of her head, and performed a stunt that Galt had never seen before, and would never see again at the many rugby post-games he would have the pleasure of attending.

All the guys clambered to the outer ring of the circle, all sixty or so, as the ring of a dozen or so women kept singing choruses of weird old English. Then, her cup on the center of her head, she slowly removed her wet and muddy jersey, shorts, and undergarments, all by her own hand... while never spilling her beer!

She then took a bow, and proceeded to finish the ten or so ounces in the cup, and put her clothes back on. This was not a dirty thing, it seemed to Galt; in fact, the guys all were cheering too, but not gawking, as they would also perform their own forms of ritual nudity as the night would approach. But not with a beer on top of a beautiful, braided strawberry hair, with blue eyes staring over the ring at Galt as she did it.

She returned to him with an empty glass, didn't say anything, and waited for our Galt to speak. He could only say, "It would be my honor to refill your cup for you."

Now her friends found the two of them, and began to talk up going to downtown Madison to State Street or party a bit more, once the guys had finished their versions of rugby post-game traditions. Will had also moved over to be with the crowd of female ruggers, and stuck up his own conversation. Then Annie said, "I am going to the bathroom, Galt, don't leave, I will be right back."

Galt took her cup of full beer and smiled back, but with a new-found sense of fear. Yep, he feared what might follow. Why was unclear, but this was Galt, who wanted to expand himself to manhood here in Madison as was advised by SHE, but this seemed beyond expansion, though most likely not.

He then turned to Will, who had struck up a deep conversation with another Blue-Jersey Illini women, and said, "Let's get out of here."

Will said: "Galt, what the hell?" Are you kidding?"

Galt only could raise his voice quickly and speak into his ear. "Now, or you can stay and I am gone up Park Ave., back downtown, on my bike, now."

Being ever the loyal pal, Will said, "OK, Galt, but you are *nuts*."

Galt then heard SHE in his ear, just a moment after Will approved of their rapid escape. SHE quietly said, "It is ok, this has been beautiful, and more beauty shall come to you here on the isthmus. But go if your heart tells you, for it is nothing to be ashamed of." And so off they went on their beat-up bikes, buzz-biking as was the way in Madison, and rambled back downtown in their muddy reds and bloody foreheads.

Galt would reflect on that afternoon many times in the months ahead, always wondering what may have been with Annie, and if he would ever see her again. If he did, would she even give a shit about this goofy tight head prop from Badgerland who ran off after she made her team proud and humbled so many men.

Between the Villa and the bar scene, as well as classes, Galt received more signals than perhaps he knew how to read. Although Annie the rugger was no subtle messenger, he was beginning to imagine he might be missing many "signals." However, he also felt the guilt that a young man can on a college campus that was in the throes of a sexual revolution. The level of participation seemed to be the measure, rather than the level of love. As was the case, he let this lingering concern stay with him for a week or so. But it was on his way to his American Institutions class one spring day that he understood his own perspective on this.

American Institutions was a class he attended due to the agenda that the professor and study group TA seemed to want to promote. This was simply that all American institutions were born out of some amount of power-seeking and perhaps less than noble intent. Not that the function did not have a noble outcome or role in American political history, but that man's greed and thirst for power drove many to being a working organism, be it the original founding fathers, the extensions of federal departments and cabinets, and also political parties. A cynical position, and one that Galt felt had little objective analysis at its core. Ultimately, he would fail this class and it would serve as the marker for his continued separation from classroom academics to his own pursuit of knowledge and wisdom, on campus and off, modeling what in later life he would come to call a mosaic or stained-glass window of learning or experiences. He would attend and monitor pros and guest speakers who came, hipsters, poets, and even Buckminster Fuller, who left a huge impression on him with his worldly view of Planet Earth, Inc.

But that chilly April morning walking up Bacon Hill towards Abe Lincoln's statue (yes, at Wisconsin's center-point of campus, donated by an Illinois alum), he realized on his own that love is the purpose. That again, that memory of friendship with a woman can sometimes lead to love and sometimes not, but that our path, when it does happen, is the best form of intimacy, rather than intimacy alone, for intimacy's sake. One could have multiple female friends in various stages of depth, and share mind, body and spirituality with them at various levels of intensity. He concluded, there should be no shame in running away from a strong personality like Annie if you had one mission in mind, to find those you know to be friends and someday may be beautiful lovers. In this way he would discover that he would not be experiencing unprotected sex as much, but would have deeper relationships and a much better physical and emotional relationship. Some would be so deep as friends, without ever crossing the threshold to being lovers. Sometimes this was due to his not seeing the signal. However, he also knew that he could feel that mutual moment when two people know that it's time to take their shared experience to the physical plain and their relationship to much higher ground than ever felt with a one-night rugby fest.

That awareness hit him in a proud way, and suddenly he turned and headed away from socialized American Institutions bullshit and toward the union, where a new friend was working a card table that morning for NOW. Next to her was another Villa lady, who desired the physical as a way to friendship with Galt in the past. She was staffing the Students for An American Communist Party table. This was Club Thursday in the Union, and the various groups could set up and share their organizations down the main hall. Of course, there were running, sailing, and the debate clubs as well. But these two tables were staffed by the only two people he knew in the Union that day.

He had no regrets about his new-found independent study method, but did have a bit of guilt, and felt he owed his folks an explanation. But he also knew they would have no understanding of this parallel track with no goal, other than full life experiences to his objective SHE had helped him to set. He was almost twenty-one, yet that had very little to do with it. It was his desire to achieve deeper understandings of love, communism, democracy, eastern religions, Christianity, the environment, transcendental meditation, self-reliance, teamwork, rugby, beat writers, the depth of rock, folk, bluegrass, and now jazz, as well as Ayn Rand. . . *all* seemed like a rich curriculum and noble academic pursuit, as he wandered past the tables of agendas.

CHAPTER 14:

Into the Mystic of Beliefs

As he walked through the union tht club day, he broke a short conversation with Ruth, from New Jersey, a beautiful woman who made you aware in the first words of her proud Jewish heritage. She was a Villa woman who was quite sincere, and despite her family wealth lived for the American Communist Party. They had come to have some nice debates over coffee after dinner, or in the kitchen as he cleaned up. She would find a way to take the simplest of requests from Galt, such as if he could clear her plate, and respond in a complicated way. Her response would never be, "Ok, thank you." It was always something like, "Do you think this is true labor, or do you need this labor? As there are others who deserve this work and this food?"

She was very thin, standing about 5'5", curves he had noticed, and a huge brain. Galt knew from her curriculum she carried that she was a junior. She didn't eat much, was a semi-vegan, and also liked meditation or transcendental meditation. Her music was jazz and classical, no rock, but folk protest songs, including Joan Baez but also Laura Nyro. All this complimented her odd position on so many issues, and had Galt fascinated. Today, Galt felt the pull to her table and stopped to watch her work with a guy who was as much interested in that long hair, narrow curved hips in that hippie dress, and her breasts in a t-shirt that held no secrets either. Her steel-toed work boots were under that dress, as Galt had made the mistake of wondering why she wore them at dinner one night.

As she was wrapping up with her pitch to the obvious preppy from a frat up Langdon Street, who had only one thing on his mind, she brushed him off as best she could when seeing Galt approach. She then locked her deep brown eyes on Galt and that amazing smile became very wide, and she finally said, "Good Morning Galt. I could use a cup of joe. Would you mind, while I do the people's work here?"

Galt was not ashamed by what others might see as condescending, or her potential vision of him as merely a kitchen slave boy. He went ahead and accommodated. Upon return, he saw her in a heated debate with some tough grad students who were pushing her to the edge on her passion and religious verve for the socialist state. These graduate students, who Galt recognized from his philosophy classes as TAs last year, were all about teaching her the difference between religious beliefs and a true logic. Galt saw her fire arising, and stepped into the fray and debate with only one comment, when there was a pause in the air between Ruth the law-school gangsters. He said: "All politics require some faith, and don't you think that with all political arguments, one can find something of value for the formulation of one's own thinking? As opposed to just attempting to be a winner and the other a loser?"

The wanns be lawyers turned at this new entry in the fray, and said almost in harmony, "There are only winners and losers in logic, and this shit is a religion, and won't work without faith."

 Galt knew they must have had the same philo class, and also knew they didn't have a clue about the difference that a little faith can bring to any dialectic or belief system. But he pushed on until Ruth cut him off, and said, "I have learned from you two, as my friend has said, so why don't we call this one tie for now, boys?" They had lost the sexual drive that Ruth could draw out of men at first sight, not knowing she was also the daughter of a former Israeli freedom fighter, as Galt would come to learn later. Her mom and dad had been there on the beach with the exodus and had moved to New York to raise money and support for Israel. Both were teen-aged children of the holocaust, and both of their stories Galt would hear in terms of their beginning, their time during the holocaust, and after life, and how that shaped how the world must be seen according to Ruth Goldstein.

Galt finally stood between her and the two legal minds, and said, "You guys are all about win or lose, and we here are about *and/also*. So take your either/or crap and walk it down to the poetry club."

They both looked at each other, Galt's broad shoulders, her voice now shouting, "Fucking assholes," and realized this was a no-win, and she wasn't a woman who fell for law students.

The Delts, now ready to practice law in a few short months, moved on with no desire for the crap this wild woman with her red-headed white knight had just brought down on them. She walked around the table and gave Galt a huge hug, whispered in his ear, "You are a remarkable man, Galt. I admire your approach, your understanding of my views, as well as the fact you don't always agree with me, but do listen to me. I see how you have evolved and truly admire and respect our friendship." Then she backed off from him a step, still holding onto both his hands, as the mid-morning classes masses were now streaming through the union behind them, starving for coffee. She said, "I would ask only one thing today, Galt. Would you join the American Communist Party with me? For one reason, for you, to help you truly understand what it is we do and why we do it? I don't expect you to embrace it, but in my own way, as my parents do doubt my commitment here as well, your rational perspectives on this effort and its members' integrity would be welcomed by me, as I also continue to explore for my purpose, and I know you for yours.."

Galt was now in a very curious position. She was a developing friend, but also a very smart and philosophical woman, who was ready to share in his personal mission on the isthmus, if only for a while, but in an arena he had only considered to be the end of the world. No doubt his Vietnam vet pals at the Villa would think he had lost his mind. For they had seen much, but they did not share much, just enough that Galt knew that the spread of communism was very anti-American. He, if anything, was a proud American, for the ability he had been given to build his own education and life's freedoms here. Many great faiths had sprung out of oppression and the lack of freedoms for the individual. But his consideration of being both a studying objectivist of sorts, and also an observer and advisor to the American communist movement, did carry with it her exotic beauty, and thus he responded with a whisper in her multi-pierced ear, "I will join for the purpose you have shared, but also for the purpose of my own parallel tracks. Know that this can only be if we both understand that it be kept very quiet and our information only. I will attend as needed, but will not promote or advocate with others. Last, if either of us sees the other to be too distant and our growing friendship is tainted by this, we can call for the other to withdraw."

She pulled back and again those rich brown eyes went deep into his, and she said in her New York accent, "Galt, I agree with your terms," and then gave him a kiss on his mouth in front of the entire mass of the student body at the U of W, in front of a card table with the American Communist Party on the sign above her head, and a fist pointing up in the air.

Cesar Chavez, Che Guevara, and the like were where her heart was, and those were the pictures on the wall. There was none of the Chinese leader Mao Zedung, as the party was wise enough to take the labor bent versus the Vietnam War direction. As it was still unknown what had actually happened in that war, and that the French had put the fear of God into Kennedy. Thus he leaped in with LBJ, going in as a fool would to make his mark, all due to the need of the people to get out from under a dictator, and find their own form of democracy away from French oppression and definitely from the deep desires of the Chinese to continue their assault on the Pacific Orient.

The U.S. had blown it there, but little was understood by all, and thus Galt felt it ok to understand for now this revolution in labor, and it would pay off for him as he found his ways beyond "Mad-town" and out of the mystic to his first steps as a grown industrial man, following the examples and designing his own Ayn Rand character in his early years of manhood.

These discussions would come back to him on future occasions as the union would want his commitment, and he knew this didn't just stop at workers' rights. His memory of *Animal Farm* would forever stick in his head as the reason this socialist whole was only meant to work if a few took advantage and thus formed a dictatorship, under the camouflage of "all for one," and "all are equal," versus fair. That is, *all animals are equal, just some animals are more equal than others.*

So he and Ruth would become a couple of sorts, but they didn't date as such. She was not a dater. She would call upon him to discuss very heavy topics at night, they would in turn maybe go out for a beer, even though she wouldn't drink alcohol, but to accommodate his need for air after hours of back and forth intellectual dueling with her, then walk back, no hand-holding, to the Villa, where they would without words climb the stairs to her single apartment, and with only eye contact begin a beautiful night of love making, often till dawn. He rarely got anything done with class, but wow, did he learn with her. They both taught each other about beliefs, this protestant suburban kid, with the all-American goy criteria, and the classic New York Jewish women who looked best in her khaki shorts, boots, and t-shirt, as if ready for a Palestinian invasion at any moment. New York and Chi-town, mixing it up on all dimensions of learning. It was to end as fast as it started, but it was largely due to Galt's immaturity, which still would arise from time to time. She felt he should be more engaged in his college work and extracurricular activities, as she was. He did not have a disregard for her view, but his pursuit of other lessons was also underway, and even though she respected his passion for rugby, the ultimate sharing game, and his lessons he would share with her, she wanted him to go in directions that he was not willing to do. So they began to quietly separate and it ended the night Kohoutek flew through the sky that spring.

Into the mystic also means into a place of no home or bed for a while.

Burning Down the House 2.0

It was the night of a huge Badger playoff on their way to the national hockey championship and his team was good. Ruth had no interest in this violent game where sharing did take place, but it seemed to be a game where the individual was the hero, unlike her tolerance of rugby. So Galt and a group of pals and their girls held a pre-game before the Michigan final to launch the Badgers hockey into the NCAA quarterfinals, with a tequila and grass event. Plenty of Steve Miller Anthology, New Riders of the Purple Sage, Doobie Brothers, and plenty of limes, salt, crappy tequila, and Wisconsin ditch weed.

Harry, the manager of the Villa, had brought the ditch weed over to Galt's 2nd floor student ghetto flat he shared with two wonderful pals from high school. They had some very tired furniture and a mattress on the floor, all right in the middle of the block that was called the COOP Town. When saying it, anybody on campus would know what and where this was. It had been the root foundation of the riots in the 60s, and HQ for the weatherman and SDS political radical student groups, some violent. It had also been a block where the co-op food store was, a grocery store where cats walked above the vegetable coolers, and you could share in food and barter. It was also now the center of the last of the hippies in Madison, but was changing rapidly, as the two-flat houses were being fixed up by the slum lords of Madison, and actually nice students from engineering and pre-med were moving in. It had been Galt's second COOP Town apartment, and due to proximity and the wild nature of the hood's people, he liked it there. There was something about this street. Like no other in Madison.

He was to have one more crash pad in Madison, but it wasn't going to be easy to get to the next address. For on this night, after 8 future leaders of America were flying high on bad tequila, beer, and that crappy ditch weed, it was off they ran to watch the puck drop at Dane County Coliseum, as many as could possibly be jammed into Johnny Knack's 1965 Chevy Impala convertible. Johnny and Galt had shared high school for two years, but really had become good friends at the university. It was his car that got them around, and was how Galt had actually gotten the job at the Villa in the first place. It was Johnny's K.s roadster that would be their way to hockey, and ultimately to the best road trip ever, a return to the West and a run with Johnny's older brother Jerome.

The game went well, and the Badgers were headed to their first of three national championships under the coach, Hockey Bob Johnson. Yet this night, the night Kohoutek came roaring over the Isthmus, was to also be the night of proving life can hand you a bag of shit at any moment. After that it's up to you if you let your shitty luck, either with relationships or your mission, to be an excuse to be a shitty person. Galt would learn that we all have shit that happens or that gets dumped on us. You can either let it define you, or you can define your own version of what shit was and never, ever get trapped by it again.

Shoulda-coulda-woulda when shit comes raining down. As always, it is up to you. You "gotta wanna", then the shit gets put in the toilet and flushed as shit should.

But that night, it was different. They returned from the victory feeling four beers more, to find all their belongings on the front park-way, along with the four nice girls from the engineering school, who lived below them crying. The frame of the house smoldered but still stood, but all their things—books, records, clothes, all on the park-way, smoldering, too. The fire officer and police officer asked Galt and Johnny if they knew what had happened. All they could add was that the bunch next door, of what appeared to be a group of all ages and no academic commit, were always burning a big garbage fire in the back near both houses. Using any-thing they could find at night, and chanting till all hours. Johnny added that they often saw embers flying all over the alley. The chief just shook his head, and said all these two flats are kindling waiting to burn, and he was glad everyone was ok. Years later, as Galt would begin to better under-stand risk and liabilities in the business world, he would reflect on how the landlord was likely concerned he would be at risk for falting wiring. As lord knows there was plenty of stuff that didn't work right. It wasn't said, but it was in the air, and likely he knew it was a slum and was way below code in more ways than one.

What did the three roomies do, Galt, Johnny, and Pauly, these homestead high school alums now whacking their way through an education in Madison? They suddenly remembered that the Kohoutek party was starting to cook at the Villa dining room that evening. The only request of the girls was that any and all bring a bottle of some booze and a mixer to throw into the 55-gallon garbage can to make what was called appropriately Wapatui Punch. *What? What?*

Ruth had already broken up with Galt, and as the dozen or so various fifths of booze and ginger ale and fruit punch was guzzled to music and flashing stars on the ceiling, Galt, dancing to the Stones and Moody Blues, would fall to all he said he would not do with Angelina that night. She was like a guy who had kept marks of the men she broke and dumped for the next experience. She was to the staff one of the most giving Villa women, and one of the coldest after. A frequent visitor for free food at night in the kitchen, higher than a kite.

This experience was not his proudest moment. For three days she let him live in her one room place on the roof of the Villa. He would sneak down early in the morning and the boxes of his belongings, that stunk like a forest fire, were stored in the garage of the Villa. The cooks had been kind enough to let him keep his stuff there. As the days went by and he knew the crush of Angelina dumping him was the next experiment, the old landlord came to Johnny and offered the boys a two-room no furniture, about three miles east of campus on a dead end, a house he had half renovated on a forgotten street off of east Washington, and a half block from the Crystal Corner. It was a hood where the PhD students who had enough of the undergraduate behaviors near campus went to hang out, study and drink. This was their distant neighborhood where bikes were the only transport back to Bascom Hill. .

Galt was to skip his classes as the move and Angelina took up all his time. He was also feeling the pain of the loss of Ruth. They saw each other, but once Ruth saw him with Angelina, that was it. So it was a few weeks of just floating, riding a bike, working and reading the writings of more classes, and off to a deeper dive into his self-ordained education and reading of the *Naked Lunch* and the *Nova* trilogy by Burroughs. It was a dark time, but it seemed like a reasonable retreat for him. The smell of the clothes, his books all destroyed but Burroughs, and the few albums he could salvage were enough. It did his academic formality no good, but he was already on his own agenda at this point, though he had neither recognized it nor been willing to admit it to his pals or folks. It could be said, he had let the shit stick to him for a bit longer than what was healthy.

CHAPTER 14 (CONT.):

Into the Mystic Isn't Always What It Seems,

Yet It All Will Matter Later. . .
. . .for karma assures it will

The next year, and his final of the last eighteen months of this self-declared education on the isthmus, was to be one of even deeper experiences and further migrations away from his commitment to his parallel path to his folks. The financial risk wasn't as high as it had been when he was single-tracking with lousy results at Mackey, and the pile of credits he had accumulated with As and Bs at the other schools were beginning to indicate he could if he wanted to, yet he struggled to define the age old question from Mackey Why and to what end is this liberal arts curriculum for. The opportunities to grow in other ways kept coming at him. The list was long, but we will share the high points here, as Galt is about to break on through to the other side, and this lack of directions from the outside looking in will soon become history; life lessons he is about to apply very rapidly and in great depth. It was all

184 | Higher Ground

much different than was expected of him as a member of the National Honor Society, four-letter athlete, all-American boy back in high school. He would ultimately get all he needed from those 5 colleges, and go to grad school, but this was not an objective by any means.

The list of classes he had not requested, but that became his academic hedron, is as follows:

1. Highland Park boy, radical-turned-mayor was a night for politics and the end of the revolution that many had wanted
2. Ankle gives out, and a cast and complete immersion into his books follows, and he goes deeper
3. Healing in the country with David, and his love of the earth and written word become a life-long goal for Galt
4. His depth of love for his East Coast buds of a different culture, but not really
5. The path to industry grabs him
6. How is it we find balance and then assure we are able to help others find their way?
7. *Life* magazine and being homeless
8. He learns to love hard work

Galt kept hearing these words in connection with the events he would find himself engaged in or curious to dive into deeper:

> "When the human spirit is taken to a worthy goal, nothing can stop the achievement thereof. You can choose to prove it to yourself and gain the human race. But first to yourself."

It was SHE. SHE was whispering into his soul in a repetitive way he had not yet experienced from her. In the past her words and meetings had been short but powerful. This was different, as it was almost relentless in its repetition. He knew that the get-out-to-vote campaign for the radical Paul Soglin for mayor was an exciting moment. And he knew that when he rolled and tore his ligaments during rec league basketball at the armory, the sedentary life on crutches, almost three miles from campus in the dead of a miserable Wisconsin winter, was not his end, but it was the end for the formal academic time. He had pivoted, and the usual pals from rugby and high school were moving to graduation and real-life next steps. He found friendship and amazing experiences with David, the son of and sibling to a dairy family of ten kids, and his sidekick and now good friend. All came from the farm, in the hills of the Driftless region.

He also found his fascination for the beauty of a great newspaper, which became one of his daily habits during that time, while he sat in union, drawing and observing people as his crutches sat next to him. But his classes were passing, and his reading was going deeper into Karl Marx, Ayn Rand, the teachings of Buddha, Kesey, the Bible, and Steinbeck. All were shaping him for the pending launch. He did move out of town when he cut his cast off, and dropped so many hours that more time would be needed to make the traditional objective. The women of the Villa, both profound and physical in his experience, were now only a memory, as were the vets, the campus buzz, the friends, and his pursuit of attending the UW law school, the last fallacy of his father's mantle.

He never held his dad in a dark thought, but he finally understood that law school was a fallacy the day of his LSAT boards, a Saturday morning in the spring, what was to be his last semester. He had taken a job on a farm as a dirty hand, doing any lousy job the owner would ask for a small fee, then moved to nights to pay rent by working in a Dr. Pepper bottling plant, feeding sugar bags into a hopper, and coating himself in powder every night. These were his works from that spring, as was attending one class, a freshman law class that would also serve as a 500-level philosophy credit. All other classes be damned; this was even worse than he could have imagined. The lawyers argued and fought over the use of "and," "also," or "perhaps," "if then" and "only then," etc.

He knew that cold spring morning, after being out till two a.m. with buddies downtown. He'd been sleeping on a borrowed couch, as he had not had a rental unit or room since Kohoutek came roaring through, and the east Washington month-to-month had become inconvenient for its distance to campus or the country. He sat down with the exam, began to read through, the clock ticking by, with a hangover as big as he had ever had. Lord knows what he had ingested the night before, but it was not a cocktail he would do again. Galt was not a big drug user, but his tendency these last days, as his ankle healed and the mission of spring rugby loomed, was to make up with various options that would enhance the beer and tequila. The Oasis and its world were long gone, as were the other bars, as he now saw himself as an older guy on campus with nothing but kids all around him.

Knowing the Oasis was done, and it couldn't have been any better than a break up. He had just finished one of his last nights at the Villa cleaning up the kitchen, and a beautiful and very smart woman, of his age and readying for graduation, too, Emily, approached him. As the late kitchen man he had been told by his predecessor, they would come just to visit. He had been visited a few times before by other women, usually not for late food, but to see if he would come to their room and help them with their loneliness or other needs. Emily was not one of these lost souls. She was more like an Ayn Rand character, with her determination, business school honors grades, and determination to succeed in business, but a loner, still.

She asked him that Thursday night, "Galt, would you join me for a beer at the Oasis, as it is my twenty-first birthday, and I am a Wisconsin girl, and it only seems right that tonight of all nights, I don't go to the library to study, but get my fair share of PBR with a friend."

Galt has been always friendly to Emily, and she had always found his pocket copy of an Ayn Rand treatise of interest as well, but the two had never spent any time together, other than some deep, late-evening talks on objectivism and life, but never for more than thirty minutes. Emily always had a purpose for studying. But this night, there she was, and so was he.

He asked her to give him fifteen to wrap up, and he would gladly escort and share in her birthday celebration at the local watering hole. They left, with a very light and spry step together. She looked at him, and he looked at her. It was as if this was brother and sister who had not seen each other in years, they were giggling, too, but knew there was some time ahead for both of them to get to know each other again. It was a memorable evening that unfolded, but not as one would have expected in these declining years of free love on the isthmus.

Emily and he moved into a very crowded Oasis, and with an army of students jamming the bar. Galt muscled his best rugby moves and courtesy of "excuse-me" over and over as he worked up to the bar, and there was his favorite bartender, Tim, who had originally turned him onto Ayn Rand, and that fateful paper that snapped Galt's naivety of U education and was one of the major vectors that called for him to pursue his own as best he could.

Tim said to him, as Galt asked for a pitcher of PBR and two glasses, "Galt, tonight you want to drink Bud, for it is being poured free. Can't you see this madness here at the moment?"

Galt responded, "Yea, but what the heck is going on?"

Tim said, "Look down the bar...over there..."

Galt did make a twist of his head and brushed his now-long locks of red hair back, and there were two journalists, one with cameras strung down his neck and the other with a lighter. The one was taking snaps, as fast as he could pull up the next camera from his neck, of the kids climbing over the bar for the free beer. Galt asked, "Who are those guys?"

Tim said, "*Life* magazine, here to do a photo shoot for an annual themed issue to come out in a few months. They gave us $200 bucks and said to pour beer until it's gone, free."

Galt had his first taste of bad journalism, as this was a prop, not a genuine news scene or real life, but life in promotion by a commitment for free beer. He turned as *Life* went on snapping, and the photographer saw Galt's eyes and just picked up a fresh camera and began to snap off one photo after another, as Galt and the woman next to him stared at him down the bar. They were close and had the appearance of dating and hanging on each other, when the reality was it was just a crowded bar. With all kinds of odd looks and caricatures Galt and she stared back at the camera, and Emily, who was just behind him, also was captured in the photos. It was to become the double truck of a center spread in a major distribution of a *Time Life* picture book, called *A Day in the Life of America*. They had sent out freelance photographers from coast to coast by the hour to take thousands of pics of America, waking up in upper Maine coastal towns to going to bed in Hawaii, and beyond. Galt and Emily would be in it, and many thought, as did the *Life* folks, that they were together. In fact, more fake journalism exposed itself to him at that moment, as the caption in the magazine said: "They are together...NOT, they seem worlds apart. As students enjoy a beer after hours at the University of Wisconsin...

Well, she approved the photo, but not the caption; there was no question on that, as did Galt. But Emily did not approve; as Galt was to learn, she was engaged to a much older guy from up north, and had great fear that his level of jealousy would take over if he ever saw the photo. She became suddenly sullen, as he explained what had happened at the bar with the photographers. She changed on him, drank her two beers, and asked him to take her home.

Galt was a bit surprised and as they left the bar, on their way back to the Villa, he asked Emily, "Did I do something wrong?"

She said, "No Galt, I have an issue," and explained it to him. She said, "I wanted to lead some of this college life you lead, and I desire it to be shared with me. I am a senior in accounting with almost a 4.0. I live a boring life, and I see your free spirit. I admired it. I truly hoped we could share in this and more tonight., but this picture in the event has reminded me of my commitment to my fiancé, and I just need to get back. I am ok with all we have done, and will always wish I might have been able to share more with you this evening, but I am committed."

Galt understood, as not only had he begun to move away from the cheap evening Villa escapades, but his heart had awakened to what true love was even more, knowing that to love was to also be a grand and trusted friend and partner, that only love can truly blossom, and the physical dimension have staying power and feed it, if two people are committed to each other in body, mind and spirit. This allowed for true expansion. Emily was one of those people who got it, and Galt only could think he wished he had been better at understanding this earlier in his life, and that a woman like Emily would come to him in the future.

She hugged him, and gave him a warm cheek kiss and tugged on his hair, as she went upstairs to her room, and he got on his bike to ride back to the country and that crazy farmhouse, his last stop before returning to Chicago. That night he wrote for the first time, he wrote a lot, for it was what David had told him to do. He had scribbled down some lyrics to a few songs, but as David, who was to become a published poet himself and the person who introduced Galt to one of his deep spiritual authors, Gary Snyder, said, "Write, Galt, write. Don't let that resistance stop you." So that night as he sat on the floor on his mattress by candlelight with a pad and a pen, her voice came to him. It had been a while. SHe spoke quickly as she was wont to do.

"Get off your ass, Galt, write it out, then pack it up. The City of Big Shoulders awaits you."

This order of sorts was to be one he ignored for a bit. He wasn't done drifting. It was like a mug of beer he kept filling up despite how drunk he was becoming.

He could get around from the farmhouse he found refuge in, as he did have his bike. It was a 10-speed Motobecane French racer, likely twice what a bike of its kind would weigh now, but an amazing machine. It became his primary vehicle for moving from friends' couches to library stacks to read and research; getting to sit in on advanced Eastern religions classes; attending free classes at the Buddhist temple; and getting to work, no matter the weather. This French bike could cut through light snow, rain, and almost any Madison beat-up street or curb. He did find the need for extra tubes and tools a fundamental requirement. So he and his French friend rode the roads of Wisconsin. Some weekends he would take off west to the peaceful regions past Madison into the Driftless Region and the shores of the Wisconsin River near Spring Green, a fifty-mile round-trip from David's trailer in the hills outside of Mazomanie. He grew leaner, as he was cut off from free meals at the Villa, and his training regime of sorts, along with his deep time spent reading, was his happy place. His ankle no longer was an issue and if he wanted, he could play rugby, but he was done, as Galt's wide framework of purpose would say to him; this is done, and this was good. Time to find the next piece of stained-glass window, the window will shine the light of life through. A true labor of love. Someday that window will find itself to be the half to another stained glass that will tell a great and wise story to those who chose to stand in its light. For it was SHE again who was quietly inserting herself to his world, but not in the way he came to know. More subtle, but SHE now seemed to always be there, as was the beat of his heart.

It was on a Saturday morning, late spring, when he saw a light coming shining through to him. He stood up at 10 a.m., about two hours into the four-hour LSAT, picked up his exam and walked it up to the monitor, while the eyes of about thirty other test-takers looked up from their intensity of figuring all the "if/then, and/or, also/or, either-if-then-maybes," and they watched as he put the exam down on the front desk. He said "Thanks" to the test monitor, who had no words. Galt threw on his blue jean coat and ball cap that said Dekalb Corn, and walked out into the spring air with his hangover gone, with a spring in his step, as he mounted his bike and headed for Oregon, Wisconsin, down the shoulder of Park, to the bike path around Monona Bay, and over the beltline. Onward down County NN, to the farmhouse he had heard some friends were staying in. They had kept badgering him to come live with them, had an open bedroom and mattress on the floor. Chickens out back and a garden the prior renters had planted, full of cucumbers and zucchini. Some of them were graduate students and the other half dropouts who were lost souls themselves. It was a coed environment, in a four-bedroom old farmhouse on a distant road, almost fourteen miles from Madison. It seemed like the right launching place, as it was also pointed in the direction of the city with the big shoulders to the southeast. He went to the road, and went with his intuition on where to turn, then suddenly there it was with an old Corvair and mini bus parked on the front lawn, and the flag of Nepal waving. Nobody was home. He walked in the open door and saw some remnants of the night before on the kitchen table, and picked up the old dial phone and called his father. He explained to him he was not going to law school, and in fact he most likely would not play any more rugby, or likely not be able to graduate that spring, as his parents had hoped. He did say this, and it surprised him a bit, "Mom and Dad, I am planning to come home in a few months, as soon as I wrap up some of my affairs here, and will find a job."

His father said, "Don't bother coming back until you get that damn degree," and soon his mother joined and calmed Dad down. But Galt knew this truth was tough love for him and for them. His younger brother was doing well, of sorts, in Montana, and his sister was also planning to go to a nice liberal arts college. Yet for Galt the promise that high school graduation made, turned out to not be the standard predicted experience that all Americans wanted for their kids, but for him it was all he could have asked for and was finally feeling like he was done with the isthmus, with just a few things to wrap up.

As he hung up and sat down on the old farmhouse porch overlooking the fields of corn, now turning brown, he knew exactly what he wanted to do. He owed a lot to so many, and yet it was probably David, the brother of nine, from the dairy farm, who didn't realize that Galt was going to take that experience of getting to know that life, and the few trips to the family farm, with its passionate commitment, and then transpose it to an industrial, hard-working environment, a combination of Ayn Rand and Midwest work ethic, be it in a factory or field.

Yep, work was the new purpose he saw ahead, not as a white-collar worker, or clerk, but as a true industrial worker on the factory floor, for he wasn't a farmer, but he sure was from Chicago. He would learn more about people, hard work, tough lifestyle, machines, noise of metal and parts running, and the pure desire to find his next purpose. He was sure his folks wouldn't understand, and he had some doubts himself. He knew what he received from his parents was a wonderful launch, and the lessons shared with his dear friends in Madison had been worth it all. He also knew that his folks would be ashamed of him for a bit, and his friends wouldn't ever understand how he threw it away. He could see in his developing intuition that this choice would lead him to a fine place of helping people, striving to be as good at facilitation as one could, to taking on only the most challenging of circumstances and objectives, all aimed at the simple outcome of serving to achieve the best outcomes for all. A place that he came to call the Higher Ground.

Not an easy choice, and most certainly not industrial engineering, but his education of all varieties of the political spectrum led him here. *Here is where he would go, back to the industrial city of Chicago, back, back, back…but also forward, forward, forward.* The end of the Man Child was upon him.

He sat now on the floor of the farm house room, as was Galt prone to do, he would sit and not jump into the new conclusion. He knew it was right, but he would just sit for a few days before beginning

The Journey from Isthmus to Cork Floors

It was cold in that old farm house in those Wisconsin November nights, where anywhere from four to ten people could be sleeping under the roof on a given night. It was the place to crash, all of fourteen miles from the center of Madison. A core group of old high school pals from Milwaukee were here, along with some graduate students, who owned the lease. Some were artists and had come back to Madison for a Masters in art, and needed an escape from the center of energy. Others were undergraduates or PhD candidates, and there were those who just knew somebody who knew somebody who was road tripping and needed a job to refill the gas tank for their trip to the coast.

Galt had his own room, and often it reminded him of a mini version of the Titanic in Missoula. But all were painted in the artist's emotions of the time, or so they claimed. He did crave the privacy of the land walks he would take into the corn and down to a stream, brown corn rattling in the fall winds, and from time to time a sugar coating of snow. There was no heat, and at night the temps were reaching the high 20s to low 30s. A few years back, Galt had purchased a Snow Lion mountaineering sleeping bag. This was to become his comfort wrap on cold nights on that dirty mattress in the room over the kitchen. Often he could smell the natural gas seeping up, as the artists would turn on the stove and leave the door open to heat the lower level, where many were sleeping in all forms of rest. It was weird for sure, but he didn't socialize with them. He was very straight and was taking longer and longer and longer distances hiking the fields and riding on the county trucks, often arriving at a small, family-owned cheese creamery, where he would treat himself with his dwindling funds to cheese curds, stuffing some into his pocket to keep in his room. Any food inventory that went into the fridge in Oregon would disappear quickly.

He may have been too much into his belly button these few weeks, but somehow the reflection he was to make was not a random experience. He felt that this big choice to move to higher ground, and begin to rebuild his body, mind and spirit, was to be enriched by what the industrial world of Chicago would bring him. He had no job prospects or abilities, beyond working in a bottling plant, and a box factory during the summers in high school. He just knew it; as he would discover, this "knew it" would come to him over the coming years.

He did, however, have a beautiful escape of his own, one that the artist may have pulled out of him. He and David in his trailer had begun to have poetry-writing sessions. Both would sit quietly, with no words for a few hours, and just write their own rough versions of what they felt were the messages and pictures of words from their hearts. David was good at his, very good, but Galt also learned from his family dairy farm that his folks and siblings had helped to raise a brilliant and wise man. David had an old friend, who was also a good buddy to one of his older brothers, who had spent some time at UW as well. "Indian" was the nickname they had given him. He was older, like three years, also full of life and aspiring to find that thing he would work on for the rest of his life. Weren't they all?

Indian would stop by to have coffee or want to rap about what was next for the end of the line at UW, but Galt had already become absorbed in this spiritual and intellectual connection that poetry brought him, so he was hard to distract. Very hard.

Enclosed are poems he wrote with David, in that cold and late fall, all just before he loaded up a truck with his pack and a small trunk, and caught a ride with one of the artists who was Chicago-bound in mid-November to look at the Art Institute. She was one of those friends from the Villa, who helped Galt come to understand women as trusted friends. To know her beyond this bond, was a fool's errand. The lesson that female companionship can be as good or better than male friendship, a friend who is beautiful, but a friend first and always. This wisdom would bring him great success later in life.

His heart longed, his spirit was ready, and he was about to jump into being an adult maybe for the first time in his life, taking what he had learned from the many institutions and life and friends that he could. It was with this longing and lost sense, but with light at the end of the tunnel finally arriving, that he wrote and wrote.

SHE has always been there, in his journey from Child to Man, stumbling along his way to the Higher Ground. SHE chooses to share his poems here, so as to help understand what was truly inside his body, mind and soul as he transitioned. This was as she saw it. SHe knew that these poems provided some of the girders of the bridge from Man Child to Adult.

First group of 7 are of the love and joy he had felt, as well as the heartbreak he had shared with Madison; "The Good, the Bad, and the Beautiful."

Second group of 6, for love of the country, where he captured his desires to always remember this special land he was now going to leave. This place where SHE had told him he would grow, and Lord, had he ever. No as most college students in their fifth school would, but how many are there who attend that many ways? He was bursting with words. She knows he is moving rapidly now"From Learning to Purpose."

Third is……..Get Off Your Ass was not to be shared with the two prior themes, as it was of the industrial visions he was beginning to have from his days of visiting the Chicago industrial corridor. Galt's great-grandfather was an early Chicago industrialist, an engineer from Denmark, and developer of early fluid power and cooling mechanisms for food storage. He had come and built his own company and manufacturing business in the Chicago brickyard neighborhood, a business now no longer in his mom's immediate family. It was in the hands of her cousin, an industrial genius and entrepreneur both, one who Galt would connect with years later. He would just come to call him Uncle in book II. All this would come to pass in a good time.

Part I, Good, Bad, and Beautiful

#1: Easy, Ode to the Villa Maria

RUN JUMP AND HIDE
Slow down young fella
It's not a one shot deal.
We all know it to be true,
But you ain't gonna catch a thing
flying like a cock pheasant
From the hunter's gun

"Living ain't living alone"
A wise man tells me,
But the trees and the fields keep coming
Back to life every spring
It's a big circle game
So just downshift quickdraw,
but don't turn off the key

RUN JUMP AND HIDE
there's a lot of different ways
to reach the end.
But everybody's trail has a different bend
If you don't like the early morning hum of energy burning,
then get out of the game
And find a different rock to stand on

If the quick glance of pretty eyes
Grabs you by the soul,
buddy your life is empty.
Keep it Full!
and let those glances

serve their simple
entertaining ways

and don't fret about it happening
cause they'll come
and go through your life.
then one day
She'll just come
and you'll have a better old time
then you ever had before…
if lucky enough…
forever.

Part 1 (cont.): The Good, Bad, and Beautiful

You Know Who You Are

Will we be there
as we are now
in twenty years
after so much love
and career?

Anxious loving and
Still full of growth?
Wanting your body still
Still, always giving my best
to you?

The desire for the road
now over

Will to not always think of it
But never sacrificing me
Because that's what brought us here.

two brave people
Opening up the value of
Their souls
ready for the day when
they can say,
"You are my best friend"

#2: The Good, Bad, and Beautiful

IN ME
So good to be alone as I am now
Running, Running so damn fast
a Whirlwind of wind joy fear tears love and growth

Sometimes fighting for air
Feeling like a newborn child
But never feeling so high and mighty with every new breath

You make me dance and smile
Tears flow, as they never did
Patience flex and strength of heart, believe in me
Believe in us

#3: The Good, Bad, and Beautiful

Hang on Tight
I don't want to walk away

I won't let my pride get in the way
when you say "it won't work"

When we irritate each other
I will stop to listen and
I will expect the same of you
But never will I shut the door

And when you won't listen to me
then I Know it doesn't matter what I say
For you will have lost what we have,
As will I

It is in our ability and heart to accept this challenge
Leap the hurdles, for you know the joys that can lie in between
This is where respect, and confidence come home root

It was just plain vanilla, that we had
Who in the hell would care what happens down the line?
Hang on girl, for ours is a love so strong
Towards our goals we shoot so hard and straight that our lust can be
deadly

#4: The Good, Bad and Beautiful

Ink on Paper
Pen in Hand Again
Here I am again
back with pen in hand
Always as before
Transition brings me to this place

So much time seems to slip by

Large gaps in the printed word of Galt
struggling to find the comfort and familiarity
But I don't think all this is motive force this time

My dream is real this time
my truth flows from my soul
Confidence and familiarity with all
A creative urge to print what she makes me feel

#5: The Good, Bad, and Beautiful

Sweet Jane of the High Ground
 Wondering if our eyes
Could ever see into each other's
as they once did
Wondering if we'll ever get the chance
To study ourselves,
Once again?

It was a formal education
Loving you,
Yet to the highest level of understanding
Both of us
Not quite able to grasp
Our small oak taking root

That oak
Has still not matured
It has not been given
The Fair chance it deserves
We both have allowed distance
To stunt its growth

Was the sea we both planted so shallow?
That it could withstand the test
I felt I had to yield
Was I being too objective
Or was I just running
again?

You really help me to stop
and try to make a stand
but it must come
from within
and I was not big enough
Yet
to realize

It was always my role
to make the big decisions
As to where what we both would do
you are so great at letting me fly
Almost amused
but I think I hurt you
the last time I took to win

So just to see if the oak
will die
and with the soil
or grow
to mighty strength
I must now find out

S I am coming back to see
if those long hours of learning

should be laid to experience
and growth
to your doorstep I am bound
I'm coming back to you, Sweet Jane of the High Ground

#6:5 The Good, Bad, and Beautiful

Like Touching the Sunrise
Big of Blue Eyes
A voice and smile
like an early morning sun
touching you was the morning sun

then suddenly
one evening
when we were alone
Word and thoughts came
to such common ground.

Things became a bit rough
with truth from both of us
Other thoughts of other ones
Stood before us

We are at the edge.

We both held ground
so close to it
The rain began to fall
As we stood so wet
we both then gave shelter
to each other

confident of our song
We both sang

#7: The Good, Bad, and Beautiful

Believe Me
Another person to see as my eyes open
The dawn brings it to my eyes first
The light brings you to my eyes
an untold joy for me until this moment

No doubt the feelings inside
do not fear the permanence that your heart demands
To brave with your love is for one to soar with a Red Eagle

Never before have I woken in the middle of the night
Reaching, feeling, making sure that you were still safe
A peace of mind that is always

I have a long way to go in my life
Many goals to achieve
Person to me and ono me to be met
it is in your sense of this news that makes us so important

Even though I have not stood on the rock and
shouted our love forever to the world
The wise and close see it in my eyes
as our time of public joy will come

Believe Me

Part 2: From Learn to Purpose

All are written by Galt as he begins to pack his stuff and say goodbye to so many good memories of the mission to the isthmus, preparing for the purpose he believes he has found.

#1 Great Land All

A boy so full of wanderlust
A desire for the open highway
He had heard of Big Skies
Massive white caps dressed with tall pines

It is Colorado first
With ugly words for the heartland
Illinois Iowa Nebraska what a bore
Nothing to compare with canyons and aspens

So he had a lover
of the East Coast and beautiful spirit
Tragedy was their theme
As was their time of the mountains

Again he returned farther north
Big sky without a doubt would provide his shelter
Wide rolling valleys cut by beautiful rivers.
As the wild west and its clear-cuts were the higher he got

Through another dream he cased
To Seward's folly and northern world so wild
Glaciers so powerful he was at a moment afraid
Clean power unsettled, still he did feel free

AWAKE YOU FOOL!
It is the heartland that moves to the contrast you desire
Black earth giving, seasons so radical
Valley below so subtle and prairie so ripe with colors
Take time to look and reach for the whole
It is in this understanding of all that beauty abounds
and your hearts freedom flows

Part 2 (cont.): From Learn to Purpose

#2 From David's Trailer

I see the old crippled man
He struggles to rise
There's dirt all over
His faded levis.
He's been workin on that chevy
For three years now
He used to spend them
Driving a tow hitch plow

His home is so proud
Is leveled to the ground
He refused to ride the train
That was progress bound

His life is a 3 room existence
In an old frontier trailer,
With high bank payments
His only jailer

His back he believes

to still be strong.
None worked harder,
"What in the Hell went wrong?"

The wife had died,
The kids now live in crowds.
His dreams move on
With the passing clouds

If he were twenty
He'd do it all again
To the crops all his life he would tend

Then his frown turns to a smile
on his cold day in November,
He knows that the land
Will always remember

Part 2 (cont.): From Learn to Purpose

#3 November
So many shades of brown
From the tan buds of the trees
Waiting their chance in the spring
To the rich black
of the late turned soil

With its gray backdrop,
or bright blue so rare
This earth with its flow of beauty
Takes on such a deceiving luster
Under the skies of November

The land seems to be so desolate
When the first full Moon brings its shine to sky
To look over the field and the distant woods
With their lunar glow,
Is like seeing another dimension grow

it the death of Octobers reds and yellows
There shouldn't be a tear,
For even they for tell of fierce winds and longer nights
There is still so much beauty in the waste of late fall
Just out of reach of winter's claw.

Part 2 (cont.): From Learn to Purpose

#4 8,757 Day Reflections

In three days
I will be 23
A crazy age to be at
and feel life
is a bore

There are bright moments, yes
with friends
and myself
but surely
there must be more

I try like hell to find that experience
Which will enrich my life
and point me
in the direction of

that elusive door.

My eye is still keen for the task
I have no plans for ever slowing down
There's one thing
I must know
How long do I spend treading water
Before I find a lemon with whom I may grow?

Part 2 (cont.): From Learn to Purpose

#5 Waiting for a Train

I was just thinking about
How easy it would be to
hold you tight
to hold you for a long time,
all through the night

Between the two of us
There would be no fright
no fears, no doubts
just you and me
Making it right

I've spent near what seems to me
A lifetime drifting
from challenge to challenge
To spend my time with each way of life
I wonder, did it mean anything?

Reach for my blind eyes and easy
Show me the tunnels end

And the beginning of the light.
just you and me
Making it right.

There's only one way in this world
to be alive
And this to always follow your heart
through the dark
and the doubt

I don't believe we're all here to fight
others
or ourselves
There are so many doors
They can all be opened

Part 2 (cont.): From Learn to Purpose

#6 Not a Clue
Now 23
A crazy age
to be at a
and feel life
is a bored

I look everywhere
Trying to understand
all I see.
I listen to elders
and the very young

I have tried so hard

to be that
which would help all
But I still wallow
In the dung

Part 3

#7 GET OFF YOUR ASS

The days are getting shorter
frons on my east window,
Dims the early light.
I think,
Now is the time to meet the day
But why?

I grab the old quilt
and role towards the shadow
of the cold wall.
The new beauty of today
Becomes and
Ugly now.

It's in the darkness I find
Most comfort
These days.
Solitary and quiet
the wind blowing,
with good down pulled to my chin

The bright moon shown last night,
as only it can
On a cold November night.

But it was only a strange friend
Whose meaning
Had somehow been lost.

Hells Bells! Who knows what's right?
to jump in the madness,
or stand here and fight.
A wise man cries out loud,
"it's a cinch the combine will suck you in, so
never give an inch"

There will be no compromise
 on the road to my horizons.
The dawn beckons now you fool,
So rise to its call.
And understand
There is no better moment than now

CHAPTER 15:

Walking on Cork Floors

He sat on the porch when all was quiet in the house, and thoughts rushed into his head.

It was always about Madison in those days, and why didn't he put it all out there?

They knew and he knew, the "I am still wondering" was deep in his gaze, and was, for some, scary, and for others, a curiosity. He needed to defend it himself.

Nobody else would! He now will tell himself the truth.

Galt was able to pack all his belongings into a large pack with his sleeping bag, which hadn't been washed in a long time. His few pairs of shoes he tied to the bag, and his only burdens were boxes of his prized books and albums. His stereo had been stolen, and his bank account empty, but he had eighty-three dollars he could share for gas, and a ride who would pick him up in a few minutes. There was a landline in the old farm house this morning as he awaited, with no heat in 40-degree temperatures that November morning. He had just turned twenty-three in October, and suddenly realized he had spent two years post-academic disciplines, living off the land from couch and mattress to friendly bed, in a holding pattern for a long time. But he had his focus now, he had this strange aim at the industrial backbone of America back in Chicago. He suddenly realized he had not shared any of this with anybody. Even SHE had chosen to stay quiet, and he did not call upon her. He did remember, SHE had said if he needed her, to call, but would no longer come without his request. For it was his time to find it on his own. SHE would have been a large help, but he then realized he had his good friend, Peter.

Peter was now out of college, with degrees and on his way to marriage to a beautiful person, and with a real job, all back in Montana, as he pursued his MBA as well. Galt had no idea how anybody could get the motive to want a more academic environment, but he also knew his issues were only his, his to bear and his to advance through. It was clear to him that Body, Mind, and Spirit, though hungry and maybe a bit depressed, were all working together, striving to find the balance of an equilateral triangle. He was being led by the heart, and the mind was trying to catch up. But it was a good place, best he had been to in a while, a Higher Ground, though many might debate it, as he awaited the pickup from an old pal on her way to Chicago to attend and show her weaving at the Art Institute.

He looked for his watch, and realized he had hocked it, and thus had no idea what time it was. He just wanted to be ready for her arrival that morning. He picked up the receiver of the house phone, and dialed his old friend in Missoula. After friendly exchanges of family and current situations, it became clear that Peter was a bit shocked with Galt's move, and his new purpose; but knowing him as he did, it soon settled in, and he had always known this was Galt, and he just wanted some feedback, not a decision. That had been made. Odd as it was for Peter to grasp that role, he did it so well.

Galt quoted Helen Keller: "Life is either a daring adventure, or nothing, Peter."

Peter: "Couldn't agree more, Galt, if you don't scare the shit out of yourself every now and then, you start becoming numb."

Galt responded, "One can get comfortably numb."

Peter: "Can't find higher ground in a two-dimensional world, Galt."

Galt responded: "Good personal mission, Peter, moving to Higher Ground."

Peter: "I have been deliberately seeking and luckily finding higher ground literally and metaphorically for the last eight years, and don't expect that to change for me in the next sixty, my friend."

Galt: "I like it, Peter. 'Deliberately Seeking Higher Ground.' I, too, have continuously been seeking through the power of my own way of enriching and developing my body, mind and spirit. But I'm beginning to realize you can't aim at just one and hope the others will maintain their maintenance and repair as well. All three have to be working together, led by the spirit. Or so I am beginning to think after all this religion and deep dives into every damn social, relations and cultural element the isthmus has offered, some on campus and some from just sharing by the many we befriend in this life."

Peter: "Galt, your pursuit is surely unorthodox, but it always has been. I think it is good for you that you have followed these tenets, but not for me, my friend." He added, "For me, it is when the hair sticks on the back of my neck. It can be when I hug a loved one, or have a day to be proud of, or playing music, riding my moto, skiing wild terrain, or hearing something beautiful. All of these have risks."

Galt: "Risks, the quantity we aspire to sense how intense before, during and after."

Peter: "Again, only speaking for me, I have great fear of failure, I am also understanding it can change but it can only be good if you have something you have learned and loved in the first place. Loss is the greatest fear."

Galt: "Loss is hard, but I do believe we must strive for higher all the way to the end. Like I said to our old friend Patrick, when talking about the death of our old pal. It's like being an offensive lineman, don't know where the goal line is, reached until it is. So make sure every second and play you have is all you can give. Think about whistling and you will stop climbing and seek that place of 3-D, joy and higher ground."

Peter: "Couldn't agree more. Go for it, Galt. It is our way."

Galt: "I am, and if you hear of anything or anybody who wonders, just say for me that I am following my heart, and have found the path to my next phase of life. We have talked about it, and we both agree, it is like hockey, with three periods. I am about to start the second period with a very different rink and puck, and you are already playing your second period. I admire you, Peter, and as always, I appreciate our friendship. See you, brother . . ."

Peter: "See you, brother, and if you run into an Ayn Rand character, say hello."

It was at this moment when he hung up the phone and put a few dollars under it to help pay the bill of what he owed the house, that these words came into his head, as did these poems that represented his third phase of crossing the bridge to the second period.

"I want my kids, if I am fortunate to have them, to want to say they would want to be as good a father to their kids, as I am to them."

No clue why this popped, but he was starting to fire on all cylinders.

The truck was pulling up the dirt road to the old farm house in Oregon, Wisconsin, and Galt grabbed up his poems of his future state, and stuffed them into his paperback copies of Gary Snyder's and Richard Brautigan's books.

So we know SHE has shared Galt's words and feelings, as he now enters his Industrial Phase of the quest for higher ground, tied crossing the chasm to being an adult. SHE knows of his dreams of diving into the Industrial Strength of Chicago.

He finds it is best if he captures some of these exploding emotions and feelings in words that have a raw resemblance to poetry. He finds that by having them hand written down in a file, that he can keep them close and permanently lock them into his learnings, so he may draw upon them. .

He grabbed the blank pages out of a paperback and found an old pencil. He began to write as he waited for his ride back to Chicago.

#1 "New WAVE"

The rivers and the corn, the rails and Iron Ore.

Who'd ever thought
They'd all come here
And form such a beautiful whore.

no stage and no lore
no old money and no bore

WE showed New York the way
to open a red-light district door

 # 2 Chicago Geometry

Is it the clean air?
Noway!
Is it the skyline?
Not really.
It is a neighborhood of like minds?
Probably not
Is it four seasons to bear?
Definitely not.

A better job market?
Probably yes.
Higher wages for all?
You can bet on it.
Friends who have done well?
That's the key.

We all bring our own along
I am a rapid growing geometry

Harlem Howard and 115th
From Rogers Park to Pullman

Harlem Howard and 115th
That really covers it all

Draw it from the map
and you've cut away the heart of the sprawl

The arteries to the burbs
The life lines to America.

The home for the ore
and the World's futures price wars

#3 360 Halsted
We are color and stamina
With an industrial spine
of pure cold steel
The system rocks through strikes,
and the people rise for their work
Demand one more hour
and one more trick.

Trains overhead
Cars underground the lake say stop!
and we climbed the for the sky

The guns yell "fight!"
The mayor yells "no!"
The people scream "Move the damn snow!"

But no one ever seems to go
Never on a Sunday

Not cowboys
not hillbillies
not eastern sophisticates
not country hicks

Chicagoans All

Full of crap
And full of grit
Sing to the sun and cursing the sow.

Fight for rights
higher wages
and better
neighborhood schools

NEVER satisfied
NEVER totally broke
NEVER leaving town
and NEVER EVER DONE!

CHAPTER 16:

Steel in Your Day, Shoes, Heart, Body, and Lessons That Last Forever (Graduate School 1.0)

Galt envisioned the city and not the surprise his folks would have when he was dropped off in the driveway and rang the door, with a pack, a sleeping bag, his books and records, and the ceremonial paper. He had not spoken to his folks for a number of months; in fact, he couldn't remember the last time. To him it seemed like they would be ok with all of it if he explained his purpose.

They were both happy to see him, and so was his youngest brother, now having moved into Galt's room and ten years old, too. Sister was off to college as a freshman, and his brother B was in Montana or Colorado or some other place. He had completely disconnected from all of them, but held no remorse for some reason. He had been on a six-year retreat to learn and get ready for this purpose, or so he expanded it to his folks. They had no idea what he was saying, and his father kept saying welcome, we will find you a great job and you can get your career going, and pick up those last eight credits, too. Very excited, even though he had walked out of the LSAT board exam.

As the goal in his six-foot frame was to continue to ease below that rugby-beer and post-Villa Maria weight. His pants were tied together to his hips by three extra punch holes from his pocket knife. His blue-jean coat only fit his shoulders, as his weight from the high of 240 was now below 200, and he was smaller than he was when he graduated from high school. He was hungry and his mother knew exactly how to welcome her number-one son back for as long as he wanted. His father's talk of the future could wait, and yes, they actually wanted to hear of his goals. Mom said, "but first how about some hot homemade meatloaf and scalloped potatoes. OK?"

Big hugs and kisses for Mom, and not much talk from Dad. Years later, he would think that Mom had asked Dad to stop putting his mantle on him. That he had to find himself, if this crazy zig zag he was on was any indication that just making them happy was not working.

He went for the next year living at home and wondering where that next purpose in a factory would be. Though that feeling of desire to wander the world was chewing at him, the strength of the purpose of working in the industrial world was taking control. Come that first Monday he was ready to go. Two days later, he was in an interview in a metal plant, called TechCoat Metals, located inside the city limits just next to an O'Hare runway. It was a huge facility with strange fumes and massive steel looms running at high speeds of 300 feet a minute, along with overhead cranes and lift trucks. Men worked in green uniforms with first names and department or level of supervision embroidered on the pockets. He was meeting with Dr. Jack Stranzio, an old friend of his family, who was a chemist for metallurgy at the company. He was the chief scientist who ensured the coatings were applied properly to the many forms of narrow-gauge steel as they rocketed through the lines. Coating or laminating tin plate, aluminum or galvanized. These lines or steel rollers built two stories hgh, running in sync on a line almost the length of a football field. Extremely loud noise came at you from all directions, and the magic of people everywhere working hard to make a good living. . There were four lines in the plant and a huge warehouse. The primary purpose was to take the fresh milled steel rolls that looked like giant oiled paper and feed them with massive automation into a line that was already running, via an amazing device called an accumulator. The set of rollers would rip and shrink the line as it kept running at the full speed of 300 feet per minute. As the new roll was fed up onto a gigantic sewing machine or stamp, it would then be pressed with interlocked steel stitches to fold sheet and nest. The call would echo out across the plant at a very high decibel when the new coil had been attached: "Stitch online 3!" warning all that the-newly formed marriage of one coil to the other was finished and headed their way somewhere down that football-field to the end coater. The oper-ators who ran devices with big pans full of chemicals and coatings, some just plain old paint to produce white, would then open their offset rollers that were pressed to the steel, allowing the steel stitch to pass through to the end, back home where it started, a few seconds later. The finished coils would be cut with their fresh baked paint or coated tinplate for mason jars, lids, etc., would be strapped with powerful signode hand scrapers, and locked with paper to afford little damage to the two to three-ton coils. The finished coil would be taken by a large, phallic-looking device on the end of the lift truck that would enter the center of the coil, gently, then get taken to the warehouse, and finally onto a large truck. It would be delivered to maybe a Frigidaire plant for refrigerators or washers or dryers, or maybe a Ford F 150 plant for fenders for a Ford pickup, or to a shelving manufacturer or to Mason Jar company for finally packaging after being stamped or cut and shaped to fit the top of their jars. Many uses, many changeovers and much chaos, as Galt was given his tour.

Dr. Jack took him back to his office and clean air, as the doors of the 600k facility were closed in the winter, thus fumes were special to work in for forty to eighty-four hours a week. Some as much as Eighty-four, which was a seven-shift, seven-days at twelve hours, max, work-week.

The shop was under contract with the United Steelworkers of Amer-ica, a stormy union by any measure. The firm was owned by a local Chi-

224 | Higher Ground

cago private equity fund, who would have professional managers running it to achieve a return to their investors. Beginning as a service to the major steel mills of Chicago's south side, it had grown exponentially and now employed over 500 people, many of them Latinos, or Kentucky migrants to Chicago and a better life.

Dr. Jack asked him the big question. "What was it you wanted, Galt? A first step. I find it amazing you even have any interest in this type of career. A young man of your quality and background could very easily get into our sales department or work in customer service, and we could see if you were management material in a few years."

Galt just looked Dr. Jack in the eye, and was never so clear, as his heart was in heaven in this hell hole. "Dr. J., I want to work on the factory floor."

He said, "Ok, then we may assign you to the quality control department."

Galt said, "NO, sir…. I want to be in the union, working on one of those coating lines or major slitters. Want to learn it all, work any shift and commit to that purpose."

The doctor was a bit taken aback, but said, "Ok, Galt, I will work on a program for you."

Galt interrupted him. "No favors, don't want plant guys to think I am a chosen one or special treatment. Give me the worst of the work, start at the bottom."

Doc said, "Don't worry, Galt, I will get what you are looking for. You are like no other I have seen here from the North Shore college boys, but you are truly authentic. I wish you luck, and I will check in on you. That is a commitment I make to you and your folks."

Galt smiled, and thanked him. He went home and shared his new-found purpose, cork floors and the smell of steel and chemicals, mixed in with weird hours and danger at every corner. He would be sharing this new education with people who spoke little English, or had an east Kentucky hard ass accent.

He told his folks these were to be his peers for the foreseeable future, or what the future entailed. Not the expected college white collar gang he considered still his good friends. The traditional academic approach was not helping them, they were just spending money. Life lessons were everywhere, and he was sure ready for this one. It was to be his adventure for the next six years, and until he met the woman who would become the basis for the family they would start, grow and complete.

Galt was sitting in his room, the one he never really lived in, as this was his folks' new home they purchased upon their return to the Village on the Bluff. But his stuff and his little brothers' things were stacked up there. His sister and his youngest brother were down the hall, and found it a bit curious that he had found himself back home in this new retro tour of the Village. They gave him his distances, as he seemed almost like a distant crazy uncle. But they also shared in pleasantries and small family events together, but Galt never connected with them as he had with his lost brother, and Ben.

He had a few hours of quiet, after a shower or nap of four to five hours before another shift would begin (for he was finding that the eight to ten he had come to enjoy on a college campus was not what this life would require). Working nights, afternoons, and weekends, he was making it work with the curtains closed and the darkness for a few was enough. Weird, but also very different. Darkness of daylight was not his joy. When the evening light began, he would find himself awakening and getting excited for this bizarre work and experience he had asked for and now had.

One Sunday morning around 8 am, when he arrived home after a twelve-hour Saturday night, he had a hard time sleeping, despite his mom being kind enough to serve him part of her amazing Sunday breakfasts she would prepare for the whole family. He had no regrets about moving home, or why he now found himself at home with his folks at age twenty-four, but he also liked this bonding, albeit from a distance, with his folks and his younger siblings. Meals and time with his failing grandparents was also special, and probably made this whole crazy industrial grad school experiment worth it. More important to him was the tie with his

Marine grandpa and his Moms folks, all who were fading fast. Time with them was priceless.

It was in one morning of reflection, as he sat on the edge of his bed after a much-needed shower on a very hot August Sunday morning, that he came to the realization that SHE had been very quiet of late, and he was finding that her silence was to be expected. Was it that SHE seemed to not need him, or he her? He found himself still dreaming of her. He did not know SHE was now alive, and of this planet, coming to the world at a younger age than he, but still here, not far from his old haunts in the Forest by the Bluff. SHE had explained her youth as the youngest of seven and of a wonderful mother and father. SHE was to see her own tragedy, but also grow into being one of the strongest living souls on our planet. SHE would endure and persist, despite family death, wealth collapse, and PHD graduate studies interrupted. They would find each other at the right time and right place. For her, the plus and minus were the reflection of what they shared and what SHE could have never known in her life's path. Her life as a descendant of an American Tribe of Native Americans, with the obligations that brought was so very different from his. They both had family life that was ahead in the next third of life; almost 10 would pass, and not allow them to cross till then. But at this moment, he became calm and assured that her promise was always there for him. Not today, or tomorrow, but it was to come for both of them in a very different reality of time and space, with purposes that aligned. Providing opportunity for both to share in true joy and bliss on earth. They would find this place in the future. . . but the details of how they would find each other through time and place to this destiny is to be found in future writings of the tale of Galt. Strange as it all may seem to our reader today, he only had the image SHE had left with him of a strange rock formation, a roaring river in red rocks. A rock formation that almost looked like a Mexican sombrero.

CHAPTER 16

Part II

Galt was so engaged in this industrial experiment that he couldn't help but constantly remind his mom and dad that he had found his next purpose, and they would laugh a bit, knowing this was probably another Galt crazy adventure that would end soon. They hoped, yet he was pleased they would smile. What they did not yet understand was that his custom program of growth was so unorthodox to anything they would see as healthy and productive, that it was understandable they would wish otherwise for him. But it was his, and as we now are beginning to understand, Galt's growth in the journey to Higher Ground was an authentic one for him alone. It needs to never be forgiven, as they gave him all he needed and wanted, even at the age of twenty-four and by all appearances, from the outside looking in, still figuring it out.

His parents gave him a room and a short-term loan cosigner to buy his first car, an orange Ford Fiesta, a German-designed, Spanish-built, hot clone of a Volkswagen Rabbit. He loved this rig. It was to be paid off in months by the big checks he earned as he lived at home that first year back, while taking a membership in the United Steelworkers of America union and a job on the plant floor at TechCoat Metals as a coil slitter operator. It was a crazy job on one of the smaller machines, where a very sharp blade, run at high speeds, set very exact measurements on a grease set of bars and gears so a new, fifty-inch-wide coil of fresh metal of many types could be run through and then reduced on a rewind to many narrow coils. All were originally set for dimensions of a finished product stamping machine. Each of say four coils would come from the big mother coil, taped and wrapped carefully, and then be transported from his station, where he was trained for a few weeks before being let go on his own. These would go to a gigantic station of four coil coaters that would run as far as a football field through washing tanks to get the steel as clean as a whistle, and then through offset rollers coated with inks and coating that would allow for the finish for the final product to be endurable to the engineered specs required by the ultimate end manufacturer. As mentioned, this could be for Rheem water softener tanks, Kenmore refrigerators frames, or Ford F 150 pickup truck fenders, even the 007 thin plate of the electro metals used by Ball jars for their lid coatings. The metal would run through very hot ovens that didn't give off the smell of fresh cookies. Instead, they produced steam, fumes, and noise. Lord, he loved it at a shift of three to eleven, or even when the change and pay upgrade came to be on the big line working for Frank Rangy. Frank was the toothless foreman on the big line two, and Galt was to be his second, running the gigantic rewind. Basically, this was a guy who would receive the coils painted baked and finished, coming at him at full speed. Later Frank would move him to the gigantic payoff device. This was Galt's favorite in those days following the move from the slitter floor job shop. That machine, you stood high on a platform of cement and looked over the entire plant with your microphone, unwrapping the mill's fresh metal and feeding a new coil on an existing coil running through the line a hundred yards away. This web of steel would be put on temporary hold, by an accumulator. A device that was a wild set of huge hydraulic rollers that would actually shrink the length of the line by collapsing in a synchronized way to achieve a dead coil's tail to be married to the new coil tip. Then Galt would hit the huge stamp machine down and would bring tons of pressure to the old coils and the lip of the new, in a way to bring metal together, like two huge toilet paper rolls. One was now being finished with fresh paint on the rewind station at the end of the line, and the other new at the payoff where Galt stood tall. Once the power and straight metal forge from the crushing stamp pressure was complete, he would restart the retreating accumulator rolls above his head and release the new stitch and nose of the new coil into the line. Declaring with a loud and appropriate announcement out over the plant microphone to the back coating stations of three there was a "Stitch on line 3", and then echoed by foreman Frank the same damn thing, "Stitch on Line 3!" A certain precaution for all, to protect any of the very expensive high speed rollers from being destroyed by the stitch, or a web break causing all to work for hours to restring a coil of steel from front to back of the 100 yard line.

As it traveled through the line, the operators with the coaters and painting automation in offset mode could then open the roller and let this rough-edge metal fly through, only to collapse back to allow for more finished product and minimize wasted product. The metal waited unpainted to be caught on rewind by Frank and then cut and scraped to the recycle. The finished coils with white pre-finish wrapper would be trapped by the amazing huge signode strappers and sent to the warehouse via an insertion to the center of the coil with a gigantic forklift nozzle, to be set onto the warehouse floor gently. The overhead crane would then either load onto a truck, or stake the load and wait for a truck to come for transportation to the manufacturer of the finished product. There, it was finally made and then sold to us for our home shelves, canning, cars, fridges... you name it. What Galt would later learn to be the supply chain!

All in all, it was an amazing process, with measurement, speed, danger, quality control, union issues, smell, and hard work all going on in the middle of the evenings. Galt would come to really appreciate the third shift, where men are men and the dawn brings with it taverns full of those who can't wait to serve those who come in looking like vampires, first entering into the early morning light. All after twelve hours in a steel factory.

Rollie, the night shift leader, was also the pal to Steve, the union and quality guy. Both were brilliant and both very different, but were to become Galt's new professors. Frank, his second-shift foreman, was pure entertainment, hollering with his toothless mouth and yelling to Galt after a fresh coil had been loaded, "Hey, you dumbass, get your boss Frank a fucking cup of coffee...unless you're are a cheap fucking prick and can't even find the money to take care of your foreman?" Yep, it was that crass, sometimes on the mic over the plant alert system.

So the days would pass, as his money and prestige and experiences would build in this darkness of the United Steelworkers' world of brotherhood, but also industrial entailed long hours into his weekends. Rarely did he go out, and his folks were beginning to actually believe he might be into this job, as he took more and more hours and shifts on different lines, as the options for his shift picks rose up and the summer hot months went on, with vacation openings to more senior workers. Any line, any shift, twelve hours, even up to an eighty-four-hour week from time to time. He slept, he wore that green uniform, he would wash every few days, and he made that long drive down into the industrial park west of O'Hare Airport.

Some evenings on break he would find himself outside on the roof with his Mexican American colleagues, who sat together away from the Anglos. Unknown to Galt, they seemed to see him as different, and invited him to try their wives' tamales out on the rooftop as Jets from O'hare would roar just a few feet over into a landing next door. There was a small fire staircase behind the paint tank storage and cleaning room, where the many trays of primer, wash and finish coatings would have to perform in huge tubs with rubber gloves and methyl ketone. The smell of this was deadly to the brain, bringing on a stoned feeling and headaches that even aspirin from the food machines wouldn't eliminate. But those wash-ups for big job changeovers fortunately were only every six to seven days, as most of the job runs went on for seven days, 24 hours a day; or 168 hours. Cleaning was something nobody liked, but the methods were quick and fast to get the gigantic pans and rollers washed up for the next project that would run. But Lord, that room was the seventh gate of industrial hell. Discriminating as it was, it was the Mexican-Americans who ran this room and the paint warehouse. One would get the job and then others would follow. The original was Papa Ruiz, who did such a good job of inventory and controls, and also kept the chemical-intense environment as clean as possible, that his family and their families were hired to fill the ever-expanding world of the TechCoats Metals workforce, numbering over four hundred employees. Just to the back door by the fire escape, they would find their way up to the roof above the cleaning room, and open up their tin wraps of tamales of all kinds and share with Galt this amazing, corn-wrapped delight. Lunch at 2:30 a.m. on a Sunday morning couldn't have been more exotic dining.

It was on this rooftop that Galt began to socially resurface. Ruiz and his men all lived close to each other about twenty-five miles south into the city, in the intersection of Whiskey Point and Back of the Yards. It was a Latino neighborhood, and where the family restaurant was, as most of those he hung out with on the roof were all related. It was up there at night when he was raving about how good the shared food was that he actually bought some dozen Pascal had brought wrapped in tin for sale. He took them home to his folks who wouldn't try them at all. A dozen pork or chicken would sell for a dollar.

Pascal and Galt were talking. Best guess, Pascal was about forty, and the quiet leader and, Galt later would learn, the nephew to Papa Ruiz: The father or uncle to most of the workers in the paint room. It wouldn't be long either until Galt realized the brotherhood of the union did create the Animal Farm dilemma.

As in, "All animals are to be equal," but for the pigs who then moved into the house, and changed the sign above the door to say, "All animals are to be equal, just SOME animals are MORE equal than others."...The Latino family of Pascal would never get their shot to work the line or the slitters, much less get out of the paint-room clean-up jobs, but were all the same happy to enjoy their union wages and this steady and unlimited number of hours to work in the great region of Chicago. He saw how wrong it was, but also how much he appreciated this high paying work, with no complaints. The shit had fallen on them, but they kicked it off everyday and flushed it down the toilet.

It was on a second shift, Friday night. Galt knew this was to be the first midnight end of shift and beginning of a weekend he had in a while; he would get a chance to actually enjoy a Saturday in a number of months since starting. Pascal and his boys would be off in a few hours, too. So on break at nine, he asked Galt, while they discussed the simple pleasures of life in American versus their old home in central Mexico (Durango was the place he heard so much of), and the benefits of making a good living for your family, and the freedoms that America brought them, "Would you like to come into the city to my family restaurant and enjoy some fun with our family tonight?"

Galt was flattered, and asked, "Where is it, and won't it be around one a.m. when we get there off shift?"

Pascal said, "This is no big deal to us, Galt. We own it and all the women will have a huge feast for us to begin the weekend. We do it every Friday or last day of the work week, usually Saturday evenings, but tonight's last shift is before Sunday night again. We are having our weekly family fest tonight. We go as long as we want. We dance, we laugh, drink Dos Equis and Patron, we talk about the work week, we hug our children, and we eat like Mayan Kings!"

Galt was in. It had been maybe four months since he had any social experience back in the Village on the Bluff. Love-making, much less sex, he couldn't even remember. He had laid low from old grade-school friends, most of whom now lived in the city of Evanston and had other work they were pursuing or, if they'd dropped out of college, they were doing construction, painting, or city work in the Village. They would ask Galt out, but he was always too tired, or had another shift on the weekend he couldn't seem to get enough of. His cuts on his fingers, and his stitches from the sharp metal edges of scrap pick-ups, strapping machines and just steel everywhere, had become numerous, but his thick gloves kept him safe from any major cuts of tendons. His scars were his signs of pride and workers who had been there a long time would show off how many scars they had on their hands and arms from major metal cuts. One of the foramen had one hand, and a claw prosthesis, due to one mistake he made during a moving-rollers clean up, when he shouldn't have been near the pinch point. So Galt knew he was now part of this, and felt maybe not with his old grad school friends, but with this crazy warm and friendly crew of Mexican colleagues, he would finally get some social life, in who knows what dining establishment...or a living room, or...?

He followed them into the city from Elk Grove at midnight, in his dirty factory greens. It was a warm night and the windows were down and traffic was light as they turned off the Kennedy to the Dan Ryan Expressway, the gateway to the south side of Chicago, and hit the off-ramp on the 47th Street exit, just past White Sox park, following Pascal, Papa Ruiz and their family of men in one old van. They parked in front of a bar with Mexican lights all around the outside. The streets of the city were bright, but the neighborhood was quiet, beyond car, motorcycle or gunshot in the distance. The bar, though, was lit up like Christmas, and signs in the window flashing. He parked on the curb, and followed the gang into the bar where three dozen or so family members were gathered. On the loud juke box Mex-pop was playing, and the smell of that great Mexican buffet emanated. Pitchers of margaritas and beer were all over a long table that had been set up in the light of the bar. Pascal locked the door behind him, and winked and said, "It's a private party, and el bar esta cerrado!" People laughing, beer flowing, and Galt sure had his share of all. A nice two a.m. glow was now his, full of tequila and beer; the food consumption was now moving to full speed ahead of the liquor, as the family sang, and the many more new names than he could recall, much less pronounced, had been introduced to him.

Pascal and his wife Maria then saw Galt's eyes lock in on a woman, who couldn't have been older than twenty-one, or maybe younger? It was Pascal's oldest daughter, Carmen. She was of long black hair, pulled back into a side ponytail, huge eyes of brown, and a Mexican dress with a lower summer cut, sharing more curves than Galt had even begun to think about over his last few months of monastic industrialization. She walked over with her father, who then introduced her to Galt, and asked if he would dance with his daughter. Galt, of course, as the good guest, said yes; they went out onto the small bar-room floor, and began to do steps of slow waltz or was it cha-cha or was it just swing? He wasn't sure, but she and he had a pace on that floor for two people who had never met that was in some way remarkable, and could be construed as them having known each other a long time. She led him and she smelled so amazing, as she pulled his head into her jet-black long hair. After two songs, she took his hand and walked him back to the family table where in much Spanish the older woman and her brothers and cousins all smiled and laughed at the two of them as they sat down for more food and margaritas. She spoke English, and also shared that she was working the family restaurant here, but was also a sophomore at Washburne Culinary, studying to be a professional chef, and hoped to run her own high-end Mexican dining establishment uptown in the loop someday. She asked what was his dream working at the plant with her brothers and father, and why had a man with college experience chose to do what he was doing?

He was unsure how to explain it here, other than to say it was part of his education and what he believed was its purpose. This was his form of graduate work and finding himself for the next phase of life. No longer a child in a man's body, he was rather one who respected this work ethic, and desired to understand and become good at what could help others in gainful employment, as industrial jobs paid well. He was coming to understand how so many Americans found their way up the ladder to Higher Ground in this country. She smiled at him, and said she understood. He wasn't sure she did, but her smile was powerful and full of trust.

She then grabbed him around his neck and with her lips went after his left ear with a kiss, and then placed one on his forehead, then moved to the lips quickly, before her family might see in the midst of what was now a three-a.m., loud celebration of the weekend. He didn't move, but picked her hand off the glass, and stood up, and asked if she would go outside with him for a minute for some air. She said yes, and Galt could see her mother and Pascal's eyes on them as they unlocked the front door and walked out to the cooler evening. At this time, all the street lights were on, as were the stop lights, but the traffic had gone, as had the sounds of a busy city for just a few minutes in this darkest hour just before dawn.

She squeezed her arm around his waist and escorted him around the side of the building to the alley, where Galt didn't seem to have any concerns, foolish or not. She and he then began a round of passionate and fondling embraces and kisses, deeper and deeper into each other, as they did with each other's hands into each other's clothes. Galt was beginning to get that U of Illinois rugby feeling again. Was this what he wanted? Was this what was right, was this just good old fashion passion, that should be ok? Shit! He was much hornier than he had even stopped to think over the last few months, and truly she was a round, warm, and willing woman, who seemed to have only one agenda for the two of them in that dark alley…against a brick wall. She said: "Forgive my lips, for they enjoy themselves in the most unusual places."

Then his brain went into that Galt other dimension, where logic and what-if began to play out. What will Pascal expect, how will this change shit at work, what if he breaks up with her, what if she gets pregnant, what if he is to be the one chosen by Pascal to take his daughter north to the suburbs of the good life in America with a baby bump. . . What if… What the fuck if!

He then held her back with a soft push of both hands on her amazing hips. She looked back and let go of where she had gone down his pants and smiled at him as if the world would be any better than at this moment. He said to her, "You are a beautiful woman, and one any man could desire as his dream, but Carmen, please understand, I must go, for reasons I cannot explain at this moment, but I must go."

She couldn't believe it, but stormed back into the bar, and he walked quickly to his little orange Ford Fiesta a half block down the curb, started up his engine, shifted into first, and pulled away, headed up north as the time on his dash said 4:14 a.m. He was drunk, but also very alert with body rushes, and only knew his retreat in the Village was his destiny for this day and hopefully before dawn broke open.

Pascal was cool about the evening on that Sunday night when they bumped into each other at the break truck, but his sons and nephews did not give Galt the best looks. Galt had no guilt, but appreciated Pascal's words of friendship and understanding, that if he wants to visit and date his daughter again, he would be welcome, but she may not understand his intent. But it was ok to choose not to also. He was sincere, disappointed but sincere in his words, but their friendship would never be the same, as Galt would migrate to another social circle in the plant. It was what the brown brothers call "The Billy Rats", or Ridge Runners, as they called themselves. These were Kentuckians, who made up most of the foreman and longer-term workers in the plant. These were experienced guys, who only stood one level below the shop's highest ranks of the old Chicago white guys with most seniority in the union plant, Chicago guys who fathers had worked there before them, and had seen how the old family who owned it at one time had built this huge family-owned steel plant, and had grown to hiring the southern migrants from Kentucky, and now Mexicans as well before selling it to the Private Equity gang. The three social classes were to be his friends and then not, but all would bring to Galt lessons and experience he would remember for life.

The layers of social infrastructure were fascinating to Galt, as he saw these segments, each to be part of a union whole, not of the management in white collars, but each of their own clique, akin to his high school days, but without women. As he had in high school, he made friends with all, at least in a way that would make the workplace a better place to be. But each had their roles, and each had their social circles. Galt was good at moving in between these circles, and felt that this education demanded he move between and dive as deep as his moral compass would allow him into each, be it the management, the Mexican-Americans, the Kentucky boys, or the old City guys. All brought an all-male chemistry, but diversity of culture, to the ring of this experience.

As Frank, his line three foreman, and Rollie, his line two foreman, both of Kentucky origins, both with their split-level houses in Elk Grove, new fridges, new vans, lawn, patios, grilles etc., would say to him, that was what they loved about America. Here they were making 40 to 50k a year in the late 1970s, working sixty-four to eighty-four hours a week: the *American Dream*. Every day one or the other, Frank or Rollie, would walk in and tell a story of how their spouse and mother of four and six in either case, would have purchased something else for their home—unheard of in the eastern Kentucky hills. Frank, with no front teeth, when at work, was the funniest of them all, and had a kind heart despite his foul mouth. Rollie was the wise man and the one that Galt has some interest in getting to know, because he seemed to have a passport that was older than many, always a draw for our Galt.

Galt would work for both of their crews in multiple shifts, as he had now all but mastered every function, but he had huge overhead cranes in the plant. He became the ultimate utility man for the plant manager, Alphonso Gara, a Mexican-American himself who had worked his way through the paint room, to the line foramen, onto the rolls with the Kentucky gang, and finally into the union, and the old-Chicago hierarchy. Al brought with him great influence and authority with his brash style, cowboy boots, and sound leadership across the plant. Alphonso was a playboy, and women his downfall, but beyond this sad fault in his armor, he proved to be very good at getting all that was possible for the white-collar ownership and senior executives, who by all measures were highly impressed with his ability to produce productivity gains, quality, and also to find a way to get more out with the same assets over time. A trend in American manufacturing that would come to dominate: in the 80s, migration to southern lower costs would first arise on the horizon, then plants would move to Mexico for even cheaper production. Then there was the Japanese miracle of quality and productivity, and finally the China trap that holds Americans hostage today. It took Galt only a few months of getting to know his colleagues, their life, and their joy at being in a dirty plant at all hours to make a living as a critical dimension of America. One we would dump like garbage someday when consultants would tell the equity and board rooms, it was cheaper overseas…but never what was good for America or that it was not for long that it would tear our blue collar middle class to shreds.

Alphonso liked Galt, and thus there was a shared opportunity for both. Galt filled every shift and every hole in the vacation schedule, to Al's delight he got one quick learner, who would bring a fresh set of eyes and a curious lift to the culture machine that Sal so embraced due to his climb through the ranks. Diversity in its truest form.

Now in his second year, Galt was getting more money, higher rank in the union, moving ahead of some of the longer-term folks as he bid for jobs and proved himself through his quick learnings of skills and outputs. Seniority would drive him ultimately out the door, but more on that later.

His dive into the culture was just getting started, with a few experiences worth sharing, as they all help us to understand how he developed in this place and came to find his true love for being a learning leader in a heavy asset environment.

As the third shift would wind down, a week for the weekends were covered, and a Saturday morning dawn would break, with all feeling fat paychecks. There was a gathering of the men from the plant in a special place that today still stands in Elk Grove. The bar was called the Korner House, a center point for all the millions of square feet of flat roofs in Elk Grove Village. Understand that Elk Village was a place of endless warehouses and factories. From an airplane, one could see miles of flat industrial rubber roofs. The jets would come in low over the tops to land at O'Hare runways, just past the bordering road. Galt was invited up on the roof for smoke breaks and would sit with Rollie and watch a late-night arrival of a 747 come pounding in, just a few hundred feet above the roof, rocking their whole body and what seemed like the whole planet's foundation. Amazing to see this in the night lights, and the power of all of it, as the jet engine fumes mixed with the gaseous split off from the paint-cleaning room vents on the roof.

God help our Galt, for he was falling in love with this madness again and again. He had already had his three finger cuts where one seemed to be threatening to lose a tendon, but all came back, and all were functioning as he needed them. As this steel and tinplate had edges as sharp as any knife, handling it all night long meant being very careful. The benefit of a deep cut and few stitches at the industrial clinic meant one could cut out of the paint line, clean up, and go run a larger machine for a week or two. It didn't matter, as all the jobs were his and his personal productivity was very high.

This evening Rollie said, "Galt, you haven't done a Saturday morning weekend bender with the Kentucky boys yet, have you?"

He had not, but also had heard of these amazing simple events with a dozen or so foremen and their key cousins from Harlan County, Kentucky. "I am in," said Galt. "This morning?"

"Yep, Korner House at seven, right after Alphonso Gara passes out the fat overtime checks."

This was culture at work, and a piece of how the people expected and wanted you to share it with them. Galt was coming to know that these invites went past just being social. It meant you were accepted and trusted as a fellow comrade-in-arms in the industrial career of a high school dropout who was living the American Dream.

So at seven, after Galt had seen his biggest two-week check yet, he asked Rollie how he could get cash (these were the days before ATMS). Rollie said, "No worries, Galt, the Korner will cash it for you. Just hold on tight to eighty percent of it, or it will be gone by 10 AM, I guarantee it."

Galt easily slid into a dirt parking lot spot across from the bar, and was in awe of the number of vehicles in this lot, with its windowless building, on a Saturday morning. There were pickups, beaters, and new vans everywhere, some with Kentucky plates, some with Texas plates, and some with Illinois. He walked through the heavy door to the smell of beer, onions, Greek spices and loud country, and a bar that was packed at every stool.

Rollie spotted the new recruit immediately and, like the gentlemen and host he was, he signaled for our Galt to come on over and join him and Frank and the others. Frank just turned and said, "What the Fuck Rollie, you invited my boy?" Immediately a cold PBR and a selection of bar whiskey was in front of him, bought by Frank. Many more were to come; dice games and money were flying everywhere. Galt had no idea how much he was spending, but it turned out to be very little, as the foreman and Kentucky gentleman took care of most, including his dice losses. Like big brother on his first time, they really showed him an amazing time. He finally took a few minutes to get to his center and find the toilet to piss, and realized it was 9 a.m. already, and he was damn hungry. On his way back from the toilets he saw plates of Greek eggs, feta cheese, olives, gyros meat, and Greek carousel of pistachio and spinach pies all over the bar. Men were chowing down like it was their last meal, after most had probably been up for over twenty-four hours now, and we're sharing it all with each other. Then out of the side of his full mouth, and one more beer and shot from Frank again, came the Greek music, and the finale to this dawn patrol: a woman with a belly of soft tissue that didn't stop wiggling, with bells in between her fingers, belly dancing, with men stuffing money into her purple sequined top and belly bottoms. Five-dollar bills, ten-dollar bills, it didn't matter. This was no strip tease, just the capstone of the owner sharing his culture with these Kentucky boys on the beginning of their weekend.

As the dances ended, and the food was almost gone, Galt had seen enough to know he was not as drunk as he had been, but it was time to get out of there at 10: 30 a.m., or live in the parking lot till his next shift on Sunday afternoon was scheduled. He gave a huge thanks to the boys, and Rollie grabbed him by his long red hair in the back, and said, "Get this haircut, boy, and you may make a good redneck yet. You did good this morning and know something about running the ride with good ole boys. Be careful, and we will see you on Line two at three p.m. Sunday. Get some rest and don't spend it all in one place tonight."

Shit, Galt was burned, and as he stepped into the morning's 90-degree August heat and humidity, in an industrial wasteland of dirt parking and overwhelming bright lights of *rah*. He knew he was going to have to be careful heading home. In those days driving drunk was not the taboo it has fortunately become today. It was a man's job to get home, and be proud he had done it no matter what condition. What fools' thoughts these were, but he and his trusty orange Fiesta with the four-speed quickly exited onto the tollway ramp, and off north to the leafy suburbs of the Village on the Bluff, and his bed. He played his rock-and-roll cassettes in the dash as loud as possible with all his windows down, and for Saturday, fortunately, the highway was pretty empty. He was able to pull this off. His survival gear kicked in finally, as it had and would some many more times in his life to come. He pulled off two exits early from his home turn and found his way into a small reformist college parking lot, where he had never ventured before; on Saturday in August it was pretty empty. There he just parked the car, and rolled his seat back, and felt only a few minutes of quiet, and he could muster the sense and focus to drive the last seven miles home. He rolled up the window, as he didn't want to be hassled by anybody, foolish as that was, and then passed out in the truest sense of passing out. He awoke, and had no clue where he was. Two hours had passed and now the heat was closer to 100, and in his orange car with black seats, it may have been a bit hotter. He was soaking wet, and felt as awful as any hangover hell could bring. Basic survival instincts kicked in. He rolled down the windows and started the engine, and slowly, very slowly, began to roll down back roads to his folks' house. Fortunately, nobody was home, as he stumbled upstairs to his bed, closed the door, closed the curtains, and fell into his industrial dream in his filthy uniform on top of his bed.

He had passed the Kentucky initiation without destruction or death.

CHAPTER 17:

Organized Labor, "The Good, The Bad, and the Ugly"

T he good was Galt's willingness to keep taking the shifts and job upgrades that nobody wanted. He was trying to help, and was making great money. He was naive about that, but seniority had chosen to not take a Saturday twelve-hour from seven to seven, or a Sunday double back after at three p.m. to three a.m. But he kept signing up for the money, and his skill set made him capable of any and all jobs in the plant.

It became bad when he found himself in the middle of an issue with old union cats, but then the Kentucky men would quietly tell him to go, man, go, as they, too, liked his challenge to the old union city rules that had never met a cat like Galt.

The Ugly came when he was approached by his mentor, Dr. Jack, with an opportunity to work in the quality labs from 8 a.m. to noon, three to five days a week after his third shift on the plant floor. The lab and chemistry of coatings was not something he saw as interesting, but Dr. Jack was intent on showing him the office ropes up front.

The issue came with the union rep, who dealt with this work with one-hour intern shifts. This was wrong—the position should be paid, and due to Galt's status in the union, should be paid as a union job if Galt was doing the work.

They began to give him the short talks, the senior old Chicago union leaders: You have to commit to the union or the office, but not both. You should take it and then sign up folks in the office with union cards for representation. You can be our voice and spy.

Despite how the money rolled for Galt, the union hierarchy and aspirations were squashing his interest. They were beginning to threaten the office with a slow-down if he took the position and was paid separately. He was aware of the issues as they increased, and suddenly the joy of this madness wore off. As fast as it came, it was gone. He had hit the old Chicago labor wall.

It was time for a retreat after this amazing 18 months. It was a kindergarten pal who came calling for the rescue singing: "Canada, Galt; Canada, Galt; let's get out here?"

CHAPTER 18:

The Wanderlust or Career Dilemma

Galt Holds Back From the Second Third of Life.

e had just gotten home from a long Monday night, a twelve-hour shift during which he worked on two different lines, and did three chemical change-overs. His head was splitting from the smell of the MEK, and his brain was a cloud. It was a Tuesday, a late summer morning, when most had just gone to work, and here he was making scrambled eggs and staying out of his mother's way, a twenty-four-year-old living at home with his steel-toed shoes resting at the door to the garage, his siblings off to college, and his youngest brother at grade school. Had he run the gauntlet with this first semester of Grad School of Hard Knocks. The union was fighting his move to work in the lab with the white-collar folks and support sales proposals in the morning after his shift. Dr. Frank had suggested this as a good step to make the jump to the outside salesforce while remaining in the union for his shift, and coming up to learn for three to four hours. Seemed like an arduous task, but he was ready, until the union had pushed back, claiming that the office work had to be a union job if Galt, a union employee, was to work it. Such bullshit. Galt had heard enough of the rep and his logic, which was to use Galt as a political tool to gain more power. Jack just wanted to help, and Galt was quickly growing tired of his headaches and, despite a fattening check book, the hours and the "no more to learn" dilemma he was falling into. Ever a seeker, he was quickly seeing this as the end of things at the metal plant. So, with some regret, yet a clear sense of the open horizon ahead, he said goodbye to Dr. Jack and the three diverse groups of friends, whom he had developed a true camaraderie with at the metals plant. All were sad to see him go, but none were surprised.

And so that Tuesday morning, at home after his shift, he shared his decisions with his mother. She had been unloading groceries, and asked him to help; and she mentioned that Jeremiah Carson (JC) had called and left a message to call him back at a number in the Village. Galt quickly recognized this as his old kindergarten pal's home phone number, a few blocks away. Jeremiah had also attended UW and was the former tennis team captain, an amazing athlete packed into a 5' 6"-frame, and also a guy who followed the rules forever until the Isthmus converted him to a radical shift in his way, in much the same way as had happened to Galt. They were the all-American boys in high school, who discovered they were not so sure of the path that had been painted for them. Rather, a path they must cut was the way. Jeremiah had dropped off the earth last year, and it was discovered he had been wandering and working as a bum of sorts between skiing in the winter out west and teaching tennis in the summer, with a little time helping his dad with his book-publishing business. Jeremiah quickly picked up after Galt had spoken for a few minutes to his mother, Mrs. Clark. She was an amazing story unto herself. She never drove and rode her bike to the grocery store and all errands, and fed Galt and all her three boys healthy food and all other forms of modern hippiedom, despite being a woman of WWII generation. After she and Galt spoke, she put Jeremiah on the phone. They had a quick "What's up, man," and "Cool, dude," exchange, and then J. got down to it:

"I am headed to the Boundary Waters in Canada, and plan to do two weeks in the wilderness in a canoe and Duluth pack before the winter falls upon central Ontario. Need a second in the canoe to make it happen with me. Want to go?"

What he didn't tell Galt that was he also planned to return and then make a few bucks to head to Western BC and ski all winter at a distant village in the Canadian Rockies, to the town of Red Mountain, Rosalind, BC. But what about this canoe fishing thing? How would this work? Our Galt was never a good camper unless with a friend overnight, or a short weekend in the woods with plenty of DEET spray!

"You in or out?"

Galt was never a fan of either/ors, but this one seemed like an easy conclusion to draw. "Yep!" He then asked, "Where is this, again?"

After he hung up, he told his mom that he was headed to Canada via canoe. She said, "What is your plan?"

"Mom, after Canada, I will decide. I need to do this."

Ever being the support for her son's heart, she could instantly tell he was ready for this wilderness, and that this could be the retreat and time he needed to figure out his next step in life. He had not taken a vacation in 18 months, and JC was a good kid, alway. He should be ok in this wilderness region of western Ontario, as JC's older brother James owned the outfitter in Atikokan. James would supply the food, the canoes, the maps, the Duluth pack, the dry food and fishing gear as needed for protein.

So, Galt packed what he could of outdoor gear, though he wasn't sure what that was, then headed to JC's, where a 1968 RV awaited, with JC and another pal, David. Both were ready to go, and pick up the other three folks they would travel with to Atikokan, in the Boundary Waters of Canada. The RV was old, but it was a grand place for all to talk and share the stories of what two years out of college was like for all of these boomers approaching twenty-five now. All three were still trying to figure it out, but the Milwaukee three had all become career people. One was a teacher, one an engineer, and the third a social worker. All were taking advantage of their UW education, unlike Galt and JC, who were taking their education in very unconventional ways. David, the third wheel, was a drop-out from sophomore year in Texas at SMU. He was smart, but had wild hair and a knack for getting in trouble and pushing the envelope. His true desire, he said, was to be an engineer, but he also was wandering. So the six departed from the Kinnickinnic Valley in Wauwatosa, headed northwest to Superior, Wisconsin over the John Blatnik Bridge, and St. Louis Bay into Duluth. From there, beer made for a lack of pure recall, but the images of the huge, open-pit mines of Robert Zimmerman's home in Hibbing, Minnesota, would always remain with Galt and his old Badger pals. Holes in the earth where iron ore had been pulled in large order, trained to docks in Duluth, loaded on freight ships, and dispatched to the steel mills of Chicago. There many types of metal would be formed out of the raw earth's materials, and finally cut, cleaned, painted and rewrapped by Galt's former colleagues. There's that supply chain thing again.

AS the RV crossed the bridge, JC reached back and said, "Time to put out the pipe, you guys, and let's open the windows and have some lunch. We need to air this rig out before we cross the border through inspection."

So they stopped, but hid the pot in the toilet tank on some hangers.

As they approached the crossing in the big pines of northern Minnesota, all were a bit nervous, as they all were truly stoned. Galt himself wasn't much of a pot smoker, as it always made him paranoid. But he was the first to admit that his spirit, seeking experiences in life with an endless road, was to try just about everything at once. One unforgettable time, he'd even experienced the "brown sugar," when he was unaware.

It was the summer of his junior year, Brown Sugar had been placed into a reefer at a lower-level apartment. It was the season when hippies would find their way into Madison and get cheap sublet rentals when students typically headed home. Galt himself was drunk on beer with Charles that night, a summer roommate and good friend from NYC he had met at the Villa. They were invited into the den of iniquity, and with a warm set of eyes of one of the hippie chicks, he sat down with her partying with the coach.

"Sit here, Galt."

He passed the doobie, harmless enough, and soon his whole body began to weave and sway. He and Charles got up and both looked at each other. "Let's get the fuck out of here, there is something weird going on." The crew downstairs was run by an old hippie who wore overalls and called himself Papa. All of the kids, probably ages sixteen to twenty-four, were his family and wandered the earth, stopping in Madison every summer. This year they sublet the second floor below Galt and Charles.

As he lay in bed that night, he knew he was in for a bad night ahead. He threw up multiple times and finally found a bag to set next to his mattress on the floor. He filled it too. Dry heaves, and finally rest. Next day they both knew it had happened after comparing notes. As they went down the stairs to get on their bikes and head to the Villa Maria and serve brunch to the summer students there, and get their own meal as payment, the old Papa guy saw them over the railing. "Far out, you cats came in last night to party, man. Seems you lost your shit...ha, ha!" They both just looked up at him, said, "Thanks, it was great," and made sure their doors were locked tight on the third floor of the three-flat old house on Mifflin.

So it was Galt and his experience with drugs. All forms once, and very rarely twice.

This pot they were smoking in the RV was bugging him. He had now learned how to make money, save money, and was a steel worker, and had visions of being something else professional, though unsure of what, and that being arrested at the border was not his top priority. The paranoia began to creep in.

They did get inspected, despite their hard work clearing out the RV's atmosphere in Bemidji, in front of Paul Bunyan's restaurant and his forty-foot statue and his fifteen-by-twenty-pal, Babe the Blue Ox.

The Canucks made them unpack everything, but no luck. Good thing the engineer, an extremely brilliant guy by all definitions (including his membership in Mensa), used the craper for the hideout. While most Canadian inspectors would have thought to check the most obvious of hideouts for pot in a toilet tank, Alex did what any genius would do. About ten minutes away from the border, he took an awful-smelling dump, that only a Cheesehead could after eating the kind of crap this brilliant graduate of the UW school of electrical engineering, cum laude, could.

The inspector had no interest in the john. When he opened the door, in fact, despite their perseverance to have us download all the camping gear, they also wouldn't step into the RV for more than two minutes. So it was worth the unpack and repack to not be busted, and take pot into Canada.

As the RV pulled into Atikokan, Ontario, a very old mining town that had now semi-transformed into an outfitter and one-night lay-over for adventurers, the fuel tank said empty. The van stank of beer, THC, and that richness of twenty-something adults who needed a shower soon.

CHAPTER 19:

We Begin to Understand the End of Book One of the Higher Ground Trilogy.

They returned from 10 days in the wilderness with no motor or electricity. Just a few batteries, fishing gear, dried food, a good tent and sleeping bag. Galt had hit his sub 200 weight, and was as fit as he had ever been. He was not at home, and time to reflect and get moving forward......

A Man Child now knows he can work hard if need be. He now knows he can adventure outdoors, he now knows he can buy his own car. He now knows he is not quite indestructible, he now knows enough of short- and long-term love affairs, he now knows how important friends are, he now knows how lucky he was to be raised in his family, but as relates to the future, he now knows what he wants in his passion for the next phase.

He recognizes he won't ever be done with the arts, as he will carry forward painting, theater, music and writing with him into his passion for industry. Long-term only seems relevant to how he can choose to dig in with the factory seduction, with its cork-floor smells of machine oil, weld-

ing gas, and the clangs of metal and Jeep propane and crane movement.
It is here he is able to see that all people who are either forced or choose
to chase this American dream through a factory are the core of who he
loves to spend time with, and how he wants to learn, and this infatuation
has now become a juice for leading. He didn't know it was leading, but he
knew it was about helping others to get a job done and assure they, too,
were enjoying it half as much as he was. But even with this juice, something still got in the way. . .

SHE had been gone now for a number of years, and he was sure he
wouldn't see her, if ever again, in his dreams or visions at the big lake. But
suddenly, there SHE was in front of him, waiting with her smile and what
he now saw was long black hair. Wanting his body as close to hers as is
possible, with his arms and hers tightly squeezing the air out of each other.
So very real, but it couldn't be. SHE was standing there when he returned
from Ontario and got a phone call.

The call came from a family friend who truly wanted him to come to
work in the factory. Learn in the plant, then take over their service desk
for the global dealer network, a maker of hydraulic gas- and battery-pow-
ered machines that propel people up and through job sites and factories,
to do maintenance and construction in situations ranging from simple to
the most complex and dangerous. Some reached as high as 160 feet with
people running the machine from that metal 42-inch basket. O'Hare
Tool was where three of his old high school friends from Chicago also
worked, and he knew after this trip with Jeremiah to Canada, and after
the last gig, he would take the gig. Salary was only $16 k a year, but with
his shared house on an old estate in the woods with two friends, and his
car paid for, he figured he could make it work. He had no budgeting skills
outside of his know-how, but knowing if you had enough had been a true
outcome of his adventures traveling. After all, wasn't this another trip with
hard work and the miles collected?

So he took the gig, and was to start in two weeks. As he had also
acquired a motorcycle that spring, he had the ability to run around a
bit and enjoy the last spring of Illinois. Country drives and all sorts of

highways that led to no place in particular, but he had ten days to let his freak flag fly behind him, and his bike to burn some miles across northern Illinois and southern Wisconsin. His folks were happy he had finally chosen to be in the region and find his own place with credible pals, and that he was still single and hadn't gotten into any trouble. For they had their hands full with the other three kids. The loss of the little one had never truly gone away, but that was the way it just seemed to be. Galt knew his deceased brother would always bring him a vision and purpose, along with his love he would never lose.

He found himself one day very far from the Village by the Lake, in the southern Wisconsin small town of Monroe. He had just settled into Baumgartner's Cheese Shop for a retro experience from college at the bar. Ordered a Huber Bock and a swiss cheese sandwich on rye, with brown mustard, all locally sourced in the beautiful county seat in southwest Wisconsin. It was about 1:15 p.m., when she walked up to him to ask if he wanted another beer, the one in front of him being only half finished. She was not the older woman who had and delivered his first order. She was stunning, with blond hair braided down her back. Small waist, a silk Mexican wedding blouse on, unbuttoned too far, and no bra. Her jeans were classic red-tag Levis, and her old farming boots had obviously been worn in the barn to milk, feed, or clean up, as folks did in that part of the country, with cow herds to milk seven days a week, twice a day. Her face was long, but perfect, her eyes bright blue, golden hair pulled back to reveal a long forehead, with earrings set in turquoise, and he couldn't believe how beautiful the "who" was. She then repeated her question about the second beer. He wasn't sure what to say, but he knew it had to be something other than the stare he was now locked into.

She then took his mug and almost began to ask again, when he finally said, "What is your name?"

She smiled and said, "Amanda." But as soon as their mutual smiles locked in, he saw she wasn't just a Wisconsin dairy gal who could stop herds of cows and was the one the guys in high school wanted to dance with if her height hadn't scared them off. Rather he knew it was SHE, but not as he had thought.

He said, "It has been a long time since the lake when you said good-bye."

SHE didn't say a thing for a long time—more like ten seconds—then said, "Yes, you don't need or want me, and I had to find my way back when it was right and at a time we both could start to share again. You knew it and I knew it."

He said, "Where were you?"

SHE said, "Here, in Wisconsin now. I have been able to leap out to you, and it was a strange feeling, and was something I never understood. This sense of us, of this ability to be here and in spirit, and to have thoughts one who is very old would have. It was confusing to me at first. It would happen when I would walk out into the field or the woods behind what is my family farm, or when I would be alone in my apartment in Madison at UW, I could begin to jump out of this reality and travel time and space. It was never easy, until we began to see each other and those moments we started by just speaking to each other with physical presence. Then as our youth passed, it became a lonely time for me, Galt. But I, too, found others who I could grow and learn to love so that when we met up again, I, too, was ready for this powerful connection we share. This place isn't the only one I know of. My heart and mind holds a place in red rocks above a raging river, shadowed by a rock formation that is shaped as a Mexican sombrero. I am in these thoughts a woman of color, and of a very different race. But I am here now, and through this vessel, I can say I was expecting you to walk into my uncle's cheese deli and bar, but we Baumgartners have a way of knowing a lot of strange events before they happen. Guess this is our first real event." She paused, then said, "Want that beer . . .?"

"No." Galt finally spoke. "I want you to get on the back of my motor-cycle outside, and let's go for a ride to the place we both know we will find."

She was a bit unsure for a second, as she knew both Spring Green at the beach by the bridge at Highway 23, and the top of Blue Mound, were spots they had dreamt about, though so far apart.

He knew what she was thinking, and said, "Blue Mound, to the top of the world. OK?"

She smiled and said something to her aunt in the cheese department, and grabbed her blue-jean coat off the hook behind the bar. He stood up, with half a sandwich and half a beer left, and walked to the end where she emerged. He was in awe of the fact she was as calm as she was, but also that this somehow was not the physicality he had imagined through their spiritual communications. But that hardly seemed to matter, as she vastly exceeded anything he could have imagined. Plus, her voice, oh that voice, just climbed into his ears, his mind, his heart every time she spoke.

He kicked his orange 750 Honda sportster over with an easy Honda kick, and the four cylinders roared across the block to the county seat at the old elms that lined the Monroe square. He kicked out the pegs for his rider, and she climbed on behind him like she had done it a thousand times before. Off they went up Wisconsin state highway 69 to Monticello, Mt. Horeb and beyond, following the old Badger Trail and the Sugar River. Green country and short corn for as far as anyone could see in those rolling, Driftless hills, perfect roads and perfect May day, with She on the back. He wasn't sure it got much better than this.

It was about a fifty mile drive to the Blue Mound State Park entrance, as one turned off 151. They climbed up the 1,200 feet of elevation to the park's butte summit, where two towers stood at either end of a beautiful grassy lawn and circle road on top. One tower faced east, and Madison, and the other faced west, and the Mississippi and Spring Green, Frank Lloyd Wright's place of peace. The bike was built for both of them as it wound up the switchbacks through the oak forest where leaves were just getting started to spring out and in a few months a very colorful fall. These hills were special, mainly because only the farmers and local service-economy folks knew how beautiful this region was. Not significant enough to attract any but those who loved and lived there. But oh, the beauty, the woods and the field laced together into a patchwork that was a cousin to the mountains of New England.

He would see her a few more times, on long weekends, and they talked for hours, usually in between long talks and rides to beautiful places. They drank, ate, laughed and talked about the future in this life. They had so much in common, yet there wasn't that feeling they both should go further together at that time; and the physical part was not as we all have come to expect of two young people. It wasn't abstinence in the religious way, and neither were declared to be celibate. It was respect, it was a sense of, this was only the beginning of something that had been crossing time and what we know as spiritual here. That patience and a time in a desert far off, under an unusual rock formation in a place of native people—it would happen.

He left her at the family store in Monroe, and she said, "I will see you tomorrow, above the river just north of Mazomanie. I have to visit a dairy farm of ours, and we can meet up at the end of the trail at Cactus Bluff. It has a wonderful view over the river. He was unsure as to why they should spend this day apart, but maybe it was a good time for some time apart. Again, they had not consummated the relationship in the physical way, and yet they had seemed to come about as close as two people could. They had slept together, just holding each other, nude, throughout the whole night. He wasn't mad as a man can be, and she just was perfect there in his arms. His dreams were rich with visions these few nights, visions that seemed impossible. At his age and in this state of running away from this life, what purpose was this red rock formation, akin to a hat? There was that huge cliff and that raging river, so unlike Wisconsin itself?

He came to actually believe that this was what they would share someday, yet it wasn't to be for a while. He had a lot of roads to run and lessons to gain and then share before they were to meet up again, and begin the greatest adventure two people could share.

He parked at the path and walked to see her standing there, overlooking the beautiful Wisconsin River, with the green hills, and the water winding to the Mississippi. Her hair was braided in a beautiful silver and turquoise stone. Something from a different place. She and he said simultaneously the same words: "It has come to an end, my love." It was like harmony.

They both laughed, then hugged very tight. They sat on Ferry Bluff over the river. SHE said, "When life brings us back together again, then so be it, but we have different paths for now." But SHE added, "I'm betting my life that we will find our way back together again. I want you to promise me one thing, Galt."

He responded with silence and the eye-to-eye they had come to share in the evenings together over those few days.

"Don't be afraid, for I will always be with you, Galt. Now you must go to the big city on Michigan, it calls for you."

He then smiled, and they kissed long and slow. Not patiently, as two who would want to remember this moment. As she walked away, he didn't see the splendor of the Wisconsin driftless region, rather he saw an image of a desert, a huge rock formation again, shaped like a MEXICAN HAT. He was so awed by it, he was unable to speak or gesture. He just watched her walk back into those red rocks.

It was a day and final moment he hoped would last forever, but it wasn't to be. The climb to the Higher Ground would take a bit more effort than he had given to date. It was only the beginning, and he was no longer afraid.

SHE and He were to make a difference to each other, a difference a few times, then many. Some of those, they would come to call family. The Higher Ground, the exploration thereof, are like no other experience. The Higher Ground is not a place, but a state of mind, one where the body, mind and spirit are in balance, and where you, too, can help others to join in the path to that state of mind.

THE END

INTRIGUE AND DRAMA AWAITS IN BOOK TWO!

Here is a short excerpt:

Galt kept his eye on the road as he turned into Mazatlan from Highway 40 D, and to the beach as quickly as the Jeep would take them. Galt longed for water, the vision of open water, and AJ was herself interested, as it had been a long time since she had sat by, seen, or swam in anything beyond a river or hotel pool.

As he maneuvered his way through the city center and past the Cathedral Basilica de la Inmaculada Concepción, a beautiful church, he saw a road that looked to deadhead straight into the ocean. He saw a park on his right and car spaces across from the beach, and pulled into the Parque Ciudades Hermanas, and the beach. As they locked up the Jeep and began to walk to the shore, despite the condition of the red Jeep and the layers of desert that rested on it, there were four young men who approached it as they turned the corner to cross the street. As advised back in Puerto Palomas, they both looked back at the same time. The four had begun to cut their way through the top of the Jeep. Galt grabbed AJ's arm and felt she was doing the same. Both then ran like lightning back across the traffic, not waiting for a light, and began to scream as AJ pulled out of her white skirt a huge knife that Galt had no idea she carried. He would find she was good at keeping "tools of defense" under her skirts. She began to scream like a wild animal as she waved the knife over her head at full gallop. He was struggling to keep up with her. At this moment he was more worried about her than the potential for all their belongings to be stolen. It was bright midday, as the ride down from Durange had only been 180 miles through a ton of switchbacks. As the gang of what was no more than teenagers, turned to see these two adults running at them. It was then Galt also recalled the gun he kept under the front seat. It was a Smith and Wesson .44 he had bought in Chicago. He had built a small lock case under the seat before he left. He was trained, but had not used it in a long time, and only at ranges.

He knew it was there and maybe even the box was unlocked, as he had done that when they crossed the border, just in case. As the youth's faces turned to horror at this 5 '10" woman, eyes burning down, in a white native dress with a sleeveless white Adidas top, screaming at full attack. They turned and ran like hell, but as soon as the two had reached the Jeep, the gang leader, who was now no more than 30 yards away realized they had not stolen anything. He turned and yelled at his peers: "You mother fuckers, we will be cooked and ass-raped by the big man if we don't come back with something. This mother has lots of stuff, we need to have the balls to go back and attack."

With that he pulled his own .38 out and the others gathered up the strength and pulled out switch blades and another pistol and began to run at the Jeep as AJ and Galt were just catching their breath. Having just begun to think verbal rapid running efforts had worked.

Suddenly two shots flew by their heads and the next beaded into the tailgate of the Jeep, just missing the spare tire and gas tank, which Galt guessed he wasn't aiming at due to this interest in what they had inside the dusty Jeep Wrangler. He reached under the seats and popped out the box on release button, and on a simple track it opened and the monster pistol was there for his taking. AJ was behind the front fender, and was in awe of what Galt was doing in rapid speed, and a smile of some kind creeped quickly from her cheeks as he pulled the .44 magnum out, pulled off the safety, and let two shots go over the boys' heads. Compared to their pop guns, this cannon on his two hands scared the shit out of the gangsters, but they feared retribution from their bosses if they came back without any goods from the innocents, thus driving them even closer into his cannon's range. Galt then took aim as they got within thirty feet and were missing with their wild shots, and put two more down at their feet. He then realized that one bullet had shot the foot of the leader, and the other sent chips of stones up into the other's faces.

People in the park were far away, so there was no fear of any other damage to the innocent. As the leader was falling down and took aim at AJ within not a few feet, Galt saw he had his pistol ready to put one right in her chest. He found that same anger and defense he had felt before in the bar in Colorado, in the football game senior year when, after whistle, an asshole had bloodied his nose, and when the jerk in junior high came at him...His logic and contingent thinking went out of balance, and the animal came out. He took aim and put one more into the gangster's thigh, and he fell like a water buffalo. He was a big fellow, and he hit his face on the rocks of the parking lot. His pals were now picking him up and begging for mercy.

AJ was now behind Galt and, hands on his shoulders, squeezing, whispered into his ears, "That's enough, they are done. Please stop, Galt." She sensed he might just put more bullets into the boy's vitals to end it.

The gangsters picked up their wounded buddy, screaming "Gracias, gracias," carried him off to a van across the lot, and tore out with dust flying under their wheels.

Galt took a huge deep breath and turned to her.

"Are you all right, AJ?"

She was quiet, but eye-to-eye he knew she was, but here was a look in those eyes he had not seen, one where she was unaware of who this guy was for a moment. She saw a man who she didn't know was inside the make-up of this kind human, a man she had fallen for like no other before.

She said, "I am, and it will be alright if you are ok to set the gun down on the seat for a minute."

He did, and with a small grin of pride. Chicago slang came out. "What the fuck was that? Sometimes it happens, and I don't even know what the hell I become, but it's rare. When he went for you with his pistol, that was it."

She kissed him on the forehead, then the lips, quickly, then jumped in the driver's seat and put the gun back in the cabinet. She quickly turned on the Jeep and shouted in his ear: "Get the hell in, my turn to drive, we have to get out of here before the cops, who are likely on their side, get here soon!"

Off they burned dust and down the road. She carefully weaved with her easy touch the back streets of Mazatlan till they found a two-lane and headed south. Then once past the city, turned down the ocean and on the Isle del Bosque, where she hoped she could find the small and remote village of her extended family on the southern beach and jungle.

ACKNOWLEDGMENTS

- Family
- Lifelong Friends
- Mentors & Colleagues
- Tish Thorton, Edit Captain
- Chris T 3Dog Creative, Captain All Things Creative and Crossing the Goal Line
- Authors of Boise Idaho who opened up to me
- Steven Pressfield's Books
- Navajo Nation, to the visits, places, and people who shared their world with me
- Sky City, Acome Pueblo to the visits and peoplewho shared so much
- A list of other authors far too long to share.

ABOUT THE AUTHOR

My journey began when I had heard enough close friends, colleagues, and family encouraging me to write a book. Blessed with enough succes to turn my retirement's excess time into something special. I spent my early days serving on multiple non profits, reconditioning my body and spirit, and reading across many genre of literature. I languished a bit, and then was given Steven Pressfield's book *The War of Art*.

It literally kicked me in the tail and gave me the ground rules for sitting down and doing "it". Doing "it" is how I describe the pounding the keys of my lap top. Throwing all I have inside into words and tales of life. What began as a business leadership book of lessons I have gathered and recorded over 4 decades, to be told as a fairy tale, morphed significantly. My work quickly became an outline of a Trilogy. Capturing the 3 stages of life for a young man, the love of his life, some wild adventures they share, and the good they aspire for Always with a purpose.

Our world seemed to be missing a belief in a common place or mind set that we could all embrace. Thus I conceived from my many studies of religions a place I came to call "The Higher Ground". Over the last 4 years I have written of characters who Discover, Share, and ultimately Defend Higher Ground. With a foundation formed from an understanding their own Body Mind and Spirit. They learn one must strive to keep this trinity in balance. For when Body Mind and Spirit are in balance the path to Higher Ground becomes clear. It is then, through the virtue of being self focused in development, and relentless, we can become altruistic. Able and fulfilled in our ability to offer to others a hand to the Higher Ground.

I sincerely believe in these principles. Told with enough modern adventure, across America, some intense drama, and violence as is called for in history(when evil knows no other response), I could best write and share this story in 3 books.

Made in United States
Troutdale, OR
11/21/2024

25133809R00169